15 Stitches

Rita Baorto

iUniverse, Inc.
Bloomington

15 Stitches

Copyright © 2012 Rita Baorto

All rights reserved. No part of this book may be used or reproduced by any means, graphic, electronic, or mechanical, including photocopying, recording, taping or by any information storage retrieval system without the written permission of the publisher except in the case of brief quotations embodied in critical articles and reviews.

This is a work of fiction. All of the characters, names, incidents, organizations, and dialogue in this novel are either the products of the author's imagination or are used fictitiously.

iUniverse books may be ordered through booksellers or by contacting:

iUniverse
1663 Liberty Drive
Bloomington, IN 47403
www.iuniverse.com
1-800-Authors (1-800-288-4677)

Because of the dynamic nature of the Internet, any Web addresses or links contained in this book may have changed since publication and may no longer be valid. The views expressed in this work are solely those of the author and do not necessarily reflect the views of the publisher, and the publisher hereby disclaims any responsibility for them.

Any people depicted in stock imagery provided by Thinkstock are models, and such images are being used for illustrative purposes only.

Certain stock imagery © Thinkstock.

ISBN: 978-1-4697-9093-0 (sc)
ISBN: 978-1-4697-9094-7 (hc)
ISBN: 978-1-4697-9095-4 (e)

Library of Congress Control Number: 2012903747

Printed in the United States of America

iUniverse rev. date: 4/6/2012

Chapter 1

Frantically looking behind me, I realized that I hadn't evaded my pursuers. I willed my legs to go faster as I struggled to run.

An alley came into my peripheral vision, and I turned down it—not noticing the No Outlet sign at the entrance. The two buildings on either side of me seemed to press in as I sprinted down the narrow alleyway. I heard their heavy footfalls over my rasping breath, and I knew I wouldn't be able to run for much longer.

In the darkness, I didn't notice that there was no escape until I reached the large brick building in front of me. I looked up at the lifeless black windows in terror.

I turned around to face them, flattening myself against the wall. Seeing that I was trapped, the four of them slowed their run. I gazed at the face of their leader, and his betrayal cut like a knife.

I never thought that his face would be one I should fear.

As the four of them approached, they snickered menacingly. They all wore large, dark sweatshirts, despite the unusually warm weather. I could hear their jeans scraping against the pavement as they sauntered closer.

"Hey, sweetheart," the leader said. I knew his voice, but it seemed unfamiliar and far away as it slurred. "We warned you to stay away," he said thickly. I pressed myself closer to the wall.

Feelings of betrayal and disloyalty coursed through me, and a cry broke from my lips, "No, no!" My voice rang down the alley, and even I was surprised by the way the sound carried and reverberated against the walls. "You can't do this," I whispered as they got closer.

I couldn't believe that my once good friend was about to hurt me this way. I shuddered as I felt his body press up against me.

"Harmony!" The angry yell broke the silence of the night. My eyes flew open, and I felt Robbie freeze against me. He turned to see who had dared to interrupt him.

An unusually tall man was sprinting toward us. The wind blew his dark hair away from his face as his shadow grew closer and closer. He didn't sound like he was much older than I was. I didn't recognize his voice, but I felt a rush of relief when I saw him. There was no menace in the way he shouted my name.

My attackers slowly moved away from me. The stranger was tall, but his build was nothing compared to that of my captors. They stood confidently as he approached—until he was close enough for us to see the strange transformation he was going through. Even though I knew he had come to save me, I shied away from him in terror.

Huge membrane-like wings grew from between his shoulder blades. They lifted and extended until they were nearly the width of the alley. In the dim light, I could see the shadow of scales as they slowly emerged across his collarbone and spread up to his jaw line. His sharp eyes took in the situation, and a low hiss escaped his lips. Horror and disbelief flashed across Robbie's face as he quickly looked back at me and then turned to take in the monster before him.

My fear slowly dissipated and was replaced by relief; as horrible as he was, this strange monster had come to save me.

My eyes flew open to see the darkness of the early November morning. My entire body was shaking, and my hands were clammy with sweat. I struggled to repress the memories that came back with that nightmare, but I couldn't help the thoughts that came next …

There was no strange monster to save me that night. The most horrible night of my life was not just a nightmare.

It was real.

As my pounding heart slowed, I felt a hard yearning for revenge flow through me. The anger and hurt burned like acid deep in m[e．．．］ longed for vengeance, to return the pain that Robbie had caus[ed．］

I thought that he loved me like a sister and that I was s[afe no matter] how many times he warned me to stay away. I felt betrayed by my parents too; they refused to believe that it was Robbie, the son of their good friends, who had done this to me.

I sat up in bed and looked around my pale yellow room, resting my eyes on my white comforter, which was in a messy ball due to all my tossing and turning during the night.

I looked at the bright red numbers on the clock by my bed. It was 5:30. My parents wouldn't be awake yet. I decided to hide my appearance from them by taking a shower before they woke up.

If my parents found out that I had this nightmare, there would be hell to pay. There would be no direct anger toward me, but an increased tension between my parents that encouraged the never ending circle of blame.

My parents would never say it out loud to me, but I couldn't help but notice how their relationship deteriorated shortly after I returned from rehabilitation. My actions shed light on the fact that my father was never really there to support his family. When my mother and I needed him, my father wasn't there. Of course I never really knew what his job actually was, only that he worked for some mysterious "company."

I walked swiftly down the dark, carpeted hallway until I heard the faint creak of my parents' door as one of them walked out of the room. I froze in place, debating whether or not I should turn around and go back to my room.

"Harmony?" I heard my mother's soft voice and felt my heart drop.

"Yes?" I answered, clearing my throat to make my voice sound normal.

"Are you all right?" I could see my mother's head peeking around the corner.

"Yes, Mom, I'm fine." I wiped my forehead to disguise any signs of stress. "I'm just a little nervous … first day back to school after five months is pretty nerve-racking."

I could immediately tell from her suspicious expression that she hadn't bought the lie that I had told her.

"Harmony, I need to know what happened. Did you have a nightmare?" she asked, gradually raising her voice. I winced, not wanting her to wake my father.

Too late. I heard the door to my parents' bedroom squeak again, and my father's heavy footsteps echoed in the dark hall.

"What's wrong, Harmony? What happened?" he asked. Honestly, I was surprised by his concern. It was the first time I had heard it in a very long time. His features were soft with worry, and I almost didn't recognize him.

"I swear I'm fine," I said, trying to keep my voice even.

"Did you have a nightmare?" he asked, his features hardening as he read the truth on my face. He didn't even need to hear my answer.

"Yes," I said, frustrated that I was unable to hide anything from him. As the words left my lips, my father's frame stiffened to throw an accusatory glance my mother's way. She shrunk away from the onslaught of his gaze. Anger rose up inside of me at the way he looked at her. Since last May, my mother had realized that she didn't know anything about my father's job. She was finally able to see that he was rarely home, and their relationship flew into a downward spiral that seemed to never end.

"Was it the same one as always?" my mother demanded.

"Well … it started off the same but ended differently." I shifted uncomfortably as they waited for me to continue.

When it was clear that I wouldn't answer on my own accord, Mom asked gently, "How was it different?"

"Someone saved me this time," I said, the words spilling out of my mouth in one big jumble. I struggled to repress the frightening picture that formed behind my eyes as the dream came storming back.

It took a second for my parents to process what I said. My parents looked at each other, confusion in their eyes.

"Really? Who was it?" my father asked.

"I don't know," I said, and I caught my mother and father eyeing me critically, as if debating whether or not they could believe me. This time, however, I was telling the truth, and they seemed to suddenly realize that.

"Try and get back to sleep," my mother said softly, squeezing my hand.

As they turned the corner to head back to their bedroom, I heard their angry whispers.

"I told you," my father hissed as they stopped by the doorway. "She didn't need to see the therapist. Dr. Andrews hasn't made the slightest difference. For that matter, I don't think she even needed to go to rehab!"

"What?" my mother said, her voice rising with anger. "After she had that fit, you think we should have done anything differently? You and I both know that we couldn't help her. If you were home a little more often, you might have been able to see the change in her. But no … you have some mysterious job that you won't even tell your wife about …" And they continued, their voices fading as they shut the door behind them. I continued to the bathroom, biting my lip to stop the frustrated tears from spilling down my cheeks.

When I walked into the bathroom, I didn't even glance at the mirror. I didn't want to be reminded of how much I had changed. I didn't want to see what Robbie had done to me. I turned the shower on, knowing it would be the only way that I could possibly relax.

Finally the water was ready, and I stepped gratefully into the hot stream. I prayed that the shower would help to loosen my muscles; it was barely six in the morning, and I was already stressed.

The water beat mercilessly against my back, forcing me to relax. I gripped the slippery shampoo bottle tightly, careful so that it wouldn't slide out of my fingers. I massaged the shampoo into my sweaty scalp, letting the bubbles ooze down my face.

I quickly stuck my hair into the hot stream of water, and the foam seeped down my back. I then grabbed the conditioner and struggled to force the stiff liquid out into the palm of my hand. The strong smell of lavender surrounded me, and I let the water work through my clean hair.

I regretfully pulled the knob down, turning the hot water off. I stepped out of the shower, shivering when my body hit the cool air. I quickly tore a fluffy towel from the rack and wrapped it around myself. I darted into my room to examine my assortment of clothes, unsure of what to wear.

I opened my closet and looked up at the sweaters and jackets, perfectly organized in a row. I reached up with my hand, having to stretch to the tips of my toes to reach one of the hangers. I grumbled unintelligibly.

I hated being short.

After deciding on what to wear, I ran a brush through my hair. The natural auburn highlights were slowly revealing themselves against the darkened wet strands.

I put my shirt on, surprised by how it fit. It used to be more tightly fitted, but now it hung off my narrow shoulders like a drape, at least three sizes too large. I slipped on a pair of jeans and grabbed a belt, ignoring the fact that I had to button it to the tightest hole, and even then I easily had a couple of inches of extra room.

The sun was beginning to rise, the golden rays leaking through the drapes over my windows. One of the sunbeams landed directly on a pile of papers on my dresser, drawing my attention.

I slowly walked toward the pile of papers, my mind filled with memories of much happier times. I flipped through all of my sketches and paintings, remembering how the urge would fill me to begin to draw. I remembered how my hand had seemed to rush across the page in a blur as I created nearly lifelike images.

I felt a sense of nostalgia as I looked at the sketches and paintings, yearning for the happiness that they seemed to symbolize. I turned away from them, a stony expression on my face. Those were from a very long time ago.

I never drew anything now.

I walked down the stairs, struggling to force energy into my lifeless step. I needed to show my parents how unaffected I was by the nightmare.

I plastered a smile onto my face as I walked into the kitchen but then hesitated slightly when I saw the dark expression in my father's eyes as he sat reading the paper.

Gritting my teeth, I walked in and said in a bright voice, "So, Dad, what's for breakfast?" He looked up from his newspaper and barely acknowledged me with a nod. I felt my heart drop to my toes. I could tell he easily saw through my act and wasn't going to respond to my attempt at lightheartedness.

With a dark feeling at the pit of my stomach, I slowly walked around the kitchen to make my own breakfast. It was clear that he was going to ignore me, as if it was my fault that he was as unhappy as he was.

Guilt surged through me when I realized that he was right. Maybe I *was* the cause of all his misfortunes. He had a good life before last May. My mom never pressured him about his job or about what he did or where he was going. If I had never gone after Robbie, my father's life would have continued exactly the way it was.

The heavy silence in the kitchen pressed upon me like a quilt on a warm summer's night. His stiff shoulders and thick brow stopped me from saying anything that might lift the weight of the deathlike hush. I heard the clicking of my mother's heels on the tile floor before I saw her face.

"Feeling better?" she asked me, her eyes soft with concern. I often looked at her light brown eyes and my father's near black eyes, wondering where my blue eyes came from.

I looked away from her and nodded, trying to keep my face as uplifted and cheerful as possible. Without touching a bite of my now soggy cereal, I checked the clock. My heart jolted; it was time to leave.

"It's time to go," I said, struggling to keep my voice even.

My parents glanced at each other with worried looks; for once they were in agreement. I looked away, angry that I was unable to hide anything from them.

I used to be relatively good at lying, but that was another skill I lost.

I got into my old rusted car, holding the key in the ignition as it slowly roared to life. I barely noticed the crisp November air or the way the sky sparkled blue. When I heard the engine churning evenly, I released the key, gently easing my foot on the gas pedal.

The engine of the old car whined louder as it slowly moved forward. The barren trees whipped by me in a brown blur, but I didn't pay attention to the familiar scenery for long. I was straining to repress the wild stirring in my stomach that clouded my thoughts and deterred my focus.

As I drove toward the outskirts of Philadelphia where my private school was located, I noticed that a large part of the forest was completely gone. I slowed my car and stared in horror at the destruction.

Every single one of the beautiful trees was burned to the ground; their only remnants were the black ashes that scattered the barren earth. In my quick examination of the area, I could tell that no more life remained in the once elegant woods.

I wanted to stop the car and go walk among the lifeless soil, but I didn't. I shook myself out of a horrified reverie and continued to drive. Another urge filled me, one that I hadn't felt in a long time.

I wanted to sketch the deathly visage before me.

I was now completely distracted, unfocused on what I was doing. I couldn't get my mind off of the destroyed forest. How could I have been so blind as to miss that? I must have gone on that road at least a few times since last May.

I made a left turn, but my eyes were still fixed on the forest in my rearview mirror.

A dark blue sedan came through the intersection—just about the same time that I turned into their lane.

I wrenched my eyes away from the mirror and stared in front of me. For a second, it felt like my heart had stopped beating, before thundering loudly at the rate of a freight train.

There was about half a second of silence where I knew what was going to happen before it did. The sound of squealing metal and shattering glass broke the quiet of the morning. I felt my eyes widen as the front of my car contorted, slamming into the sedan.

I felt my body being thrown against the seatbelt, and the airbag exploded in my face. My arms twisted painfully as I struggled to hold the steering wheel and keep control of the car.

As soon as it had happened, everything stopped and grew silent. My head and back throbbed, and I could feel my body shivering. I slowly tensed my muscles to see if I was injured. Nothing really bothered me except for the aching in my head.

Remembering the other driver, I looked up through my windshield to see if he was okay. My heart stopped. In front of me, in the car that I had just nearly destroyed, was a man with electric blue eyes, so blue they couldn't have been real. As I stared, his pupils slowly began to change into narrow slits, running vertically through his eyes.

In the next instant they were gone—both the car and its driver.

Chapter 2

I sat in my car, my hands trembling as I struggled to rationalize what happened. *Did I hit a tree—not a car?*

Darker thoughts slowly entered my brain. Was I going crazy? Was I going to have another fit?

Trying to repress the panic, I pushed the thoughts out of my head. I realized I was in the middle of the road and blocking people's way. I pulled over, surprised when my car moved forward without a problem. I quickly got out to assess the damage.

My mouth dropped open when I looked at the old car; there wasn't a single scratch on it that wasn't there before. It looked the same as when I pulled out of the driveway that morning.

I could still feel the way the car shuddered as it hit the other car. I had seen the contortion of the front and the shattering of lights. I ran my hand over the front of the car, trying to detect some evidence of the accident that I was sure had happened.

Calling the police briefly crossed my mind, but without evidence, they would never believe me. I sighed and shook my head, refusing to let my thoughts get out of control.

I got into the front seat again and turned the key, surprised when the gentle hum of the engine came to life. I listened for any abnormal sounds but could detect nothing.

I pulled out onto the road again.

Had I imagined the entire thing? The sharp ache of whiplash contradicted that heavy thought. If I didn't imagine it, then what the hell happened?

I struggled to puzzle through and rationalize the crazy scenario. I went through the sequence of events over and over but couldn't come up with a single explanation for what had happened. I was convinced that I had made up the clear blue eyes of the driver. I had seen them only in my dream.

I was so lost in my thoughts that I barely noticed when I pulled into the driveway of the school. I looked around, wondering if anything had changed since I had last been there, five months before.

A large brick building sprawled across the brown fields. From where I was, it was possible to see the turf field and track behind the building. Two parking lots were on either side of the building, and I drove my car to the lot that said Student Parking.

When my eyes registered all the familiar faces around me, my heart raced into a sprint, and sweat began to break out on my forehead. What would they think? What would they say? One day I was there, and the next I was gone. None of them knew what had happened to me, not even my closest friends.

What would my friends think? Would Sarah, Adrienne, and Jen ever forgive me for not calling them or telling them what had happened to me? I struggled to steady my breathing as I pulled into a parking space. I saw a few curious glances at the car, but I knew that the minute they saw my face, they would whisper and gawk as I walked by. I closed my eyes and leaned my aching neck against the back of the seat before getting out of the car.

As I walked through the crowd of students, I kept my head down and stared at my feet. I kept myself hidden in the hair falling around my face, a straight sheet of auburn that covered me until it reached my waist. I looked up only once in a while, hoping not to be recognized, but when whispers began to break out among people in the hall, I suddenly felt angry that no one had even tried to say hi to me yet.

Once the anger coursed through me, I wasn't afraid to show my face anymore. I felt someone's eyes on me, and I couldn't resist looking up, expecting to see a nosy former acquaintance. However, the face I saw was not one I recognized. He must have been new to the school, and I couldn't help the way my heart gave a little jolt.

His hard features were softened by a wave of thick black hair that hung down and brushed the top of his nose. I quickly brought my eyes down again and didn't look up until I was sure that he had passed.

I gave him one more curious look before I turned to the office door and opened it. It was a small room with posters and bulletin boards, all surrounding a squat man sitting at a desk. I was still going to take the junior classes even though I hadn't finished any of the sophomore courses. My grades had been high enough that the school permitted me to stay with my class.

Mr. Bealer stared at me for some time before recognition finally crossed over his features. "Harmony?" he finally asked, and I nodded, struggling to repress my irritation. I really hadn't changed that much.

"Hello, Mr. Bealer," I said, forcing a polite smile. I could see pity behind his muddy brown eyes, and I could feel my anger rising again. I didn't need his sympathy.

"How are you doing?" he asked.

"Well," I said, hoping I was able to lie more effectively to him than to my parents. I kept the muscles of my face relaxed and my eyes on his.

"Here's your schedule," he said, placing a sheet of paper in front of me. "I alerted your teachers that you'd be returning. Okay? Any questions?"

I shook my head, keeping my smile. He reached over his desk to shake my hand, and I had no choice but to extend my own. The minute he let go of my hand, I turned and left, glancing down at my schedule for my homeroom and first class.

I walked through the familiar halls with their dark blue lockers and starched white walls. I checked my locker number and combination, walking straight there. I kept my head down as I tried to ignore the whispers that seemed to follow me everywhere. Even though it had been five months, I opened the locker easily. A wave of dust swirled when I threw a pile of books into the bottom. A tickling sensation crept up my nose, and I let out a loud sneeze that reverberated off the walls of the hallway.

"Bless you," someone said, and I jumped at the sound of the familiar voice.

"Sarah?" I asked, keeping my voice soft. I could feel my heart beating in my throat as I waited for a reply. She had turned around to face me at the sound of her name. She hadn't changed much since the last time I saw her. She was still tall and thin with large brown eyes and sandy brown hair. When she laid her eyes on me, there was no immediate recollection, but then it only took her about half a second to finally recognize me.

Her mouth dropped open, and she was gawking at me with a staggered expression on her face. "Harmony?" she whispered.

I rolled my eyes. That was the second time I had heard that incredulous tone today, and I knew it wouldn't be the last.

"Hi, Sarah," I said, and suddenly I was enveloped in a huge hug that nearly sucked the life out of me.

"Oh my God, what happened? You completely disappeared for months! It was as if one day you came and then the next … you didn't." I could hear the sadness in her voice. She pulled away from me, an angry expression slowly emerging. "What happened?" she asked.

I knew she deserved an explanation—so did all of my friends. That was, however, the one thing I couldn't give.

"I …" I started. She looked at me impatiently, and I could see her registering the emaciated, paler, sadder version of my former self. She was trying to hide her shock, but I could read it in her eyes. I took a deep breath to try to steady myself. "I don't really want to talk about it," I said.

Her expression hardened. "Look," she said, and she couldn't keep the anger out of her voice this time. "I actually thought we were friends. If you don't want to be friends with me, Jen, and Adrienne, then you don't have to."

"Sarah, you know that's not what I meant! If you had any idea what happened, you wouldn't say things like that."

"Well, if you would just tell me, then maybe I could have some sympathy for you. I tried calling a few times during the summer, but your phone was disconnected."

I was just beginning to see the damage I had done to our friendship.

"My parents moved after … I know I shouldn't have kept anything from you guys. And I will tell you … but it's hard for me to talk about." I felt the tears start to bud. In a vain attempt to hide them from her, I blinked them back.

"Oh, Harmony," she said, and she pulled me in for another hug. I breathed a sigh of relief; to lose her friendship would have ruined me. "Let's go find Jen and Adrienne," she said as she turned away from me and darted into the heavy crowd. I struggled to follow her, my heart thudding in my ribs at the thought of a similar encounter with Jen and Adrienne. I followed her to the cafeteria.

The minute they saw me, they stared at me in shock, just as Sarah had done. Then they were running toward me, and I was surrounded by them as they all enveloped me in a hug.

"You don't understand how worried we were!" Jen exclaimed. "You just disappeared, and none of us knew anything!"

"What happened?" interrupted Adrienne. Her dark eyes analyzed me carefully.

My tongue felt strangely thick as I gave them the same lame excuse I gave Sarah, "I can't tell you … I'm sorry," I said, wincing at the shocked expressions on their faces.

"What?" Jen said, looking almost heartbroken.

"I thought we were supposed to be friends," Adrienne said. They had every right to be angry; I had left them hanging, and they had absolutely no warning before I seemed to disappear from the earth.

"You're right," I said, and I couldn't believe the words that seemed to leave my lips of their own accord. I knew that if I said anything else, I would lose their friendship. I needed their support to help me get through the next few weeks. Guilt seemed to overwhelm me out of nowhere. How selfish was I that I would demand their support with no explanation?

"I *will* tell you," I said, keeping my eyes down. There was silence, and I could tell they were waiting for me to continue. "But not now. It's not something I can talk about here."

"Why don't we all go to one of our houses this afternoon? That way we can catch up with each other's lives," Sarah suggested.

"Good idea," Adrienne said, but I still didn't like the way she was staring at me.

"All right," I agreed, trying to keep my voice even. The thought of what I would have to share caused my heart to pound loudly against my chest.

"Whose homeroom do you have?" Sarah asked me, snatching my schedule out of my hands. "Good, it's the same as ours." We all started to walk to homeroom; they were silent, and I could feel their probing glances in my direction.

Every once in a while, I looked up to see familiar faces swirling around me. They all wore identical expressions of curiosity and suspicion. I could feel my face blush scarlet; the last thing that I wanted was all this attention.

We walked into the classroom, and I stopped by our English teacher's desk, Mr. Arlington. He was tall and bald with small, narrow eyes behind a pair of thick glasses. "Harmony?" he exclaimed. Anger coursed through me again as, like everyone else, he seemed surprised by my appearance. "Glad to have you back." He looked back down at his papers, but I could see the curiosity on his face. My parents had specifically asked Mr. Bealer not to tell any of the other teachers what had happened to me.

I turned and was struck by the sight of the abnormally tall boy I saw earlier. He was sitting in the seat in front of mine with books spilling over his desk. I studied him for a second and glanced at Sarah, Jen, and Adrienne, giving them a questioning look. All three of their faces said, *we'll tell you later.* I sat behind him and slowly took my textbooks and notebooks out.

I could tell Sarah, Jen, and Adrienne were trying to include me, but we had spent way too much time apart to just pick up where we had left off. I sat quietly off to the side while they delved into conversation. The bell rang, signaling the start of class, and we all turned to face the front as Mr. Arlington stood up to start talking about the last story the class had read. I hadn't opened a text book since last May and could barely follow the discussion. I was far too short to see over the head of the boy in front of me anyway.

"Do me a favor," Mr. Arlington said. "Keith, switch places with Harmony." Without saying a word, he smoothly stood up and scooped up his books as I did the same. We slid past each other in the narrow space, and I noticed how he pushed up against the desk to avoid brushing up against me. My heart jolted at our close proximity.

As if he could hear it, his head snapped up, and for the first time I noticed the angles of his face. I saw how his sharp cheekbones and hard jaw stood out against his pale, thin features. I couldn't bring myself to meet his eyes before slowly settling in the seat in front of him.

Mr. Arlington's dreary voice faded into a gentle hum as I once again examined the events of the morning. As I analyzed the situation again, it seemed impossible that my car collided with another car, but what had happened? Finally the bell rang, and I decided to ignore the peculiar events of the morning and focus on getting to my next class. As I left the room, Sarah, Jen, and Adrienne caught up with me.

"Who was that guy sitting behind me? I didn't recognize him," I said, keeping my voice down and scanning the crowd to make sure he wasn't nearby.

"Oh, that's Keith Draykon," Jen said.

"He's kind of odd," Adrienne added.

"What do you mean 'odd'?" I asked them.

"Well he doesn't really talk to anyone," Sarah said, and for the first time, I noticed an identical blush in all of their cheeks. It took me a second to realize that they all thought he was incredibly attractive, something I hadn't been able to bring myself to notice. In fact, it seemed impossible for me to find someone attractive ever again.

"Yeah," Jen agreed. "The only time anyone ever hears him talk is when the teachers call on him."

"Really? That is weird." I sighed, frustrated at how awkward it was to talk to my former best friends. "So …" I said, struggling to keep the conversation going, knowing I was the reason for the strange silence between us. "What classes do you have now?"

"History."

"Science."

"Gym."

"I'll see you later then," I said, and I felt a blush creep into my cheeks as I turned and headed in the opposite direction toward math. I should've forced myself to pay attention to my classes, especially on the first day of school. I couldn't get my brain to focus on anything the teachers were saying, and all of their voices faded into the same gentle drone.

After history, I wandered slowly toward the cafeteria, a headache already starting to pound mercilessly against my temples. I kept my eyes on my feet, not making eye contact with anyone. Out of nowhere, I collided with someone, causing my books and theirs to go flying in different directions.

"Oh!" I let out a squeak of surprise as I stared at the middle of someone's shirt before slowly raising my eyes and craning my neck back to look at his face.

"I'm sorry," he muttered before bending down to retrieve our books.

"No, it was my fault. I should have been paying better attention," I said as I grabbed some of his.

"Maybe I should have been paying better attention," he said in a low, raspy voice. His eyes were a bright startling blue, so bright that he could have been wearing contacts.

"Maybe we both should have," I said, taking my books from his arms, being extremely careful not to brush my hand against him.

"Yeah," he said, gazing past me before saying, "By the way, I'm Keith."

"Harmony," I said, nodding at him, pretending I didn't already know his name.

A small smile pulled at the corners of his lips, breaking the hard mask that had seemed to be in place, before he said, "Nice to meet you."

"Same," I said. "You have lunch now?"

"Yeah."

"See you around then?" I asked.

"Sure," he responded and turned and headed down the hallway. I stared at his retreating back. He didn't act nearly as antisocial as Jen, Adrienne, and Sarah made him out to be. Suddenly all three of them ran up to me, trying and failing to keep their voices down.

"Were you just talking to Keith?" Sarah squeaked at me.

"Um … yeah."

"And he like … spoke words?" Jen said, brushing her fingers through her honey blonde hair, her blue eyes bright and excited.

"No," Adrienne said sarcastically at her. "I'm sure he just made these caveman grunting noises at her and walked away." She looked at us with a completely straight face until Sarah and Jen burst out laughing. It would look weird if I didn't at least start chuckling, so I forced my lips to make some semblance of a smile.

"How did you get him to actually speak to you?" Sarah said excitedly.

"I wasn't really paying attention to where I was going, and I just … ran into him."

"That was it?" Jen said, a disappointed expression on her face. Sarah and Adrienne burst out laughing as we walked through the cafeteria.

"What?" I said.

"Well," snickered Adrienne, "she tried that already."

"What are you talking about?" I asked, and then I remembered the bright blush on Jen's cheeks earlier that morning. "Well, he was actually very nice. You guys made it sound as if he didn't talk at all."

"He doesn't," said Adrienne seriously, and I shrugged. I didn't need another thing that would make my headache worse. We settled down at a table, and awkwardness came over us again. I looked at my dish and picked at my food, not really feeling like eating anything.

"Look whose back!" I jumped at the familiar voice of my old crush, Damon. I looked at his face and remembered something that seemed from a different time. My old feelings for him seemed so far, like they were worlds away and there was no possibility that they would ever return. He sat down next to me, and I struggled not to cringe away from him.

I could feel Jen, Adrienne, and Sarah's eyes watching me, studying my less than enthusiastic reaction. I tried to ignore them and studied Damon, rationalizing his behavior. It was understandable; we had almost been going out when I disappeared.

"So, what happened to you?" he asked.

What was I supposed to say to him? There was no possible way I would tell him the truth, but I didn't want to lie to his face.

"I … I …" I stuttered, and I stared at my hands, my fingers curled and twisted in my lap.

"Well?" he asked, and I could tell he was getting impatient with me.

"I don't really want to talk about it," I said, forcing confidence into my voice even though I desperately lacked it.

"I get it," he said, and he was studying me seriously.

"You do?"

"Sure. Hey, why don't we go out later this week—celebrate you coming back. What do you say?"

I stared at him speechless. A long time ago, I would have been thrilled by such an offer.

"Maybe another time," I said, keeping my eyes down and my voice low. I tried not to cringe as his faced hardened.

"All right," he said, confidence still ringing in his voice. "We need to get reacquainted first. That's fine." Damon walked away, and my hammering heart began to slow. I would have to put him off as much as possible, since I wouldn't be able to deal with his pressure to continue our fledgling relationship right now. Sarah, Adrienne, and Jen were staring at me as if I was completely crazy, so I avoided their eyes, praying that they wouldn't ask me about it now.

I looked up from my barely eaten food and saw Keith staring at me from across the cafeteria. My heart jolted once again with the intensity of his electric blue eyes. He turned away from me, but I continued to study him, comparing him to the terrifying figure in my dream the night before, and his eyes to the eyes of the driver in the mysterious car accident that morning. I shook the thought out of my head. It was just a dream; the accident never happened.

I turned away and tried to involve myself with the conversation that was going on around me. I was grateful my friends tried to include me in their discussion, even if my heart wasn't in it.

"You won't believe this," whined Jen.

"What?" we all said together.

"Ecology gave us a *huge* project that's going to be due sometime in the spring. Can you believe that? And she's forcing us to work in pairs, and we don't even get to choose! I'm stuck with Danny Richardson."

"*That* sucks," Adrienne said. "I hope I get someone smart."

"Don't we all?" asked Sarah, and they immediately fell into a heated discussion about who the best partner would be.

"So, whose house do you want to go to later?" Jen said, and I felt my heart slowly speed up as I thought of how I was going to explain my disappearance. The bell rang, and I jumped a little in my seat.

"Why don't we go to mine?" said Sarah.

"Sounds good," Adrienne said.

"Yep," Jen said as we started to split into different directions. All three of them suddenly stared at me, and I could tell they were waiting for me to say something.

"Don't worry. I'll be there." I tried to keep my voice even, but it ended up coming out like a whisper.

Chapter 3

I headed off to Ecology by myself. Despite the discomfort with my friends, I was disappointed that we had few classes together. The minute I walked into the classroom, I could feel people watching me. I tried to ignore the way their eyes pierced right through me. Ms. Shelns bustled in, her gray eyes scanning the class. I kept my eyes down and felt my hand start to curve around the paper to form a doodled drawing.

"Okay, I'm sure you heard from the students in the morning class that you all will be doing a long-term project. You and a partner will study a problem in ecology and inform the class—" Her voice cut off as the door opened and Keith walked in, his blue-black hair hiding his face from view.

"I'm sorry I'm late," he muttered, and I could feel everyone lean forward to catch what his voice sounded like. I suppressed the urge to roll my eyes; some people could be so ridiculous.

He quickly moved down one of the rows and sat in the desk next to mine. I kept my eyes on my desk, focusing on the empty lined paper in one of my notebooks.

Ms. Shelns continued, "You and your partner will have to come up with a topic that you will be researching for the remainder of the year. By the end of that time, you are expected to present the evolution of your topic in one form or another and tell whether or not the problem was solved. Any questions?"

The heavy silence in the room reeked of resentment; nearly twenty faces wore identical masks of anger and frustration.

Ms. Shelns smirked slightly. "All right, I will now assign partners: Allison and Mike, Micaela and Emily, Keith and …" She paused, studying her list carefully.

The entire room held their breath, and again I fought the urge to roll my eyes. "Harmony." I started slightly at the sound of my name and immediately turned toward Keith. He was watching me carefully, but there was no trace of the earlier friendliness. He wore an emotionless expression, his blue eyes hard crystals in his face. I unsuccessfully tried to smile at him; his hard mask frightened me.

Ms. Shelns finished naming off the pairs of students and then said, "You have the remainder of the class to discuss topics for this project with your partners. After class, someone from your group will tell me what topic you have chosen." The minute her voice drifted into silence, loud talking erupted, and people broke into pairs. I turned my body to face Keith's and tried to start a conversation.

"So …" I said. "What kind of things are you interested in?"

"Well …" he said, and the look on his face softened. "I don't really follow current events or ecology very much, so it's hard to say."

"Okay," I said, and I could feel myself relax as he did. "I'm guessing you're not into energy conservation?"

"No," he said, and his trace of a smile became slightly more pronounced. "What ecological problems are *you* interested in?"

"I don't really follow them that much either," I said.

"This puts us in a real dilemma, doesn't it?" he said facetiously.

"Have there been any natural disasters lately? There's usually plenty of information available on those," I said brightly as he watched me carefully. I could tell that he wasn't fooled by my false enthusiasm.

Couldn't I lie to anyone anymore? Even someone who I'd barely met could hear a false note in my voice. It used to be something I was pretty good at.

"I don't know," he said, and the smallest of smiles crossed his face again. "I don't really watch the news."

"Oh my gosh!" I suddenly exclaimed, with true enthusiasm this time.

"You know those woods that are burned down on that road ... oh, what's it called?"

"I know what you're talking about. I live right near there ..." he said, and his husky voice slowly trailed off as if he were waiting for me to continue.

"Well, we could do like ... what caused it, and can anything be done to help ..." I suddenly thought of my irrational urge to draw earlier. "I used to draw. I could sketch pictures of it as it grows back." I watched his expression carefully and could see he was intrigued by the idea.

"Sounds good. I like the plan of doing something closer to home," he said, and I nodded.

"We could have done global warming," I snickered.

"No, that's too political," he said, but I could see the smile on his face. The bell rang, and we both stood up. Again I was struck by his height, towering nearly a foot and a half above me. "So what class do you have now?" he asked.

"Ugh ... Spanish," I muttered, not looking forward to what was probably my least favorite subject.

"Gym." He turned away from me and said, "I'll tell Ms. Shelns about the project, okay?"

"Sure," I said before I walked out the door, resisting the urge to turn and stare at him. I walked to Spanish by myself, pondering my friends' experience with Keith in contrast to my own. Talking to him had felt like a breath of fresh air from the constant dark clouds that hovered and oppressed me. Even though I just met him, I wanted to talk to him again as the dark clouds came storming back. I heard Damon's familiar voice behind me.

"Harmony!"

I half-turned to look at him and gave the smallest of smiles.

"So, what's new with you?" he asked loudly, and I struggled not to cringe at the way his voice carried.

Straining my tone in an attempt to be casual, I said, "I just got that project from Ecology." I forced myself to sound angry and resentful, just like everybody else.

"Ah, that sucks. Who's your partner?"

"Keith ... I don't really know his last name."

Suddenly Damon looked furious, his features twisted into a snarl.

"What's wrong?" I asked him, startled by his reaction. As quickly as it appeared, his expression smoothed over, and he gave me a look.

"Nothing—he's just a freak, that's all." I could hear the air of superiority in his voice, and I felt anger rise and burn in my stomach.

"He's not weird, at least not when I talked to him," I said, surprised at the coldness in my voice.

"Well," he said, "you don't know him."

"And you do?" I asked, not sure why I was fighting with him over this.

"I know his … family." I could hear his sneer, and I looked up at him. Before that horrible night last May, I had never noticed the arrogance in him. I sighed and let the subject drop.

"What are you doing for your topic?" I asked him, eager to make peace.

"Global warming," he said seriously, and I could feel a smirk bubble to my lips as I recalled my conversation with Keith. "The earth's welfare is a concern for everyone," he said, sounding so much like a politician that I couldn't help the smile that broke across my face. I didn't laugh. I never laughed much anymore. But Damon burst out laughing—at himself, it seemed.

"I'm guessing you have Spanish now?" he asked, and I nodded. "At least we have one class together." He sounded eager.

As I walked into the familiar classroom, I saw Sarah and Jen sitting in the back, and I lifted my hand to wave.

Sarah smiled when she saw me walk in with Damon, and I tried not to grimace, hoping that she wouldn't read too much into the situation. I immediately went and sat next to her and smiled slightly.

"So, we were thinking of meeting at my house at around four. Is that okay?" she asked.

"Yeah, that's fine." I looked away, my heart hammering against my chest as I thought of how I would answer the questions that I knew were coming. I didn't listen to a single word Mr. Scott said as he talked about prepositions and their use in a sentence.

Chapter 4

I pulled up to Sarah's house a little after four o'clock, clutching the steering wheel of my car so hard that my skin stretched tightly around my knuckles. I barely noticed when the noise coming from my engine suddenly cut off as I pulled the key out of the ignition.

Jen and Adrienne had pulled up at around the same time and were staring at me intently.

I was so dazed that I barely noticed when Sarah answered the door. We all went up to her room, and I didn't even feel the uncomfortable silence; for me, it wasn't silent.

I could barely hear Sarah say my name, but it sounded strangely far away.

I remembered vaguely when I had a nervous breakdown, not long after Robbie's betrayal. I could feel myself spinning out of control, just as I had then.

"Harmony, chill," Adrienne said, and it was her harsh words that stopped my wild spinning. They snapped me back to reality. I had opened my mouth to back out, to tell them that I couldn't do it, that I wasn't strong enough.

But I was strong enough. I had to be. If I didn't tell them now, I would lose them. I couldn't afford that in this incredibly dark hour of mine.

A dark hour that seemed to last forever.

Taking a shaky breath, I started my tale.

"You know I used to live in the middle of Philly, right?" I started off, and shock flitted across their faces.

"You moved? That explains why your phone was disconnected," Jen said, and I nodded.

"I'll get to that part. So you guys know that's where I grew up. When I was little, I had a very good friend; we were so close, it was as if we were siblings. We did everything together even though he was a few years older than I was. His name was …" I paused, forcing myself to say the painful words. "His name was Robbie. He was in high school, and I was in middle school when we slowly started to grow apart.

"He got involved with new friends. That's when I came to this school as a freshman and met you guys. Anyway, we drifted farther and farther apart, but I still cared for him like a brother … and I thought he cared for me that way too.

"Well, let's just say when we were sophomores and he was a senior, he got involved in some really shady things—drugs, alcohol, et cetera—and his parents remained blissfully ignorant, as did my parents. They were good friends.

"Sometime last May, I found out he was planning something extremely harmful, not only to him, but to other people too. So I ignored all of my instincts and snuck out and followed him and his friends.

"I caught up to him and asked him to stop." My voice broke at the painful memory, and all three of my friends were watching me with identical expressions of horror. "But there was no way that I could reason with him. He had already been drinking that night.

"He warned me to stay away from him." I stared off into the distance as I felt the tears begin to pool in my eyes. "I tried again the next night to redirect him from the horrible path he had chosen.

"He had been drinking more that night and was angry with me. He again warned me to stay away and said he wouldn't be so nice if I followed him again.

"I suppose he warned me and I should have listened, but I couldn't help but go out again that third time. To say he was furious was an understatement, and for the first time, I was truly frightened of what he might do to me. That was when I realized that our friendship didn't matter to him anymore—and it hadn't mattered for a while.

"I walked home slower than I should have; I was too upset by his betrayal to move any faster. At first, I didn't realize they were following me." I paused again and smiled grimly at the faces of my three horrified friends. "When I realized it, what else could I do but run? I sprinted as fast as I could toward my house, but I knew that they were much faster than I was, even in their intoxicated state. I tried, stupidly, to fool them by going down an alley.

"I didn't see that it was a dead end until it was too late. I looked up at the building surrounding me, and the windows were empty and lifeless; no one would hear me if I screamed." Jen shuddered next to me, and I decided to skip some of the details of the story that they wouldn't want to hear.

"You can probably guess what happened next … and then they left me there in the street. When my parents found my bed empty in the morning, they called 911 and I was found.

"No one believed me when I told them who the culprits were. My parents refused to believe that the son of their good friends would do something like that."

"Wait—did they, like, beat you up?" Adrienne interrupted.

"No, they didn't beat me up," I said quietly, glancing up at the three confused expressions on my friends' faces. "They raped me."

The stunned silence that followed my words seemed to echo louder than wild screaming. I took another deep breath as I resisted the urge to run.

"After having a nervous breakdown a couple of weeks after, I went to rehab for a couple of months, till September, but my psychiatrist didn't recommend starting school till now." My eyes had overflowed a long time ago, and the tears streamed down my face. I hadn't cried in a very long time, and retelling my story—the entire story—felt good.

"Oh, Harmony," Sarah said, and she was the first to reach forward to give me a much needed hug.

Jen still stared at me, her blue eyes horrorstruck. "Harmony, if we had known, we never would have asked you to—"

I cut her off quickly, my voice still uneven. "But you didn't know, which was why I had to tell," I said, and I smiled through my tears, grateful that they all listened to me.

"Why didn't you tell us last May about your efforts to help Robbie? I don't remember ever hearing his name before now," Adrienne said. "We could have helped you."

"We were already drifting apart by that time; he was almost like my little secret that I didn't tell anybody about. I convinced myself that it was something I had to do alone," I said, wishing I had done things differently.

"After that, it makes everything we've done seem superficial," Jen said, and I just gave her a small smile. All three of them suddenly swarmed around me and gave me a huge hug. I held them close, as a feeling of relaxation came on me. It was such a relief to have my story off of my chest. They slowly pulled away, and there was a pause. It was clear that no one really knew what to say.

"So, who's your partner for that Ecology project?" Sarah said, clearly trying to distract me from everything that I had just revealed.

I felt my smile widening as I thought of what their reactions would be. "Keith." Shock flickered on every one of the faces in the room.

"How did you come up with a topic? Did he say anything?" Jen said immediately.

"Yeah, actually."

"So, what are you guys doing for the project?" Adrienne asked.

"We're studying the fire that destroyed the woods in town, and what they're trying to do to fix it."

"That's cool," Jen said, but the silence settled over us again. As much as I wished for everything to be the same with our friendship, I knew that it couldn't. I had gone through too much for them to possibly understand me. But at the same time, I needed them to restore some normalcy to my life.

"What are you doing about Damon?" Adrienne asked.

"I have no idea. I don't think I'm ready to start a relationship with anybody right now. I better get home," I said and stood up.

"Harmony, if you need anything, just call us, okay?" Sarah said, and I smiled a thanks at them. Even though I knew that they had no capacity to help me, I was touched that they each gave me a hug as I left.

On my way home from Sarah's house, I forced myself to concentrate on nothing but the road ahead of me, frightened that I would have another mystery accident. I passed the completely destroyed woods, and I felt sadness well up inside me.

I looked across the road to the healthy forest and then back to the ashes. The grief pulled at my stomach, and my heart beat unevenly. The two woods were like my life—how it once was, and how it was now.

I pulled over onto the shoulder of the road and grabbed my camera out of my purse.

I got out of my car and aimed the camera at the desolation before me. Just as I was going to capture the picture, a gust of wind blew from behind me. It swirled the ashes from the ground, forming a black cloud that twirled around the remaining black trunks.

I pressed the small button, and the click was impossible to hear against the whisper of the wind in my ears. I looked at the miniature version of the picture I had just taken and smiled.

It wasn't too early to begin the ecology project.

The minute I walked through the door of the house, I rushed upstairs, eager to download the picture of the woods and begin my drawing.

"Harmony!" I heard my father's voice thunder, and I froze, surprised that he was home at that time. I turned around and went down to the kitchen.

"How was your day?" he said stiffly, as if even talking to me was painful.

"Fine," I said quickly, and I could feel his dark eyes X-raying my face for any signs of falsehoods. For once I was actually telling the truth, so there was nothing for him to detect. "We already got a project from school. We have to work with partners," I grumbled, hoping to make conversation.

"Who's your partner?" he said, and for the first time, he didn't sound angry, only very tired. He filled a glass with water and slowly took a drink.

"His name is Keith."

"Keith …?"

"Draykon, I think." As the words left my lips, his eyes bulged, and the water that he had in his mouth nearly spewed all over the kitchen.

"What?" he hissed.

"I didn't pick him for a partner; we were assigned by the teacher," I squeaked, terrified by his reaction. He put his water glass down and slowly rubbed his temples with his two pointer fingers.

"His last name is Draykon you said?"

"Yeah," I said.

"What does he look like?"

I couldn't help the suspicious feeling that began to crawl into my stomach.

"He's tall with longish black hair and blue eyes."

"I think I know his dad," my dad said, his angry glare slowly fading.

"What? How?" I asked, feeling shock that two different parts of my life could somehow be connected.

"We work at the same company. I see him walking around sometimes," he said dismissively, and my stomach tightened with doubt. He suddenly turned away from me, and again I yearned for the happier time before last May—when my parents were happy, when I was happy.

"Harmony, I know your mother complains a lot about my job, but the reason I've always kept it from you two is for your own safety. It would be dangerous if you knew," he said quietly.

"Why don't you just tell her that?"

"Don't you think I've tried?" he snapped, suddenly angry at me. "She keeps insisting that married couples don't have secrets. She doesn't understand … Anyway, I'm sorry, I shouldn't be telling you this. You probably have homework to do or something."

I ran upstairs, just as eager to get away from him as he seemed to get away from me. While I fought with my tears, I remembered a time when my father and I had a good relationship.

I quickly loaded the picture onto the old computer in the hallway upstairs. It groaned and whined as I asked it to print the picture in color. For once, I didn't care about the amount of ink that I would be using.

The sudden fiery desire to sketch the picture with my own hand was irrepressible. I looked down at the newly printed picture in my hands. The old computer and decrepit printer hadn't been able to ruin the lifelike image.

I could still see the way the cloud of black ash was lifted by the wind and swirled around the few black trunks that were still standing.

I pulled out a piece of my old sketching paper and one of my old, unsharpened charcoal pencils. I held it carefully over the blank sheet of paper, almost frightened that the black pencil would ruin the clear perfection.

Anguish and fury erupted inside of me so strongly, and now more than ever I wished my life was like the soft woods across from the broken ashes.

I wanted vengeance on the person who had burned me.

My pencil came down hard and fast on the pure white sheet of paper and slashed a rigid line across—my horizon line.

I continued in that way, black line after black line. The tears blurred my vision as the picture seemed to create itself out of the furious black slashes. I took my finger and smudged across the paper, creating the movement of the wind over the ashes as they lifted through the trees.

I had the base down, but all of my lines were too hard, too angry. I took my finger again and softened the edges slightly. I gently shadowed the base of a tree, allowing the soft black smudge to run together with the hard line of the trunk.

I stopped and looked at the picture again. The shadows had softened, adding grief to the fury of the picture. The pain welled up inside me again, and I set the paper down on my desk, about to rub my tear-streaked face with my hands.

I looked down at my filthy fingers; they were completely covered with black charcoal from the pencil. I smiled slightly, remembering how filthy I always used to get when I drew.

As I looked down at the picture I had just finished, there was something raw and incomplete about it. Emotion seemed to pulse from every line and shadow, and I looked at the photograph of the image that nature itself had created.

That was the difference between the two pictures. Nature's forest would heal eventually, but mine would stay in ashes forever.

I turned away from the two pictures, exactly the same but frightfully different, to wash the charcoal from my hands. I was suddenly reminded, as the dark smudges slid off my fingers, of the ashes at the bottom of the forest floor.

I slowly washed my face with warm water until all the blotchy redness was out of my face and only my gray-blue eyes showed any sign that I had been crying.

As I returned to my room, I looked at the two pictures with a slightly different perspective. Yes, creating it had been painful, but I felt much better having done it.

As if one stitch had been pulled through a hole that needed fifteen.

Chapter 5

The next morning, I quickly got out of bed, barely glancing at the picture that I had created. I turned it over and shoved it into a folder while I struggled to repress the pain I had felt the night before.

My mind was filled with questions. Was it right to have told my friends? Would they think of me as scarred now that they knew the truth?

As I slowly got ready for school, I couldn't help but feel like something bad was going to happen today. There was an uncomfortable silence that spread over the house.

When I went downstairs, I found my dad was sitting in the kitchen, his expression unreadable. His dark eyes held no light.

"Hi, Dad," I said, struggling to pull him out of his perpetually dark mood. His cool eyes shifted to my face, and he allowed a tight-lipped smile to cross his features before turning away from me again.

On the way to school, I passed by the large section of destroyed woods, the clouds above them hanging low and dark. They cast an ominous shadow over the barren, blackened trees, their silent threats a warning.

I forced myself not to look at the barren trees for too long, knowing that I would be distracted if I stared at them. I focused on the drive ahead of me, but I wasn't able to completely ignore the menacing dark clouds.

I finally arrived at school and breathed a sigh of relief. I was relieved that the stares from other students seemed a little less potent, the whispers a little less cutting.

| 15 Stitches |

"Hey, Harmony," Sarah said as we passed each other in the hallway. She fell into step beside me, and I could feel the breach in our friendship once again.

Jen and Adrienne eventually joined us, and as we walked to class together, they both smiled at me. Still, there was a huge ocean between me and each of them. It was almost harder to talk to them now than it had been yesterday. Yesterday, they sensed the rift between us, but now they realized how impossible it was to cross.

Keith wasn't in class yet when we sat down, and I didn't make a huge effort to include myself in my friends' conversation. I could almost feel the picture that I painted burning a hole in my backpack. I wished I had left it at home, but I needed to show Keith that I had already started on the project.

Keith eventually walked through the door, and his eyes showed the smallest flicker of recognition for me. I knew this was probably the most greeting I was going to get from him, so I gave him a small smile in return.

"Harmony, are you okay?" Jen asked me, and I barely looked at her before nodding.

"I'm fine," I said. I struggled to keep my voice soft and even. The feeling of intense foreboding was upon me, and I struggled to hide it from them. Keith was staring at me with an intent expression on his hard features, but he didn't say anything.

I turned around to face the front of the classroom and pretended to study so that I wouldn't have to talk to them. I wasn't focused on anything. I barely spoke to any of my friends, and I couldn't keep the image of my father's dark expression from this morning or our resigned conversation from yesterday out of my head.

The day seemed to pass by like a movie in fast forward. Before I knew it, it was time for Ecology.

"Okay, everyone, get together with your partners for the first ten minutes of class and discuss your projects," Mrs. Shelns said in her high, fluttery voice. I slowly turned my desk toward Keith's, and he did the same.

"So," he said, surprising me by starting the conversation. "When I talked to Ms. Shelns yesterday, she said that our project was fine but to make sure we have enough information to expand on." He spoke formally and blankly, without putting much emotion in his voice.

"Yeah. That sounds good," I said, and he immediately started talking again.

"Well, I started to do some research on it last night, and they don't seem to be doing much about it, maybe just a little replanting. Nobody really knows what started the fire, and nobody is really trying to figure out what happened. Everyone thinks it's just a random event, but the weather wasn't even very dry when it started."

"That's really scary. To think that someone might have started the fire is really weird though. Why would someone randomly set woods on fire? It doesn't make any sense," I said.

"That's true," Keith replied, "but it could have been an accident or some kids. Anyway, since there isn't much specific information, we could do the project on forest fire prevention in general."

"That's a good idea. Oh, and I did something also." I could feel a blush begin to creep up my neck and flame in my cheeks.

My heart started thundering in my chest as I realized I was about to share the strangely personal picture with him. But would he see the deeper side it? Or would he simply see a charcoal sketch?

"Really?" he said,

"Yeah," I said. I bent down and slowly pulled out the folder where I kept the picture.

It was almost painful to put the folder into his pale fingers, as if I were handing over a piece of myself. I studied his face as he slowly opened it. I saw shock flit across his expression as he examined the picture. I thought he saw the emotion pulsing through each line and shadow.

His blue eyes flashed to my face, and he was suddenly scrutinizing me very carefully. He wasn't looking at the picture anymore; he was watching my face. He seemed to be trying to read something, as if he knew I had a secret.

He suddenly blinked, breaking the strange focus. He snapped the folder shut and said, "It's really good."

"Thanks," I muttered. We fell into silence once more, and my flaming red cheeks refused to return to their normal color. I stared at my twisting fingers as I said, "I was thinking, we should probably meet sometime this weekend and try to learn more about the fire."

"My house or yours?" he asked me in the strangely blank voice of his. I glanced up at his intense blue eyes.

"Um …" I thought about my screaming parents and chaotic household, and the fact that my dad would explode at the sight of a boy in our house. "How about yours?"

"Saturday afternoon at around two? I could come pick you up if you want."

"Okay" I said, reacting to his earnestness. He didn't smile at all while talking. His face was perfectly smooth, as if nothing affected him.

During last period, I couldn't stop fidgeting or doodling. My eyes constantly roamed around, straying to look out the windows. The strange feeling that something horrible was going to happen settled over me again as the day finally ended.

On the drive home, I allowed my foot to get heavier and heavier against the gas pedal as the speedometer inched to fifty miles per hour, and then sixty, and then seventy.

The barren trees blew by me in a brown blur, the wind whistling rapidly past the windshield. I finally arrived home, and to my dismay, I could hear screams of anger coming through the door. Their voices grew louder as I approached.

There was something different about the way they fought this time; there seemed to be a strange finality in the tone of their voices that sent a shiver up my spine. I stopped outside the front door, took a deep breath of the unusually warm November air, and slowly walked in.

The sound of their voices was suddenly intensified upon my entry, the loud shrieks from my mother intermingling with the heavy bellows from my father. I tried to ignore them and slipped quietly into the house unnoticed. I ran up the stairs and barricaded myself in my room.

Clenching my teeth together, I struggled to stem the steady flow while the screeching grew louder with each minute.

My brain was racked with guilt, knowing I was partially the cause of their anger and fights. I heard my father's thundering footfalls when he ascended the stairs and flew past my bedroom door.

"That's *it*!" he bellowed down the stairs before storming into his bedroom and slamming the door behind him.

"Wait!" Mom called after him, her light footsteps barely audible next his loud stride. Her breathless voice screamed for him to open the door, her fists banging desperately on the wooden surface.

After the door was thrown open, I heard my mom say in a panic-stricken voice, "No, we can talk about this!" I heard him running down the stairs, and the knot in my stomach tightened with fear as I suddenly realized what was happening.

"Dad, no!" I screamed. I tore out of my room and sprinted down the stairs while he was yanking open the front door. My tears overflowed once more and streamed down my blotchy red cheeks.

I grabbed onto his jacket with a death grip, bracing myself against his heavy weight. "Dad, don't," I sobbed as he turned to face me. "Please stay," I whispered, clutching his arm with all my might. His eyes softened for a millisecond before they turned to black stone once more.

He allowed two cold words to slip past his teeth—"I'm sorry"—before he put a massive hand on one of my shoulders and pushed back, forcing my fingers to be torn from his jacket.

I stumbled backward and caught myself. I barely heard my mom sobbing in the kitchen as I shrieked at the top of my lungs. He jumped into the car and was pulling away as I ran after him in bare feet.

"Come back!" I croaked at the steadily retreating taillights. I stopped running as I reached the end of our driveway. My sobbing slowly faded as his car disappeared in the distance. After what seemed like an eternity, I dragged myself to the house. I sprinted up the stairs and grabbed my sneakers, frantically tying them with shaking fingers.

"Where are you going?" asked my mother in a broken, shaky voice.

"I need to get out of here. I'll be back soon," I managed to spill out before tearing out the door, letting the tears fall freely. I ignored my blurred vision, and the only sound that I heard was the steady pounding of my feet on the asphalt.

I entered the base of the trail, and the smooth sound of my feet hitting asphalt changed to the rough sound of crunching gravel. The clouds changed to a strange purple color, and sweat began to gather at the base of my back because of the sixty-degree weather.

As I continued to jog through the trail in a steadily darkening sky, I felt a thick raindrop hit my head. My heart sank as large water droplets continued to fall on the branches and the dead leaves on the ground. A soft pattering noise filled the forest and drowned out the sound of my footsteps.

A new kind of darkness filled the sky as the sun sank lower and lower on the horizon. I wasn't really keeping track of where I was running, randomly turning in different directions. A flicker of worry began to enter my stomach as I realized I had absolutely no idea where I was!

It seemed like hours since I had first entered the trail, but now there was no sign of a path. The heavy rain fell continuously, growing in momentum. It soaked me down to the bone, and despite the warm weather, a shiver began to creep up my spine.

I squinted my eyes as another gust of wind funneled through the trail, and I began to tremble even harder.

I turned around and debated whether I should try going back, taking the risk of getting even more lost. After quick deliberation, I continued going the same way, hoping that I would be able to reconnect with the trail somewhere.

I sprinted back and forth, totally losing track of which way I came and which way I was going. The large raindrops continued to pound mercilessly.

"Help!" I screamed. The tremors that had been creeping up my spine intensified, until my shoulders were shaking.

I had no idea what time it was or how long I had been gone. As the rain fell and the wind blew, the trees began swaying dangerously back and forth above the narrow trail.

A flash of lightning suddenly illuminated the dark sky, immediately followed by a large clap of thunder. I jumped, splattering mud on my already soaked shirt. My eyes automatically flew up, only to see the mystifying darkness.

Despite the fact that I was completely lost and sopping wet, I couldn't help the fact that heaviness began to pull on my eyelids.

I sat down on a fallen tree and looked around, the rain disguising any sense of where I was. My eyelids drooped lower and lower as I tried to keep myself awake.

I lost the battle with my fatigue, slowly sliding down the tree trunk to sit on the muddy forest ground. I rested my head against the tree as my eyelids slowly drifted closed.

Frantically looking behind me, I realized that I hadn't evaded my pursuers ...

The nightmare played out exactly as it had every other time.

Seeing that I was trapped, the four of them slowed from their run. I gazed at the face of their leader, and his betrayal cut at me worse than a knife. I never thought that his face would be one I should fear ...

Half of me knew I was dreaming, but that didn't stop the feeling of adrenaline that coursed through my veins as I waited expectantly for them.

I could hear their jeans scraping against the pavement as they sauntered closer ...

"We warned you to stay away," he snarled, and I pressed myself closer to the wall ...

I felt his body press up against me ...

Half of me was waiting for him, for the monster that was going to turn the corner any minute now and save me.

But there was no monster that grew wings from his back to take me out of this nightmare. I couldn't help the new level of fear that I felt when I realized I would have to relive the entire nightmare all over again.

"Help!" I screamed. A hand covered my mouth as he pressed my body to his. I writhed in his grip, struggling to extract myself from his hold on me.

I battled with his hold on my mouth as I strained to work up the energy to scream. He used his other hand to hold both of my hands together. His tall body pressed over me as he called his friends to help.

"Hold her hands," he demanded. I kicked out wildly at him with my legs, although it had no effect. They were going to take me—all four of them—and there was nothing I could do about it.

| 15 Stitches |

A large roar of thunder awakened me from my trance. I was huddled in the mud, tears streaming down my face. Sobs racked through my body as I struggled to stop myself from screaming. I was overwhelmed by an onslaught of memories, from that first horrible night to every night after that. At that moment, another flash of lightning, which was followed by a clap of thunder, illuminated a large figure in front of me. Fear gripped me as I dizzily got to my feet.

"Hello?" I called in the darkness.

"Harmony?" said the figure, and I felt tremendous relief as I recognized his hoarse, expressionless voice.

"Keith?" I said breathlessly, stumbling forward. I had no idea what he was doing there, only that I was so grateful to see him.

"I have one question for you," he said, and his voice was half-relieved, half-teasing. "What are you doing out in the middle of a storm when you should be at home?"

At his question, the memory of that horrible night overwhelmed my weakened defenses.

"Are you okay? You look like you're going to be sick," he said, and suddenly his voice was filled with worry.

"How can you see anything? It's so dark," I said weakly as I took a cautious step forward.

"I have good eyesight," he said dismissively. He took both of my shoulders into his hands, and I looked up to where I thought his face should be. I heard, against the thundering rain, his soft exhale as he slowly bent down. I felt his muscular arms slide under my weak frame, lifting me with ease.

"What are you doing? Put me down," I demanded as I writhed in his grip. I felt his fingers tighten on me.

"Just relax. I'll take you someplace where you can warm up a little bit," he said, and at his words, I completely relaxed and rested my head against his shoulders, allowing my eyes to slide shut and succumb to the pressing blackness.

Chapter 6

The first thing I was conscious of was a thick heavy blanket draped over me. I could feel the steady drip of my wet hair rested against my arm. I was conscious that I was lying on top of something leather; it felt like a sofa with the way it rose up steeply on my right side. I shivered again and curled deeper into the quilt that surrounded me.

I finally blinked my eyes opened and was shocked to see that I was in a place that I didn't recognize. My first impression was that almost every square inch was completely covered in books.

They didn't seem to be just any books either. They looked so old that they could have been in a museum. They were all bound with the same brown, cracking leather. The wonderful smell of old books wafted from the walls, and they seemed to whisper of forbidden secrets.

I struggled to repress the panic as I thought of where I could be. The only idea that made any sort of sense was that I was at Keith's house. But … that didn't make a whole lot of sense either; I had met him only a couple of days ago.

I sat up slowly and looked around at the ancient books, my curiosity suddenly piqued. I slowly slid myself off the edge of brown leather sofa.

In the middle of the towering shelves, my eyes were drawn to a small golden book. Ignoring the occasional shivers that racked my body from the hours in the rain, I slowly walked across the smooth pine flooring toward the book.

My heart pounded against my ribcage as I realized that I shouldn't really be doing this, and I wondered what Keith's reaction was going to be—if I were actually in Keith's house, of course. I carefully removed the golden book from the shelf and flipped it open. The binding crackled from lack of use. My eyes narrowed as they fell over the long, loopy, elegant script, and I slowly started to read.

The story that I tell is true. It is not for entertainment, but for the memory of years long gone. It is the beginning of the end of a once respected race, made out to be evil. It is the start of an everlasting war between two species, a war that would end up with one of those races gone from the face of this earth forever.

The story starts very long ago, so long that it is before the war between Dragons and Griffins began. The story begins with a young Dragon named Zylon. His scales were a sparkling blue, his roar deep and terrifying. His sharp teeth could cut bones like butter, and he could snap trees as if they were twigs.

He had a rebellious nature, and nobody in the Kingdom of Dragons could control him. He would often go on long wanderings to the territories of other races, most often the human territory. It was on one of these wanderings that he would change the way Dragons, and all other intelligent races, live forever.

One day, Zylon went to the human territory to observe how they lived, for he was interested in the unusual looking species. He looked on from a distance as they went about their business, content to watch them.

Out of the large crowd of people, a beautiful maiden stepped out, holding a basket filled with fruit and flowers. Her long blonde hair reached her thin waist, the almost colorless strands gracefully swirling around her fair, angelic face. Her bright red lips were turned up in a slight smile as her startling blue eyes examined the flowers in her basket.

When he saw her, Zylon instantly fell in love with the beautiful maiden. You may think that I jest that a Dragon fell in love with a maiden, but it is true. Every word.

The maiden's eyes were very blue, but they looked gray in comparison to Zylon's startling blue scales. His eyes sparkled with happiness as he looked upon her. He willed the maiden to approach him, hoping that she would not be frightened when she looked upon him.

As Zylon was watching her, she came upon a fork in a trail; she could either go up to the flower patches or toward him. His large heart thudded loudly as she slowly turned toward him.

She looked down at her feet, her long eyelashes brushing her cheeks. When the maiden came into the clearing, she looked up in shock. The maiden had often heard Dragons described by the elders of her race as terrifying creatures with horrible tempers. The Dragon that she saw here was not that terrifying. He had kind, soft eyes, and even though he was large and muscular, he was not threatening.

To Zylon, the maiden was even more beautiful close up than she was far away. A faint peach tone colored her pale cheeks, and her small, soft hands held the basket with unusual grace. When the maiden first laid eyes on Zylon, she smiled tentatively up at him, unsure of what to think. And when Zylon saw that smile, it seemed to him the entire world was glowing.

He and the maiden started to talk, and soon they were in deep conversation and were not watching the time. Before they knew what happened, the sun had started to set and they needed to go home.

"Can I come meet you here tomorrow?" he asked, his lips pulling back across his razor sharp teeth when he smiled.

"Yes," she answered, her soft, bell-like voice ringing through the air. Filled with joy and happiness, Zylon took off and headed home.

From that day forward, Zylon saw the maiden, whose name was Magdalena, every day from dawn until dusk. During the time that he wasn't with her, Zylon was thinking about her.

He struggled to hide where he was going from the others, but it was very difficult. He wanted to jump for joy and tell the world how happy he was, but he couldn't. For if he told the rest of the Dragons, they would forbid Zylon from ever seeing Magdalena again.

Every time he saw her, Magdalena became more and more beautiful to him. Her pale cheeks now glowed a rosy pink, and her sparkling blue eyes shined with happiness.

One day, as Zylon was flying over to the clearing to the human town, he noticed that another creature was with Magdalena. It was a Griffin!

The Griffin was strutting toward her, and Zylon could hear him hissing at her. Magdalena's blue eyes were round with fright, and her chest heaved with *fear. He felt the fire burn like acid deep in his stomach as it threatened to come pouring out of his mouth.*

He restrained a roar so loud that it would awaken the dead that had once been cold in their graves. He folded his wings and flew in a gentle arch, aimed at the Griffin and Magdalena. As he closed in on the Griffin, a growl ripped through his clenched teeth, causing the Griffin to jerk up from his position.

"Get lost, Dragon! I am busy here!" the Griffin jeered with a smirk.

"No!" Zylon practically roared, raising his wings in front of Magdelana. "You get out of here!" Zylon rose to his full height, towering almost three feet above the Griffin. He bared his ivory colored teeth, which glistened in the dazzling light coming from the sun. He felt the fire rise to his throat, but he pressed it down, knowing that if he attacked the Griffin, all peace in the world would be lost. Zylon raised his wings in a threatening posture, making himself look even bigger and more muscular than he was.

The Griffin raised his wings as well, struggling to intimidate the furious Dragon. In response, Zylon rocked back on his hind legs, now easily towering five feet above the Griffin. The Griffin, knowing he was outmatched, took off, flapping his feathery wings in Zylon's face. As the Griffin drifted away, Zylon gave him one last, resounding snarl.

As Zylon slowly lowered himself to all four of his claws, he knew that this encounter would not be forgotten by the Griffin race or his own. He prayed to God that it would not end up in war, for even though the Griffins were smaller, they had cunning that far outmatched that of the Dragons.

I heard the sound of footsteps echoing on the wood outside the door. Suddenly my heart accelerated at the thought of being discovered reading the book.

Keith stepped into the open doorway, his black hair still clinging to his head from the rain. He stared, jaw clenched at the empty couch, his hands balled into fists. He turned around to face me, his face relaxing when he saw that I was still there.

Then he saw the book that was resting lightly in my hands. His bright blue eyes suddenly widened with shock. The instant I registered his expression, it was gone.

"So, I see you discovered one of our books," he said teasingly, but the tone of his voice didn't sound right.

"I'm sorry if I wasn't supposed to read it, Keith. My curiosity got the best of me," I said sheepishly, still puzzled by the slightly frantic expression in his eyes.

"Don't worry about it. That one is one of my personal favorites," he said, his voice relaxing ever so slightly. "It's a really good story. A lot of the other ones are just boring traditions and such, but this one is great."

"Um, Keith …"

"Yeah?"

"Where am I?" I asked uncomfortably, staring at my feet.

"Oh," he said. "I'm sorry. We're at my house. I found you in the trails near here."

"How did you know I was lost?" I asked.

"Well, your mom knew that we were partners on the ecology project, so she called the house to see if you were here, and I said I would go looking for you," he said quietly, looking down at me, a slight smile playing on his features.

"Oh, well, thank you," I said, feeling a blush rise to my cheeks. Already, this person who I barely knew seemed to understand me better than any of my friends did.

"It was no trouble," he said. "You're sopping wet. Do you want some clothes?"

"I don't think anything you have will come close to fitting me."

"Yeah, well, we could put your clothes in the dryer, and you could borrow something until they're dry," he suggested.

"I guess we'll have to do that." I shrugged, looking around at the towering volumes around me.

"I'll be right back," he said and ran off. It took me a second to realize that he took the small golden book with him. I looked around at the other books but didn't touch any of them; they looked far too old and delicate. I heard the sound of his sneakers echoing on the floor seconds before he walked in the door.

"These are a little small for me … so maybe they won't be quite so humongous on you." I took the bright blue shirt, held it up to my chest, and laughed when it nearly reached my knees.

"You can stay here to change. You could rest your clothes over there, I guess," he said, gesturing to a small table and chair in the corner of the room. A small blush colored his cheeks, and he said slightly brusquely, "I'll meet you in the kitchen." He walked out, closing the door behind him.

I sighed with contentment as I slid the warm clothes over my chilled skin. I pulled my dripping hair back in a low bun at the base of my neck so it wouldn't drench the dry clothes. I laughed slightly to myself as I rolled the pants about five times, knowing I probably looked absolutely ridiculous.

Before I left the room, I looked around once more at the towering shelves. My eyes were suddenly drawn to a strange symbol. The picture was of two feathers, one big and healthy, the other burned. A deformed cross encircled the intersection of the two large feathers.

I slowly walked toward the kitchen, my feet padding quietly on the wooden floor. As I entered the small kitchen, Keith was sitting at a wooden table, his blue eyes distant and distracted. He looked up and smiled at me, his eyes twinkling when he saw my ridiculous appearance.

"I look absurd," I said grouchily, and he chuckled, the deep sound resonating around the otherwise silent kitchen.

"I called your mom."

"You did? Thanks a lot, Keith. I didn't even think about that."

"No problem. I told her I would drive you home as soon as your stuff was dry."

"Thanks again … you know, for finding me and stuff," I said.

"Hey, don't worry about it. What were you doing out there anyway?" he asked. The question was innocent enough, but I felt the color slowly leave my face. I felt my features stiffen, and I stared at my hands resting on the table. "You don't have to tell me," he said, quickly reading my response.

"It's fine," I said, refusing to look at his face. "My dad left us this afternoon," I said in a barely audible whisper. My hands trembled slightly, and I suddenly realized that they felt very cold, as if I had dumped them in a bucket of ice.

"Harmony, I'm sorry," he said, and he suddenly reached across the table and enveloped my hands in his. His firm grip steadied the quiet shivering that crept up and down my fingers. I looked up and smiled at him, grateful that he was so understanding.

"I guess I should have anticipated it," I said. "My parents haven't exactly been getting along well for a little less than a year now."

"Did anything happen in particular, or did they just sort of stop loving each other?" he asked, his tone mirroring mine.

"Something happened," I said, looking away from his concerned face. I hated sympathy from most people, but I didn't mind it with him. He really seemed to *understand*. I suddenly realized that he was probably a better friend than Sarah, Jen, or Adrienne, but then again, he didn't know my secret.

"Was it related to you at all?" he asked, and I felt my heart speed up slightly; our conversation was slowly straying into uncomfortable territory. I withdrew my hands from his and left them clasped in my lap.

"Yes ... it was *because* of me," I said, and I felt the tears slowly start to pool in my eyes. "I don't really feel like talking about this now ... it's a very long story ... and one that I haven't told many people," I said, and he nodded, seeming to appreciate my words.

"Did you tell Adrienne, Jen, and Sarah?" he asked, and I nodded slightly. I was surprised that he already knew who my friends were.

"But look what happened to our friendship—we can barely talk now," I said.

Suddenly, his pale face seemed to freeze over, and the muscles in his jaw were clenched tight.

"Have you told Damon?" he asked, and I was suddenly glad that I hadn't.

"No, I haven't told Damon," I said. The muscles in his shoulders and neck seemed to loosen.

"What's with you and Damon?" I said. "Have you guys been enemies since you were three or something like that?"

He stared at me for a second before he started laughing. "Kind of." He didn't elaborate, and something was distinctly wrong with his laughter; it sounded forced. "If it makes you feel any better, my mom left us when I was little," he said.

"Keith, I'm sorry," I said, even though I could barely keep the tears out of my own eyes.

"It must be worse for you, though. I have no memories of her at all," he said. I didn't know how to respond, so I just stared at my hands, wrapped in his.

"I'm going to check and see if my clothes are dry," I said, yawning loudly. My mom was probably sick with worry, and I suddenly felt horribly guilty at the selfishness of my actions. She was probably more distraught than I was about Dad leaving, and I left her alone in that house.

I flicked my eyes to the bright red letters of the clock, which sat directly above the stove. I was shocked when I saw that it was past one in the morning. "I need to go and see how my mom is doing."

"All right," he said, and I could feel him watching me as I walked out of the kitchen and back toward the room where my clothes were. I was pleased to see that all but my sneakers were mostly dry, and quickly changed.

I walked out of the house with Keith. Despite that the raging storm had passed, the clouds continued to hang heavily in the sky.

"Keith, I can't see anything," I said, for he had already walked forward without me. I heard his soft chuckle, and he was standing next to me again; the faded light coming from the house illuminated his tall figure.

He grabbed my hand, his long fingers completely enveloping it. Then he slowly guided me through the darkness to his car. I let out a gasp when I saw it.

"What?" he asked, his voice slightly alarmed.

"*That's* your car?" I asked as I stared at an exact replica of the car that I supposedly crashed into that first day.

"Yeah … what's wrong with it?"

"Oh nothing … just … it um … looks familiar." I didn't think I should try to explain my nonaccident to him. He gave me a strange look before he unlocked the door and we drove home.

Chapter 7

I never thought that I would miss my dad. After all, he locked himself up in his office most of the time, and when he was with us, he barely spoke to us.

Even so, I couldn't help but feel the loneliness that settled over the house. My mom was wandering around, a completely blank look on her face. It was almost as if she was lost to the world.

On Saturday morning, I ran to the coffee shop a few minutes from my house to grab a hot chocolate before Keith came over. It wasn't a long walk, even though it was freezing out.

I shivered as the cold air blew in behind me when someone walked into the otherwise warm coffee house. I could feel goose bumps rise on my arms as I stared at the menu far above me.

"I'll just have a hot chocolate, please," I told the girl at the counter.

"Would you like whipped cream with that?" she asked me, and I shook my head, my stomach churning at the thought of inhaling such heavy food.

"Harmony?" I heard a voice behind me. I jerked around in surprise and smiled at Damon. His chin wasn't held up arrogantly, and he smiled at me with seeming sincerity. His golden-brown eyes were soft and deep, not shallow with his usual teasing laughter.

"Hey, Damon," I said, and I could feel myself begin to relax. This was more how I remembered him being; maybe I hadn't been blind to his faults last year at all. Maybe he had changed, just as I had.

"Do you wanna sit and talk for a while?" he asked me, and I could feel my muscles stiffen up again. But this couldn't hurt, could it? This was something that friends did—wasn't it?

"Sure," I said. Maybe it was simply the influence of his friends that had made him cocky and proud, or maybe something else. I didn't really know.

We grabbed our drinks and sat down at a small round table by the large windows in front of the shop. We fell into a silence that pressed heavily upon us.

I couldn't help the small sigh that slipped through my lips. These awkward silences seemed to follow me everywhere, like my personal rain cloud that dampened the atmosphere in any situation.

To avoid his gaze, I stared out of the window to people watch. I watched as they hurried back and forth, preoccupied by whatever business they had to deal with.

Most of their eyes were riveted on some sort of electronic device, neither worrying nor caring about a world outside their own.

As I watched their faces, I began to wonder about the story behind each one, the worry behind each puckered brow and the secret behind each guarded eye.

"What are you thinking about?" Damon suddenly asked me.

"I was trying to come up with a story for each person walking by," I said. His eyes sparkled, and he gestured toward a man with greasy dark hair.

"Well … he just insulted his boss with his lack of hygiene and would rather be fired than take a shower." I giggled, and he didn't seem to notice that my laugh was a little forced.

"And she," he said, gesturing toward another woman whose skin was so stretched with Botox that she looked like a toad, "is worrying whether the wrinkle under her left eyebrow is starting to show and wondering whether she should go get it taken care of." I laughed at the probably realistic story.

"And that one," I said, nodding toward a woman who was talking on her cell phone and dragging a screaming toddler, "doesn't care at all about that poor kid and is wondering whether her boyfriend remembered to get her a birthday present." He laughed again, and I chuckled along with him.

"And he," he said, pointing to a man in a business suit with overly gelled, sandy brown hair. The man was walking next to a gorgeous girl with heavy dark hair and an olive complexion. He seemed to be nervous about something and was constantly glancing at his watch and over his shoulder. "He's worried that his wife is going to catch him cheating on her."

I laughed really loudly this time, for the first time since my dad left us last week. The expression on the man's face suited this story perfectly. Part of me realized it wasn't right to make fun of people that way, but I was tired of being so serious all the time. It felt good to let go a little and do something I wasn't supposed to, no matter how trivial.

We slowly settled into silence again, and I glanced up at the gray sky through the window. Small white flakes danced like fairies down from gloom. They twirled and whirled through the cold air before slowly fading into nothing as they hit the asphalt and cement. They created a temporary magic in the window as they spun, but the magic was over before it began, turning to water droplets against the window.

The temperature change since last week was unimaginable; now I could barely go outside without my teeth chattering.

"So, what are you doing for Thanksgiving?" I asked him. It was weird going on break right after I had been back in school for such a short time. For most, there was eager anticipation for the first break in almost three months. For me, it meant more monotony in a tense, empty house.

"All my family is gonna come to my house, including every one of my thirty-three cousins," he said, rolling his eyes. "You should see us all when we get together; it's insane. There's always a huge blowup between my parents about the food or decorating or something stupid. And none of the cousins really want to be there, and my sister usually fights with one of the other cousins. And then there's always an annual political debate. It's the most retarded thing I've ever heard because everyone agrees with each other, but they insist on yelling to everyone about it."

"Sounds rough."

"Tell me about it. No one really wants to be there, but we all go anyway just 'cause it's like a tradition that they feel forced to keep up."

"We don't really do much for Thanksgiving," I said, unable to keep the bitterness out of my voice. We used to have a celebration, but not anymore. "It must be nice to have a big family," I noted.

"You know, it's funny, I've always wanted a small family. But you know what they say—you always want what you can't have."

"It's hard to say, though, because you don't know if you'd still want it if you already had it. Anyway, I'd better be getting home," I said, standing up. It was already almost one o'clock, and Keith and I planned to work on the project at his house that afternoon.

He followed me out and headed in the direction of the parking lot. I was furious at my stupidity. What had possibly motivated me to walk? I sighed as the cold wind whipped at my face, so sharp that it stung my cheeks. As I was walking down the road, I heard a car pull up next to me. I looked up shyly. Damon was sitting in the car with a smug expression on his face.

"Do you need a ride?" he said. I could feel my cheeks flame redder as I slowly approached his car door.

"Thanks, Damon," I said quietly, too embarrassed to look him in the face.

"What were you thinking?" he asked, and I could still hear the laughter in his voice. "It's like two degrees out."

"I know, but it seemed like a good idea at the time." I sighed, and he laughed again. We fell into silence, and I watched his face as he stared blankly at the road in front of him. I remembered how his face used to take my breath away. Would I ever feel like that again? His face angled slightly in my direction.

"Why are you staring at me like that?" he asked.

"I was just remembering last May, you know … before I left."

"What happened to you anyway? You have no idea how weird and scary it was. Nobody had any idea what had happened to you—not even me."

"It's a really long story, Damon," I said, knowing that I couldn't tell him. It was hard enough telling my best friends; with him, it would be impossible. We were stopped outside my house now, and I didn't even know how he knew the way since my family had moved.

"I figured," he said.

"It's not exactly something I like to talk about. It's not like I went on an extended vacation or anything."

"I figured that too, seeing as you seemed to have lost like fifty pounds."

I looked down and began to open the door.

"No, Harmony, don't go!" he said. "I didn't mean that. I'm sorry. It's very frustrating, that's all. You've changed so much …" His voice trailed off.

"I know that, Damon, and I'm really sorry too. I wish that I could tell you, but I just can't." I tried to smile. "And I really do have to go now." I opened the door this time. Suddenly his eyes moved to somewhere behind me, and a sneer suddenly crossed his face. I looked behind me and then back at him. "What?" I asked.

"Nothing," he said. "See you Monday!" he called to me as I shut the door. I waved to him as he slowly drove away.

I stared after his retreating black car.

"Hey, Harmony." I heard a low, raspy voice and nearly jumped out of my skin.

"Oh my God," I said, putting a hand over my heart as I stared up at the shocked face of Keith.

"Are you okay?"

"Yeah, you just scared me—that's all," I said.

"I just have a question." There was something different in his voice, and his eyes kept darting to the receding car behind me.

"Sure."

"Don't think I'm nosy or anything, but why were you in Damon's car?"

"Oh, I didn't have my car, and he just dropped me off," I said. I watched as his face changed from relaxed to completely enraged.

"Are you okay?" I said.

Suddenly I noticed something begin to change in his eyes, and it had nothing to do with his expression. His very pupils seemed to change shape, but I couldn't see what they were morphing into. He immediately brought his hand up and pinched the corners of his eyes between his fingers.

All I could do was stare at him. What had I just seen? Had I imagined it? I must have, but there was obviously something different about him.

"Keith?" I asked, raising my hand and resting it on his elbow. At my touch, his eyes snapped open, and I could feel my worry about my sanity increase when I saw that his pupils were perfectly round. Was I just imagining things? There didn't seem to be any other plausible explanation. How could his pupils *change their shape?*

"Yeah, I'm fine," he said quickly, and I dropped my hand.

I followed him silently to his car and struggled to forget what I thought I saw in his eyes. I didn't know why he was following me to the passenger side of the car until he opened the door for me.

"Thanks," I mumbled and I felt a blush creep up my face. He didn't say anything as he closed my door and walked around to his side.

He drove in complete silence for a few minutes and then asked, "How long have you been going to this school?"

"Since I was a freshman."

"Really?"

"Yep." I refused to elaborate.

"You wouldn't believe the rumors that are going around," he said, hinting at the obvious.

He barely knew me, and he was trying to pry into my deepest secrets.

"I bet there are plenty," I said, and that seemed to quiet him for a while. Silence descended upon us, and instantly I regretted my terse words.

"I'm sorry," he said as we pulled up to his house. I hadn't looked at it carefully from the outside before. It was a medium-sized house that looked as if it were in the middle of nowhere. It rose gracefully from the ground, as if it had been there for hundreds of years. It didn't seem to clash with its surroundings like so many houses did. It was as if it grew out of the earth naturally and was meant to be there.

"No, Keith, I'm sorry. I shouldn't have talked to you like that. That's just a sensitive topic—that's all." I kept my eyes focused on his house, but I could feel his eyes on my face. "Um, Keith?" I asked as I scanned our surroundings.

"Yeah?"

"Um … what town is your house in?"

"Oh, it's the same town you live in; this is just one of the older houses. My dad actually owns most of the land around here."

"Really? That's so cool!" I exclaimed, trying to recapture some of my old enthusiasm but sounding fake. I didn't have a lot of any real enthusiasm anymore.

"Yeah, it's pretty neat." And his voice fell quiet again. His eyes were far away as he said, "I should probably warn you—my dad and I look so much alike, it's scary." His voice came out in a rush as if he didn't want to say the words.

"So? We all look like our parents."

"No, I mean we literally could be clones. I don't know if he's home, but if we run into him, I thought I should warn you." He was staring at me, and I couldn't help but let out a small giggle.

"What?"

"It's just you look so worried about it." I started chuckling again, and he started to laugh with me.

His laughter was a strangely freeing sound, and I was surprised by how natural it seemed. He had seemed so uptight at first that I had trouble picturing him so open.

"All right," he said, sliding out of the car and into the cool air. "Enough laughter at my expense. But really, people get really creeped out."

"Chill. Seriously, almost every guy I know could be a clone of their dad," I said.

We walked up to the front door, and he unlocked it. When we went inside, I saw the massive bookshelves I had seen the time before.

"You guys must seriously like reading," I said.

"They're more like a family history, you could say. My dad looks at them mostly; he doesn't really trust me to touch them."

"That's a long history," I said, staring at them.

"They're mostly legends," he said, and there was something tight and quick in his tone.

"Legends about what?"

"Nothing in particular."

For the first time, I realized I must not be the only person trying to keep a secret.

I shrugged and let the subject drop, knowing how frustrating nosy people could be. He led me through several more rooms, all completely lined with books, books that I didn't ask about.

We walked through the room where he brought me after he found me in the woods. I looked around the large expanse of shelves for the small golden book, but it wasn't there. If he noticed my pause, he didn't say anything, just leading me into a fourth room. The house looked much smaller from the outside, and I would have never guessed that all of these different rooms existed.

The fourth room contained an extremely high-tech looking computer.

"Wow, fancy," I said examining the skinny screen and tiny box that must have been the computer.

"My dad's job needs the highest technology," he said with a note of sarcasm, as if he was sharing an inside joke with himself.

"Some job," I said. It didn't look like a computer you could buy from just an ordinary store. Within five seconds of pressing the "on" button, it was ready to go.

"Tell me about it," he said, rolling his eyes.

"Do our dads really work together?" I asked him, remembering the conversation my dad and I had before he left.

"Why do you think that?"

"He just mentioned it a little while ago. He said they worked for the same company."

"Oh yeah … they do, I think."

"What do they do? My dad's never really explained it. He was secretive about his work, and … he … you know … left," I said, trying to keep my voice light despite the pain that coursed through my chest.

"I, uh, can't really tell you more. My dad doesn't really talk about it either," he said, but he wouldn't look me in the eye.

"So, then you knew about me—I mean us?" I asked.

"No, Harmony," he said, looking right at me this time. "As secretive as your dad was about his job, he was just as secretive about his family to us."

"Can I ask you something random?" I asked.

"Sure …"

"Do you wear contacts?"

"No … Why do you ask?"

"Just their color is kind of unrealistic—that's all."

"Oh," he said, and his voice drifted into silence. I watched quietly as he searched the Internet for information on the fire that consumed the woods.

"You know," I said, seeing a way we could expand our project even more, "we could research how long it should take the forest to start to grow life again."

"That's an interesting idea," he said, and his fingers flashed across the keys again. In an instant, there was a detailed environmental website. We spent the rest of the afternoon researching our project. I was surprised how easy he was to get along with, how easy he was to talk to.

Suddenly I heard footsteps echoing from somewhere else in the house. Keith's shoulder tensed up as the footsteps, echoing loudly on the hardwood floor, got closer and closer. I was leaning over Keith's shoulder and staring intently at the screen when Keith's dad walked in.

Keith had prepared me, but it was still utter shock. Keith wasn't kidding when he said that he was literally a clone of him. They were probably exactly the same height. Unlike Keith, he didn't have eyes so blue it was sometimes painful to look at. Instead his eyes were predominantly gray. Even though he didn't appear to be very old, his eyes held an ancient wisdom and sadness. His hair was a slightly different shade of black, more brown than Keith's, and streaked with dark gray. Keith's was so black it held the smallest hint of blue when the light hit it in the right way.

"Hey, Dad," Keith's voice was filled with tension, and his eyes kept flashing to my face to determine my reaction. "This is Harmony. We're working on a class project together."

"It's nice to meet you, Mr. Draykon," I said quietly and extended my hand to shake his. I could barely bring my eyes up to meet his and wanted to curse my shyness.

"Please just call me Cyrus," he said, and his voice had the same hoarseness that Keith's had. His face was much more open than Keith's, and he gave me a big smile before saying, "Anyway, I'll leave you two. Let me know if you need anything." Then he turned and left, and we both listened to his retreating footsteps.

"Wow, you weren't kidding." I said, glancing at the doorway.

"I know. It's really creepy."

"Not creepy exactly … just really unusual. What does your mom look like?"

"I don't really know," he said. His voice was mechanical and forced. "I've never seen a picture of her."

We didn't talk about his dad or his mom for the rest of the afternoon. As the time passed, he seemed to relax more and more as we kept our conversations to small, unimportant things.

"So," he said as we got into his car, "I think we got off to a pretty good start on the project."

I smiled at him. "Me too."

We drove in silence, and I turned my head to face out the window and stared as the trees blurred by us. The silence between us wasn't pressing or suffocating; it was easy and relaxing.

"Thanks, Keith," I said as we pulled in front of my house.

"No problem."

"I'll see you around," I said as I slowly stepped out of the car.

"See ya," he said and pulled away. I waited outside of the house as his taillights slowly disappeared.

Between my encounters with both Damon and Keith, it was the most interesting Saturday I had experienced in a long time.

Chapter 8

It was Monday morning. Damon waved energetically at me, and I couldn't help that his wild energy was beginning to grow on me. The qualities that I valued in him last May were beginning to show themselves again, but I detected something else I couldn't explain, almost like some intuition had come alive in me that I couldn't access before. He wasn't the person he had been, but I didn't know if that was a good thing.

"Hey, Harmony," he said. "How was the rest of your weekend?"

"It was okay. You know … sat around the house, did homework, worked on that stupid project that we have for Ecology. The usual."

"Same. I hate it when weekends are like that. They're almost as bad as weekdays."

"Well, I wouldn't go that far, but they're certainly not as fun as they're supposed to be."

"Agreed," he said, and he was quiet for once. He started chewing on his lip, as if he were debating whether or not to ask me something. "I was wondering …" he said, his voice filled with embarrassment. He again reminded me of the boy that I had a crush on last May. "Do you wanna go out to dinner or something over Thanksgiving break?"

We stopped walking, and I stared at him. I remembered what this would have felt like had this been a year ago—or even better, if that dreadful night had never happened.

I was suddenly filled with anger at myself. Where was my hesitancy coming from? I didn't even know, and I wanted to do something that would make me feel normal.

"Yeah, Damon, I'd love to."

"Great! Saturday, at around six? I'll come pick you up?"

"Sounds good!" I said with true enthusiasm this time.

"See ya!" He turned, and we walked in opposite directions to our respective homerooms. I saw Sarah, Jen, and Adrienne walking ahead of me and rushed forward to catch up with them.

"Hey, guys! Guess what?" I said energetically, and they all stared at me with identical expressions of surprise. It took me a second to realize that they hadn't seen me this lively since last May.

"The aliens from another dimension have finally broken through the dimensional barrier and are invading in less than twenty four hours?" Adrienne asked, and I broke out in laughter.

"No, but Damon asked me out!" I said, and they still looked at me in shock.

"Didn't he do that last Wednesday—and you turned him down?"

"Yes," I said, feeling my smile begin to falter. "But I said yes to him this time. It feels strangely freeing."

"That's so amazing, Harmony!" squeaked Jen. "You have to call us right after and tell us how it goes. When is it?"

"Saturday!" I said, and they talked and squealed at me until we sat down for homeroom.

Keith walked in a few minutes afterward, and a feeling of guilt erupted when I saw him. I couldn't help remembering his reaction when Damon drove me home the other day.

"Hey, Keith," I said.

"Hey. Are you ready for the break?"

"Not particularly. We don't really do much."

"Neither do we," he said. "I kind of wish that we did though—you know, those classic big families with the long table and a huge turkey."

"I know what you mean."

"You know, we should probably meet sometime over break and actually visit that forest and do some more research."

"Yeah, we probably should. I'm free Sunday," I said quickly.

"All right, sounds good."

"My house this time? Is the same time okay for you?" I asked him, trying to ignore the obvious stares of my friends as they listened to him converse easily with me.

"Sure," he said, right as the bell rang.

Keith cornered me by my locker after history class, and I had a suspicion of what he was going to ask me about.

"So is it true?" he asked me.

"Is what true?" I said, feigning ignorance.

He rolled his eyes at me. "Are you really going out with Damon?" he asked with a condescending tone, as if I was stupid for doing so.

"I don't know if I'm going out with him, exactly, but we are going to dinner this Saturday," I said quietly. I was surprised by the silence that followed. I was almost afraid to glance up at his face. When I did, he was hunched over in the same odd position that he assumed last Saturday. His eyes were closed, and his fingers were pressed into the corners of his eyes.

"Are you okay?" I asked. I was about to touch him on the elbow, as I had last time, but something weird seemed to shudder up his entire frame. I just stared at him in shock. *What's happening to him?* "Keith, what—" I started.

"Excuse me," he grunted at me before he sprinted down the hallway and out of sight. I stared at his retreating figure and couldn't help but think that Keith might have anger management issues. It would explain why he seemed so detached all the time and why he was acting so weird just now. I decided not to say anything to my friends about it when I ran into them in the hallway.

I walked through the cafeteria alone, scanning the large crowd for Keith's towering figure. I had to make sure that he was really okay, because what happened to him by the lockers was downright scary.

I saw him standing in the long line to get lunch, but there seemed to be a three-foot circle that surrounded him. His shoulders were hunched, and he was staring vacantly off in the distance.

"Keith," I said as I walked up behind him, and he turned around and gave me a ghost of a smile.

"Are you okay?" I asked.

"Yeah, I'm fine. Can we pretend that never happened?" he asked softly.

"If you don't mind me asking … What happened?"

He raised an eyebrow at me. "That doesn't exactly correlate with pretending it never happened."

"You seriously scared me, Keith. I thought you were dying or something."

"I apologize for scaring you—but, no, I wasn't dying." A smirk flashed across his features before he continued, "Sometimes, when I feel irritated by something … I don't feel very well." His voice was robotic, like poorly delivered lines during a play.

"I'm really sorry, Keith. I didn't know that what I said would …" I let my voice trail off into nothing.

"No, it wasn't your fault. Don't worry about it." He smiled more convincingly this time, and I returned the smile tentatively.

One thing was for sure: I didn't buy his act one bit. He was definitely hiding something.

Chapter 9

My mom was shocked when I told her about my upcoming date with Damon.

"That really is wonderful, honey," she said, and I could tell she was trying to keep her voice warm. I could see the reservations in her eyes; she didn't think I was ready for a relationship yet. She didn't think it would be good for me.

She turned away from me and walked into a different area of the house. I watched her retreating back, feeling the ache of guilt in my chest when I remembered that her sadness was my fault.

Saturday came much faster than I ever thought possible. I felt like I was almost normal, with normal problems, and it felt really good. I called Sarah a couple of hours before, and we talked about what I was going to wear. By the end, my entire closet was practically on my floor and I was still standing there in my underwear, at a loss for what to put on.

I finally decided on a medium length, black skirt with a deep blue top to bring out my eyes. I tied my auburn hair back into a low bun, letting a few of the shorter strands escape and swirl around my face.

The doorbell rang, the breezy sound echoing loudly throughout the house. My heart, already thundering against my chest, pounded harder, drowning out almost every other sound.

"Harmony, are you sure about this?" my mom asked as I walked quickly toward the door.

"Yes!" I said, feeling slightly exasperated at her constant hovering and worrying. I was really fine on my own, and there was no need for her to be so concerned. I yanked open the heavy door with a big smile on my face.

"Hey, Harmony!" Damon said, and his golden brown eyes slowly swept up and down my figure. "You look great!"

I smiled and gestured for him to come inside.

"Hello, Damon," my mom said coolly.

Damon immediately extended his hand and said, "Hello, Mrs. Vindico. How are you doing?"

"I'm fine, thank you," my mom responded calmly. "So, where are you two going tonight?"

"Well, I was thinking that we would go to dinner at this really awesome place near my house." He glanced at me to see if that was okay, and I beamed another smile at him.

"Okay, Mom, see you later," I said as we turned toward the door.

"Not too late," she called behind us as the door slowly shut.

"Sorry about that," I said smiling apologetically.

"Don't worry about it; she's really nice compared to some," he said. He held the door open for me as I got into the car, and then he walked to the other side.

"Just feel lucky that you didn't see my dad," I said, shuddering to think of what would have happened if Damon had.

"Is he one of those crazy overprotective types?" he asked.

"No. It's more like he just acts really nasty to pretty much everyone, even me and my mom. I don't even want to know how he would have treated you."

"Guess I'm glad I didn't meet him then." He laughed—and there was something strange about it, but before I could put my finger on why, he continued, "I have a question. That history test that we took on Tuesday—was it just me, or was it really hard?"

"No, I thought it was pretty bad also. What did you get for number ten? I was debating between A and C."

"I had trouble with that one too. I think I ended up putting B."

I sighed loudly. "Well, I guess I got that one wrong then."

"I wouldn't count on my answers by a long shot. For all I know, I could have gotten them all wrong."

"Seriously, Damon, you didn't get them all wrong." I laughed; he was one of the smartest people in the class.

"No, I guess I didn't," he conceded, and then he started laughing along with me. He casually slung his arm on the steering wheel as he drove through the streets. "Here we are!" he said suddenly, and he pulled into the parking lot of an Asian restaurant.

When we reached the doors, he held one open for me, and I looked down and blushed at his unexpected chivalry.

"Table for two, please," Damon said to the waiter, his voice etched with politeness as he gestured for me to go in front of him as we followed. When we sat down on the well-cushioned chairs, the waiter gave us menus and then walked away.

"Have you ever been here before?" I asked, sneaking a glance at him as he studied the menu. His face didn't have the hard planes that Keith's did, but he was cute in his own way. He was certainly much friendlier and easier to get along with in a superficial way than Keith was.

"Yeah, I have, a bunch of times," he said, glancing up at me from behind his menu. For the briefest moment, I wondered whether he took all of his first dates here.

"What do you suggest?"

"Hmmm … Do you like sushi?"

"I'm not really a sushi person."

"Okay, then I'd suggest the chicken tempura with rice as a side. I'm going to have the sushi."

"I think I'll try that," I said, folding my menu and putting it down in front of me.

"So how's your project for ecology going?" he asked.

"It's okay. I don't think we really know where we're going with it yet."

"Who did you say your partner was again?"

"Keith," I said carefully.

"Oh, that's right. How's that working out? That guy is such a freak."

Anger rose up inside me. "That's not true. He's really nice. You don't know him at all," I said, rising to his defense.

"Don't I?"

I was struck by the oddness of the statement. There was clearly a deep-rooted animosity between them that I had no knowledge about.

Silence settled heavily on us, and I searched for another topic of conversation. Our food came, and we both started eating.

"What do you like to do in your spare time?" he asked me.

"I really like to draw—you know, sketch and paint and stuff."

"Seriously!" he suddenly exclaimed. "Are you any good?"

"I think I'm pretty good," I said quietly, not wanting to sound cocky.

"I'll have to come to your house sometime and see some of your work. But I love to draw too! In fact, my family is having an art exhibit in the middle of February. You could enter something if you want to."

"Really?" I asked, my voice starting to rise with excitement.

"Yeah of course! That would be really cool! The exhibit has a theme of fantasy world."

"That's okay, it would be really cool just to enter something," I said trying to sound nonchalant. In reality, I had been intending to submit something that I had already painted, but the theme ruled out that possibility. I had nothing already drawn that would fit a fantasy theme.

For the rest of the dinner, the exhibit was all Damon could talk about.

"What are you painting for it?" I asked him, trying to get an idea of what would be expected of me.

"That's going to be a surprise," he said, and his golden eyes glittered. He paid the check, and we both stood up.

"So, I could paint any fantasy creature?" I asked him.

"It doesn't necessarily have to be a creature, just fantasy, like a person crossed with something else. Stuff like that."

"That's a really unusual theme," I commented as we walked out to his car.

"Yeah, well, my family is into that kind of stuff," he said, suddenly seeming uncomfortable. He didn't say anything more on the subject, and silence descended upon us. It wasn't the uncomfortable silence that had fallen heavily when we were in the restaurant. This silence drifted over us quietly and peacefully.

We drove home, and the stillness continued as I sat back and relaxed in the comfortable leather seats of his car. I looked out the window and watched as the dark shadows blurred by in an indistinguishable haze.

As we pulled in front of my house, I turned toward him. My heart broke into a sprint when I saw the intense expression on his face.

"I had a really great time, Damon," I said softly.

"I'm glad," he said, as quietly as I had spoken.

I tried to slow my breathing as it sped up with the intense vibe that seemed to suddenly fill the small car. I knew what he was going to do before he did it.

His shoulders slowly angled forward as he leaned in toward me. I couldn't really believe what I was doing as I leaned in response to his movement.

I had no idea how I was going to react to this sudden closeness, not only physically, but emotionally. Was I recovered enough to handle this after what Robbie had done to me?

Before I had made any kind of decision, our lips slowly met.

I felt my muscles lock down, but I didn't move away from him. My heart was hammering in my chest and ringing loudly in my ears. I struggled to repress my immediate reaction and allow myself to let go and act normal for once.

Damon must have felt the tension leave my muscles, because he pressed harder before slowly pulling away.

I stared at him with wide eyes, and he gave me a smile. My heart was beating so fast and hard that I was surprised he couldn't hear it. My fingers were clenched tightly in my lap, and I could feel the muscles in my arms quivering.

"I'll see you on Monday, Harmony," he said, and I nodded slightly with a smile before stepping out of his car.

I waved as his car pulled out and disappeared into the dark night.

Chapter 10

The next day, I was completely dazed about what had happened the night before. I couldn't believe that I had allowed myself to be that close to Damon—and that I liked it. Every time I thought about our time together, I couldn't help the blush that flooded my cheeks.

"Hey, Mom," I said, realizing that I completely forgot to tell her something. I walked in to her reading the paper and eating a bagel. She looked up and gave me a sad smile.

"Um, I kind of forgot to tell you, but Keith is coming over later today."

"I thought I heard something about his father knowing yours?" Mom said. It seemed as if she had to force the words from her lips; I could tell how painful this was for her.

"Yeah, I think they only met once or twice."

"What does he do for a living?" Mom said suddenly, and I couldn't help the suspicious feeling that began to crawl into my stomach. Mom obviously had not gotten over the fact that Dad never told her about his job.

"I don't really know—something super high tech, though. You should see the computers that they have at his house."

My mom eventually left me alone in the house, and I turned on the computer before Keith got here so it would have time to properly start up. I wandered around aimlessly, not really feeling like doing anything in particular.

Finally the doorbell rang. I ran to get it and opened the door to see Keith standing sheepishly on the step.

"Hey, Keith," I said energetically and encouraged him to come into the house.

"Hey, what's up?" he asked and walked in. I led him through the house, which felt barren and empty compared to his. I brought him to the computer and sat down by the old machine that was wheezing and whining.

"It's no high-tech computer, I said.

"It's fine," he said quickly, and he smiled at me.

"Oh!" I said, suddenly remembering my conversation the night before with Damon and eager to share it with him.

"What?" he asked, raising his eyebrows.

"You're not going to believe it! So Damon's family is holding this art exhibit thing sometime in February, and he said that I could enter something!"

"Really?" he said, and I could tell he was trying to be excited.

"I know! I'm so excited! But I have no idea what I'm going to paint because he says it's fantasy themed." I stopped at his expression. It looked like he was seriously trying to hold back hysterical laughter. I gave him a look and continued, "And I was going to enter stuff that I already painted, but none of that is fantasy, so I'm going to have to draw something else."

"I can't believe he asked you to do that! That's awesome," he said. He was trying to show enthusiasm but was failing miserably.

"Anyway," I said, changing the subject, "I was looking on the computer about fires and forests and stuff. According to my research, we may not start to see many signs of life until March, because that's when the weather starts to warm up. But, do you want to head over there now and look for subtle signs of regrowth?"

"Sounds good," he said and followed me out of the very pitiful looking house. We got into his car and drove toward the burned woods.

"When did the fire happen anyway? I don't really remember," I said. There was a good three months of time when I wouldn't have remembered seeing or hearing about the burning woods.

"It was around last June," he said and started to pull over as we reached the barren section of forest.

"Oh," I said quietly, lost in memories. They were less painful ones but they still sent an ache through my chest. The timing explained a lot, though; I was in rehab at that point.

It took me a minute to realize that he was studying me carefully, his bright blue eyes intense and his jaw hard.

"Let's go," I said and quickly got out of the car. I grabbed my camera and winced slightly as our feet made loud crunching sounds on the blackened earth.

We walked deeper and deeper into the burned woods, until the road and the sounds of cars were far behind us. It seemed as if the smoke from the flames never left the woods. The light from the setting sun filtered through the haze, casting steep shadows around us. The black trees swayed stiffly with the faint wind, the dead bark groaning with the small movement.

"It's kind of creepy in here," I noted when we stopped walking to look around. I stared steadily at the ground, looking to see if new life had started to form in the lifeless ashes. Keith broke a stick, looking for signs of greenness, which was unlikely considering how recent the fire was.

"Agreed," Keith said. Unlike me, he was staring up at the trees. I took a few more pictures of the lifeless forest. A tremor crept up my spine, and it wasn't from the cold. The woods were so devoid of any form of life it felt as if no other person existed besides the two of us.

It was different from the bareness of a forest during winter. In woods like that, there were signs of life everywhere, and the trees didn't look truly dead. They still had a warm brown color, filled with life, unlike the trees that were charred and black.

"It kind of feels like … I don't know … like there's no other life anywhere in the world," I commented. "It kind of brings back all those stories from when we were little. You know, with dragons and stuff." The minute the words left my lips, he stiffened.

"What makes you say that?" he asked, his voice as lifeless as the woods.

"I don't know. It kind of reminds me of those movies where you're walking through an ancient forest, and it's like so quiet that it's creepy. Then a monster suddenly jumps out with its teeth bared and claws out."

"I see what you mean," he said quietly.

My eyes scanned the trees for any sign that things had changed since the fire and were suddenly drawn to something that seemed to be etched in the tree.

"Whoa, look at that! That's really weird," I said, approaching the strange looking marking. The image was of two feathers—one was big and healthy, and the other looked burned. A deformed cross encircled the point where the two large feathers intersected. It vaguely reminded me of the etching that I had seen on Keith's shelves.

Keith stared at the etching, looking completely dumbfounded, his blue eyes wide with shock. It looked like he was trying to say something, but nothing was coming out. He suddenly walked forward and slowly ran his fingers over the etching. I couldn't help but notice the way his fingers trembled slightly.

"Keith, do you recognize that?" I asked, tempted to rest my fingers on his elbow again. He seemed to shake himself out of whatever reverie he was in and looked at me, his face blank and smooth.

"No, of course not," he said, his voice expressionless.

"There's not really anything else really to do. We're probably not going to start seeing anything until March anyway. Do you want to go?" I asked, eager to leave.

"Yeah, this place is seriously giving me the creeps," he said, and he started walking swiftly toward the road. I had to practically run to keep up with him.

"What's the hurry?" I huffed at him, and he stopped walking to turn and look at me.

"I'm sorry," he said quietly.

"It's not your fault that you're like freakishly tall," I grumbled at him. He smirked slightly, looking down at me.

"It's not your fault you're short either."

"It may not be, but at least you don't practically need a ladder to reach the doorknob," I retorted. He started chuckling, and the soft noise was all we could hear besides the creaking of the trees.

As we walked closer to the road, the sound of the occasional car echoed in the seemingly empty forest, breaking the illusion that we were the only two living people in the world. We got into the car and drove back to the house.

"There's not much we can do now with the woods themselves, but we can begin to research information on how burnt forests form new life," he said.

"Yeah, and then we could do something where we compare the signs of life that we're supposed to see in the forest to the signs that we actually see."

"You know, there might already be life in the forest because it had most of last summer to generate. We just don't see it yet."

"True," I said. "Real trees won't actually form until like five years from now. It's kind of funny—there's more to this project than I originally thought."

"Maybe we should have done global warming after all," he smirked, and I laughed.

As I stared at his blue eyes, I thought about the symbol in the woods and how it must have meant more to him then he let on.

Chapter 11

I stared at the unblemished surface, my mind as blank as the large white canvas in front of me. My brain had been empty for more than a week, and I could think of nothing that I wanted to draw. I sat there frustrated as I struggled to think of something related to fantasy.

This was part of the reason I didn't want to become an artist when I grew up. I couldn't think of anything to paint when I was directed. I had to wait for the inspiration to assail me, and then I couldn't stop. So I went to bed on Wednesday night hoping that Thursday would show a little more accomplishment.

*   *   *

I sat up suddenly, the images from my dream still vivid in my memory. My heart was pounding, and adrenaline was coursing through my veins. The half-man, half-monster had visited me once again, and he both terrified and intrigued me.

I flipped on the switch to the light next to my desk, sat down with a pencil, and slowly began to sketch the outline of his face. I forced myself not to do any shading; this was only a guideline.

I pulled his frightening image from my memory, and I couldn't repress the shudder that crept up my spine. My hand flew lightly across the course surface of the canvas as the details became more and more refined. My eyes stared off into the distance; I was letting my hands guide the image. As I worked, the sun rose higher in my window, casting an orange array of lights onto my desk and work. Unfortunately, it was time to go to school before I could finish, and I huffed out the door in frustration, hoping that this sudden flux in creativity would last until the afternoon when I would start painting.

Later, standing beside my locker, I felt an arm rest on my shoulder, and I jumped. "Jeez, Damon, you scared me," I said, resting my hand over my slowing heart.

"Sorry," he said sheepishly. "Anyway, have you started thinking about what you're going to paint for the exhibit? You know that's in a couple of weeks, right?"

"Yeah, actually. I just came up with an idea this morning. It was kind of based on a dream I had." I felt my cheeks flame red with embarrassment.

"Do I get to hear what this idea is?" he asked me, his golden eyes bright and teasing.

I shook my head. "You'll get to see it on the day of the exhibit," I teased.

"Shouldn't I get to see it a little bit before the day of? I did invite you," he mock pleaded. I grinned brightly at him and shook my head again, my auburn hair swinging around my waist.

"Nope," I said.

He sighed quietly and grinned at me again. "So, do you want to do something on Friday? We could go watch a movie or something."

"Hey, why don't you come to my house this time? We could have pizza and rent a movie," I suggested, nervously keeping my eyes down at our feet.

"Sounds like a plan!" he said. "I've got to get to class. See you around, Harmony!" He jogged away from me, joining a bunch of his friends down the hall.

Throughout the day, I struggled to keep myself focused on the painting that was waiting for me back home. I held on to the image of the monster's face and his eyes and the way the monster's wings expanded and extended out and away from his back.

"Are you okay, Harmony?" Sarah asked me as we headed toward the parking lot that afternoon.

"Yeah, I'm fine. Why?" I asked. Things hadn't gotten less tense or awkward in our friendship. All three of my friends were oddly distant, and it was getting harder to stay close with them. I was beginning to think that I should have never told them my secret.

"You just seem kind of out of it today, that's all," she said.

"I'm trying to keep my creative flux of this morning going," I announced. She stared at me with raised eyebrows. "Well," I said, "I haven't really drawn much since last May." I paused and gave her a significant look. "And Damon's family is holding one of those art exhibit things, and he said I could enter something in it. But that means I have to draw something, and I just had an idea this morning. I'm trying to keep my moment of inspiration going."

"Did he seriously say that you could enter something in his family's exhibit? That's awesome!" she exclaimed. "So that's what you were talking about with Keith this morning?"

"Yeah—sorry ... I like completely forgot to tell you guys."

"Don't worry about it. I just don't understand how you get Keith to talk to you like that. In math yesterday, we had to work together on some worksheet, and he didn't say anything," she said, rolling her eyes. I couldn't help but feel protective of him. It really wasn't his fault that he was painfully shy.

"I don't know. We kind of clicked, and we're buddies now."

"Whatever. I'll see you later."

"See ya!"

I watched as she pulled out of the parking lot and drove away. I jumped into my car as a gust of bitter winter wind swept across the emptying parking lot. It forced the barren trees to sway back and forth without any rhythm, their branches bunching together and separating.

I drove home and immediately headed upstairs. My mom was still very quiet in the house. There was a heavy coldness that had nothing to do with the weather.

I suddenly felt red hot anger deep in my stomach when I realized whose fault this really was. I wanted to paint, but thoughts of revenge on Robbie crept back.

As I passed by my bedroom, I glanced at the canvas with the lightly sketched drawing. I remembered the fury that the monster had radiated in the dream; he was so enraged that he was positively frightening.

| 15 Stitches |

I used my sudden anger to channel the fury of the monster in my dream. I tore out my old acrylic paints and my wilted brushes and sat down at my desk again. I squeezed out three colors onto a paper mixing plate. Black. White. And a hard, electric blue.

Chapter 12

It seemed as if I had pressed a fast-forward button on my life. It was already the day of the exhibit.

I had finally persuaded my friends to sit with Keith at lunch, but he didn't say much to them. Despite her obvious depression, my mom became extremely fond of him. Once, she even insisted that he take home several of her charred chocolate chip cookies when he came over to work on our project again.

Damon wasn't happy about my friendship with Keith, but he didn't say much against him. He would only grumble unintelligibly the few times I mentioned Keith's name while I was with him.

The sun shone brightly on the February morning, sending almost everything I saw into a faded silhouette. The bright sun sparkled through the still barren trees, and I took a deep breath to calm the butterflies in my stomach.

I glanced at the finished painting with a slight satisfaction, temporarily abating the nervous feeling in my stomach. It was perfect.

For the first time in what felt like forever, spring was finally on its way. Despite the crisp air, the strong smell of spring wafted through the windows and through my car.

I drove slowly down the street, my engine whining loudly as I struggled to coax it into a slightly faster pace. As I headed toward Damon's house, it amazed me how the houses steadily evolved from the smaller houses in my neighborhood to larger and larger houses until they were practically the size of mansions. I stopped outside Damon's house and stared at the driveway. I wondered why, after several months of dating, we never ended up going to his house or meeting anyone in his family.

I couldn't help feeling insignificant as I stared at the polished cobblestones. The tires of my car bumped and bounced on them, and I gripped the steering wheel all the harder.

The driveway expanded into a large circle before the immense house. Two columns extended up the front of the house, seeming to imitate the huge Grecian temples. An elegant staircase led up to the wooden double door. I slowly got out of my old car, grabbed the sheet-covered canvas, and started walking across the dead grass toward the immense staircase.

As I raised my hand to ring the doorbell, the heavy wooden door opened and Damon's smiling face greeted me.

"Hey, babe," he said and greeted me with a hug and a peck on the cheek. Damon and I were officially an "item" now, as Jen would say.

"Hi," I said.

"Can I see it *now*?" he asked, his golden eyes pleading with me. "It is the day of the exhibit after all," he said, hugging me closer to his chest.

"When we get there," I said, slightly nervous about showing my painting.

"That's not fair," he complained.

"You won't let me see yours," I pointed out, and that silenced him.

"The exhibit is at the conservatory in the back of the property," he said, gesturing for me to get into his car.

"We need your car to get there?" I asked, raising my eyebrows.

"Well, I didn't think you would want to walk. It's a little far."

"All right," I said.

We got into his black BMW, and I carefully placed the painting on the smooth leather backseat. We drove the few minutes in silence, and I couldn't stop jiggling my knee with anticipation. This would also be my first time meeting Damon's family. I hoped my painting would be acceptable to them.

"Damon, I'm so nervous," I squeaked as we pulled up to the front of the conservatory where the art exhibit was being held. Large, shiny glass windows revealed the stark white interior of the room. I could see the rectangular shape of paintings through the window, but I couldn't make out what they were of.

"Don't be," he said with a soft smile. He leaned forward and gently pressed his lips to mine, and I closed my eyes, trying to forget about my worries.

He slowly pulled away and smiled at me again. I struggled to force the muscles of my face into the small semblance of a smile. We both got out of the car, and I grabbed my sheet-covered painting in one hand and Damon's hand in my other.

We walked into the large white-walled room, and I looked up to see the ceiling stretching high above me. I clutched the canvas close to my chest as Damon led me through the room of official-looking people.

Damon gently tapped a man with dark hair. He turned around, and I felt my heart accelerate at the sight of his face. His mouth was pressed into a hard line, and dark bags hung under his golden brown eyes, the exact shade as Damon's. His eyebrows looked like they were perpetually pulled together in worry.

"Hey, Dad, this is my girlfriend, Harmony." I blushed at the word "girlfriend" as a grim smile flashed on his dad's features while he reached forward to shake my hand.

"It's very nice to meet you, Harmony. Donovan Caliego," he said, his voice rough and coarse.

"Nice to meet you, Mr. Caliego," I said hesitantly. Damon grabbed my hand and led me to an empty, wooden painting stand. I carefully placed the painting on the wooden stand and grabbed the sheet with my shaking fingers. I could almost feel everyone's eyes on me as I slowly slid the sheet off the canvas.

There was complete silence.

The painting seemed to ooze with one emotion: fury. The colors were black and white except for his eyes.

Their stunning blue color wasn't the only unusual thing about them. Instead of a normal round pupil, they had a vertical slit that ran right through the middle. His hard cheekbones cast a shadow across his hard jaw, anger pulsing with every line and stroke. His lips were curled up into a snarl, and he appeared to be inhaling, as if he were hissing.

The nostrils on his sharp, pointed nose were flared out with rage, casting a second, darker shadow across his narrow but hard cheekbones. His black hair was lifted out of his eyes by an imagined wind, softening his hard features. In the background, there were gray flames swirling around his face and shoulders, lifting and twirling his thick hair.

And it was all done with black, white, and different shades of gray.

I began to notice that the silence in the room wasn't natural anymore. I felt my heart beating loudly. Why wasn't anybody saying anything?

Finally, Donovan Caliego's voice broke the silence. "What the hell is that?"

"I … I …" I stuttered, completely confused by his furious reaction. "I don't really know," I finally muttered, finding my voice. "I pictured him in a dream I had." My voice was soft, and I was surprised they could even hear it. "The theme was fantasy, so …"

"Who the hell are you?" he hissed as I slowly pulled the sheet back over my painting. His golden eyes, so much like Damon's, were slowly growing and widening until they were practically bulging out of his head. I couldn't help but notice the way his hands seem to shake by his sides.

"Believe me, Dad, she's not related to them in any way." Damon sounded reassuring, but his tone was just as dangerous. He was trying to calm his dad down, but it clearly wasn't working. They were talking right in front of me, but they were acting as if I wasn't there.

"Do you know him? Do you know what he is?" he growled at me, and I had no idea what to make of his ridiculous behavior. I opened my mouth to say something, but Damon interceded for me.

"They're friends, but I don't think she knows," he said, and by this time people were beginning to stare.

"Do you mean to tell me that they talk together, *privately on a regular basis*?" Damon's dad said.

"It would appear so," Damon said, but his voice remained slightly hushed.

I wanted to scream and yell and question. What was going on? It felt as if everything was exploding around me, and I had no idea what the cause was.

"Damn it, Damon! Then what the hell is she doing here? Do you have any idea what would happen if they saw that? I can't believe you could be so brainless," he roared, and I wanted to be swallowed up by the earth and never return. I had no idea what was going on.

It looked like Donovan was completely losing it. He had raked his fingers through his once gelled hair, forcing it into spontaneous spikes on top of his head. His face turned beet red.

"I had no idea that she would bring something like that," Damon muttered.

"Well, you should have found out!"

I could feel people's eyes boring into me. I refused to look up and meet the probing gazes. I kept my eyes trained on my interlocked fingers, praying that this horrible ordeal was going to be over soon.

"How could I have found out?"

"Are you sure she doesn't know about him or Cyrus?" Donovan's voice was slightly calmer. *Did he just say Cyrus? As in Keith's dad?*

"I don't think so," Damon said.

"Well find out! And, Damon, I hope you're not so idiotic that you don't realize what has to be done now?"

"I understand," he said, his voice flat and emotionless.

Suddenly I felt his hand rest gently on my shoulder, and I immediately tensed up. "Damon, what's going on?" I said.

"I can't explain now, but I'll tell you in the car." His eyes had lost their frozen look, and his face was soft again.

"Does that mean we're leaving?" I asked, grabbing my painting off of the small wooden stand.

"Yes, we are leaving." He grabbed my hand and towed me out of the exhibit.

Outside, I got into his car and kept my eyes down as the he started the engine.

The door to the exhibit opened again, drawing both of our attention.

| 15 Stitches |

Donovan was standing there, gesturing for Damon to come out of the car. Damon sighed and said to me, "I'll be right back."

I didn't want to overhear their conversation, but my window was open just a crack. Their whispered voices drifted through the window with the wind.

"Dad, I don't understand. Why can't I take him?"

"Because, who knows if we have the resources to contain him without the Artrox? Just wait until I have it working again."

"You've been working on it for more than fifteen years! I know you've come a long way, but how much longer can we let him roam around uncontained?"

"You will listen to me and you won't act until I have the Artrox working. Understand?"

What was an Artrox? And who did they want to contain?

Damon came back to the car, got in, and we drove off.

"Damon, what was that? What's going on?" I asked.

"I already told you, my family is a little weird."

"Their reaction to my painting was more than a little weird," I said, trying to keep my voice from rising with frustration.

"I know, I know. I don't even understand them sometimes," he said.

"That's not a very good excuse for what happened. I was kicked out!"

"Well, what do you want me to say?" he asked, his tone rising with anger. "Do you think I know why my family is mental?" His hands were tight on the steering wheel, his knuckles turning white as he clenched his fist.

"I'm sorry, Damon," I said quietly. "I was just upset, that's all. I didn't mean to yell."

"I understand. I know my family can be frustrating." His voice was a little softer but still tense.

We were silent for the rest of the drive to his house. When we pulled in front of his house, I started to walk over to my car, but then Damon's hand on my shoulder stopped me.

"Yes?" I asked him, hesitantly turning around to face him.

"Can you come inside for a second? I want to show you something."

"Sure," I said and followed him up the dramatic front stairway and waited as he slowly unlocked the large doors.

I tried not to stare around at the ornately decorated house as we walked in. It felt cold and empty, as if nobody spent a long period of time in any of the rooms.

"Stay here for a second," he whispered, and he headed up the striking stairway that led up from the enormous foyer. I could hear his footsteps echoing above me as he walked through unknown rooms.

As he walked back down the stairs, my heart immediately dropped a beat at the sight of the small golden book he was carrying.

"Have you ever seen a book like this before?" he asked, holding it out to me very carefully.

I took it in my hands and recognized the elaborately decorated golden front, with the scripted gold lettering. I gently opened the book to the first page and recognized the hard-to-read, loopy script.

"Yes, I've seen it before," I said quietly.

Suddenly, I heard his breath quicken, and I glanced him. He looked blazingly excited, his golden eyes wide and bright, and for a second he seemed just as crazy as his family.

"Where did you see it?" he said.

My heart began to thunder in my chest. His reaction was too weird. I took a wild guess and thought it would be better not to say that I saw it at Keith's house.

"I don't really remember. Maybe at a library or something," I said, staring him in the eye, hoping that he wouldn't be able to read through my lie. Suddenly his features fell, and the half-crazed expression left his face.

"Are you sure it's the same book? Did you read any of it?"

"Yeah, I'm sure it's the same one. I read the first few pages."

"Read the first page just to make sure," he said quickly. I glanced down at the book, knowing exactly what it would say. But I reread the words just to placate him.

The story that I tell is true. It is not for entertainment, but for the memory of years long gone ...

"Yes, Damon, I'm sure that it's the same one," I said.

"That's all I wanted to show you," he said. "I really am sorry about today.

I know how excited you were." He reached forward and gave me a crushingly tight hug.

"Don't worry about it, Damon," I said, pulling slowly away from him. As I turned to walk out the door, I couldn't shake the feeling that something creepy was going on.

Chapter 13

I lay in bed on Monday morning; the last thing I wanted to do was face Damon at school. He hadn't called me since the exhibit, and I was wondering whether we ever really had a relationship.

I didn't want to have to tell Keith what happened at the art exhibit, and I didn't really want to talk to my friends about it either. My mom's shout echoed from downstairs, and a sigh escaped my lips as I dragged myself out of bed.

I slowly got ready, not even attempting to do my hair. Then I stomped down the stairs and out the door.

I drove into the school parking lot the same time Keith did. I waved hesitantly to him, and he waved back as he got out of his car.

"Hey," I said, walking up to him, and he looked down at me.

While we walked into the building, he was constantly looking up and around, his face tight and his jaw tense.

"Keith, are you okay?" I asked him.

"Of course. Why wouldn't I be?" There was a strained note in his voice that was impossible to ignore. "So, how did the exhibit go?" he asked.

"Not well," I said, turning to face him.

"Why? What happened?"

"Well, his dad didn't exactly like my painting."

"You saw his dad? What do you mean 'he didn't exactly like it'?" he said, his voice rising slightly.

"Yeah, I saw him. He's really scary. He was saying this crazy stuff at me that didn't make any sense." I decided to leave out the fact that he screamed at me. Keith had closed his eyes, and he was gently rubbing the corners with his thumb and forefinger.

"Like what?"

"He was saying stuff like 'You know about them! Who are you?' Stuff like that."

"What did you paint?" he asked, his voice tense.

"Well, I kind of had this dream. It was about this guy who had these really strange eyes, and he was like a monster … kind of."

"Are you kidding me?" he asked, his bright blue eyes suddenly bulging wide.

"No," I said quietly.

"Was there anything else besides the weird eyes?"

"Not in my painting, but in my dream he had wings and scales along his neck."

"Oh my god, I don't believe this," he said. He turned around and sprinted down the hall. The weirdness was beginning to overwhelm me. My attention was drawn to across the hall where Damon was waving at me.

"Harmony, I wanted to apologize again for what happened on Saturday," Damon said. His comment was oddly forced.

"Damon, it's okay, really."

"I hope this won't change the way you feel about me," he said quietly.

"Don't be ridiculous," I lied.

*   *   *

Keith continued to act strange all day, constantly looking around and playing with his fingers. He didn't pay attention in any of the classes that I had with him, which was extremely out of the ordinary.

That night, I thought about Keith's strange behavior and decided that I was just making a big deal out of nothing. I curled up under my heavy quilt and let my heavy eyelids shut.

Out of nowhere, I heard the loud sounds of the phone ringing. I jumped out of bed, irritation flowing through me. Who the hell would be calling us at three in the morning?

Above the sound of the ringing telephone, I heard the sound of my mother jogging through the hall to reach the phone on time.

Suddenly, the piercing sound of the telephone cut off, and I heard my mother's faint, groggy voice, "Hello?" My heart started thundering in my ears, and my blood pulsed loudly behind my temple. Why did Mom have to pick up the phone? Why couldn't she have let it ring?

I crept to the door, and I heard the sounds of my mother's heavy, anxious breathing. I opened the door to see her standing down the hallway with her back facing me. Her shoulders were hunched and trembling. I could see that she was barely able to keep the phone from slipping through her fingertips.

"Mom?" I asked. "Mom, what happened?" At the sound of my voice, the trembling in her shoulders grew much more pronounced.

"Of course," she finally managed to say to the person on the other end of the line. "I'll be there as soon as possible." She slowly brought her hands down, and I felt a shiver begin to creep up my spine.

"Mom, where are you going?"

"Something happened," she said quietly.

"What?"

"You—your father …" She closed her eyes as she strained against the words that refused to move past her frozen tongue.

"What happened?" I screamed.

"Your father was found by those burned woods. The police want me to identify him," she said, her voice a whisper.

"What?" I said for what felt like the eighth time tonight.

My mind spun wildly out of control. I couldn't form coherent thoughts, I couldn't think, I couldn't feel anything. I couldn't understand the words my mom was speaking. They couldn't be true because they were impossible.

"I have to leave now," my mom said, and I felt my brain struggle to focus on her soft words. She seemed so far away, like I was staring at her through a long, empty tunnel.

"Harmony, honey, take a deep breath," she said, placing her hands on my shoulders. Then she pulled me close and held me to her chest. "Everything will be all right," she told me, but she was wrong. Everyone kept telling me that, but those words were never, ever true.

She walked downstairs, and I forced my frozen muscles to follow her.

"Mom?" I said as she was putting on her coat.

She just looked at me.

"Can I come with you?" I asked.

"Of course," she said, and I could tell that she wanted me to go with her—that she didn't trust me alone by myself, not like this.

I pulled on my jacket and followed her out to the car.

As we drove, I could see the flicker of blue and red lights in the distance ahead of us. My mother's hands started trembling on the steering wheel.

The flashing blue and red lights ahead grew brighter as the car moved faster. We slowed down a little behind the scene, and my mother lurched out of the car. I followed her.

That was when I saw him, and the shock of seeing his face there, of all places, broke through the frantic spinning of my brain and the wild churning of my stomach.

Cyrus Draykon was standing outside the caution tape, a pained expression on his face as he raked his fingers through his hair. I saw Keith standing behind him, his face ghostly pale. *What the hell are they doing here?*

"Excuse me, but this area is roped off; you cannot come past here," the policeman said to my mother and me.

"That's my husband back there," my mom said, and I stared at her in surprise. Her voice was calm and reasonable as she extended her driver's license to the officer.

"Of course, my apologies," he said, and his face melted into sympathy. She became more anxious as she pushed past him and ducked under the bright yellow tape.

A tall man in a business suit walked up to us with a grave expression on his face. His sandy brown, graying hair was slicked back from his narrow face.

"Mrs. Vindico?" he asked my mother, extending his hand in her direction. I could see my mother struggling to hold it together, but she stayed professional. "Come this way please," he said and immediately turned on his heel and walked away from us.

He weaved in and out of people rushing back and forth. As we continued walking, I couldn't help the frantic feeling in the pit of my stomach. I overheard a voice saying, "Looks like a homicide, but I've never seen injuries like that before …" Then the voice trailed off as we continued to follow the man. I suddenly wanted to go home, to go home and fall asleep and never, ever, have to wake up.

Suddenly my mother started screaming.

I whirled around and froze. All the senses in my body wanted to shut down and repel the image from my mind forever. I couldn't look at his face; my eyes were riveted on the bloody scars and burn marks that seemed to cover him everywhere.

My mother hadn't stopped screaming.

I could feel my body shaking and trembling as I closed my eyes. I heard deep male voices as they struggled to comfort my mother and bring her back to her senses. I thought I heard someone faintly calling my name, but the sound was so far away, as if it came from the other end of a tunnel that stretched across the entire country. Despite my frantic shaking, I could feel my eyes focus on something that I had seen over and over again.

Two feathers, connected by a twisted cross, were carved into the huge tree behind where my father lay.

I felt gentle hands on my shoulders as I was guided outside of the caution tape lines again. I could feel my knees begin to weaken and shake, and I heard someone dimly calling my name again. I forced my eyes to move in that direction. Keith was standing in front of me, and he had crouched down until his eyes were level with mine.

"Harmony," he said, as if he was trying to drag my eyes away from the macabre sight behind him. I could feel my lips moving as I struggled to get the words past my throat, but, like my mother, they got stuck and refused to be heard. He stood up to his full height and looked around, looking frenzied.

Suddenly I took a step forward and wrapped my arms around him, squeezing him tight. I felt his arms wrap around my shoulders as he pulled me closer to him.

Standing there in his arms, I immediately felt sane again, and the world came zooming back from across the tunnel at the speed of light. I knew that

Damon would never be able to comfort me like this, no matter what I tried to tell myself.

"What are you doing here?" I mumbled into his shirt. The trapped words were finally released from their cage.

He didn't answer me, his hands just forming steady circles on my back.

Chapter 14

I took a couple of days off from school so I could support my mother and help plan the funeral, and after that, I just couldn't go back for the rest of the week.

I woke up that next Monday morning with a tear-streaked pillow and a tangled bedspread. My mom was forcing me to go to school. She said I couldn't sit around all day and mope, and I guess she was right. It felt like I was lifting up the world just to climb out of bed. I was sore without having exercised, and I was wound up even though I had slept.

When I got to school, everyone said they were sorry, but why would I need them to be sorry? Sarah, Jen, and Adrienne just stared at me with concerned eyes without making much conversation. I smiled at them, knowing that if I didn't, I would burst into tears.

There seemed to be increased tension between Damon and Keith. Even I could detect the way that they glared at each other from across the hallway or the strain when they both reached for the same apple at lunch. Keith refused to say why he and his dad were at the scene that night. Every time I hinted at it, he would become tense and change the subject. It seemed impossible that it could be a coincidence.

When the day finally ended, I couldn't remember anything that had happened.

I sighed and struggled to push through the loud commotion of people.

When I had reached a breach, I was shocked to see that Damon had Keith backed up against one of the lockers, a frightening expression on his face.

It seemed as if their positions should have been reversed, for Keith towered at least five inches over Damon.

I saw Damon's lips move, and a terrifying expression flashed across Keith's face. He placed his hands on Damon's shoulders, and it looked like he barely pushed. Damon stumbled back to the opposite wall and sneered something at him that I didn't catch.

Then Damon turned and walked away, calling over his shoulder, "Watch your temper!" Keith sprinted off in the opposite direction and disappeared.

The loud shouts had dissipated into quiet whispers as people wondered what was going on. I followed Damon as he walked away, struggling to keep up with the way he slid easily through the crowd of people.

"Damon!" I called out.

He slowly turned toward me, a smile forming on his face when he saw me.

"Hey, Harmony!"

"What just happened?"

"Nothing. Your buddy there was just prying into things that he shouldn't," he sneered. "I'd like the chance to tell you more," he added, suddenly smiling. "Can I come around to your house on Friday? Maybe we could watch a movie and get pizza or something like that."

"All right," I said hesitantly. Although I was feeling reluctant, he and Keith were hiding something serious, and Damon seemed to be willing to talk. Keith wasn't. I shook my head and walked to my locker.

The hall had cleared in the past few minutes. I opened my locker and packed the books I needed for homework.

As I walked out of the building, I noticed that the parking lot was empty, except for Keith's car and mine.

I walked to my car and wrapped my sweatshirt tighter around me. The early March air was getting colder as the sun moved steadily toward the horizon. Suddenly, I heard footsteps behind me.

"Harmony!"

I turned around.

"Hey Keith, what's up?" I asked, pretending that I hadn't witnessed his encounter with Damon.

"I really need to tell you something," he said anxiously. He shuffled his feet a little, and his eyes scanned our surroundings.

"What is it?"

"Well, if Damon asks you to go to a deserted place with him, don't go. Okay?"

"What are you talking about?" I asked, exasperated by the ridiculous situation.

"Just listen to me," he said.

"Keith, don't take this the wrong way, but it's really not any of your business what Damon and I do together."

"This is different," he said, glancing around nervously.

"How is it different? I'm tired of the animosity between you two. It's driving me crazy!"

"This is more serious than even that," he said.

"What's going on? A lot of weird stuff is happening, and I have no idea what to think about any of it!"

Something seemed to snap inside of him. He lunged forward and grabbed me by my shoulders.

"For God's sake! Listen to me! It's for your own safety," he practically yelled.

I felt myself start to tremble. I had never seen him lose his calm like this.

Suddenly, I burst into tears. "Keith, let me go!" I whimpered, trying to make my voice sound strong. His grasp loosened from my shoulders, and he slowly put his hands back by his sides.

"I'm sorry," he said, staring at the ground.

"I have no idea what's going on anymore," I bawled. "I have no idea what's going on between you and Damon, or his family or your dad or my dad. But you two need to sort it out and leave me out of it! I feel like everything's out of control and there's nothing I can do about it." I felt like I was going crazy.

"Harmony," he said after a second, his voice quiet. He held his arms open to me, a gesture of comfort. I couldn't resist the feeling of his arms around me,

| 15 Stitches |

so I moved forward, crushing myself to him like I had last Monday. And like last Monday, he stroked my hair and let me stain his shirt with my tears.

"Harmony?" he asked after my heaving sobs had subsided.

"Yes," I said with a sigh.

"Do you want to get together again on Friday for the project? There are some things I need to explain to you." I pulled away from him and examined his face, hating the words that I would have to say to him.

"I can't. I have plans to see Damon," I said before I got into my car and drove away. When I looked back in my mirror, his tall dark figure was still watching me.

Chapter 15

On Friday afternoon, the doorbell rang. I knew my mom was somewhere upstairs, and she probably wouldn't bother us.

When my father was still here, the house never felt warm, but it didn't have the empty coldness that now hung in the air. I felt a sadness suddenly fill me, which I fought with all my heart. I wanted to at least try to enjoy the evening with Damon.

When I opened the door, I felt a smile slowly creep over my face.

"Hey, babe," he said, bending down to peck me lightly on the lips. "It's such a nice evening. I have an idea. Do you wanna skip the movie and just go for a walk in the park?"

The memory of Keith's admonishment stood out vividly in my mind. I hesitated, remembering the livid expression on his face when he shook my shoulders with his large hands.

"It's getting dark out," I noted.

"It'll be nice to go for a walk. We won't be out too long."

Damon could be so smooth and convincing. "All right," I said, and again Keith's warning rang in my ears. I grabbed my sweatshirt, and as we headed out along the sidewalk, Damon grabbed my hand.

I squeezed his fingers and smiled to myself, suddenly happy that I had decided to go for a walk with him. Keith was being ridiculous.

As we reached the entrance to the park, Damon began walking faster, practically dragging me through the winding path.

"What's wrong?" I asked. I had to practically jog to keep up with his long strides.

"There's nothing wrong," he said tersely, his eyes darting around as we walked deeper into the park. "Why?"

"It's just that you look kind of tense, and we're going really fast."

He slowed down, gave me a comforting smile, and said, "Don't worry."

"Where are you taking me anyway?"

Damon grasped my hand in his firm grip.

"Where are we going?" I repeated as I struggled to shake my hand free of his grasp.

"You'll see," he said, and I struggled to ignore the chill that went up my spine when I heard the sharp edge in his voice.

I should have listened to Keith after all.

"Damon, what's going on?" I asked as he rushed me still faster through the winding trees. He ignored me, and I forced myself to gulp and press down the mounting panic.

Finally, the path seemed to come to an end, and we came upon a large wooden building that looked abandoned; the windows were dark and empty, and the paint was old and peeling.

"Damon, what—"

"Shut up," he snarled at me, and I immediately fell silent.

Adrenaline pulsed through my veins as my body registered a fight or flight response.

"Do you know how long I've waited for this?" he asked, a hint of insanity creeping into his deep voice.

"Waited for what?" I barely croaked out.

It seemed strange that only a few minutes ago we were laughing together in my kitchen.

"Do you remember that small golden book that you read at Keith's house?"

My heart froze. How did he know that I read that book at Keith's house?

"Ha," he laughed suddenly. "You wanna know how I know that? Because there are only two copies of that little book in the entire world. My family has one, and Cyrus Draykon stole one when he betrayed the Griffins," he hissed.

"Damon, what are you talking about?" I asked, trying to figure a way out of the situation. But my back was to the large wooden building and the only way out would be past Damon and through the path in the park.

"Well, that story is true, every word of it," he said, making absolutely no sense. "If that stupid Dragon hadn't wandered off in the first place, he would have never met the stupid girl. Then the Griffin could have done what he wanted and wouldn't have been killed by the stupid Dragon. Don't you see? The first act of evil was done by the Dragon, causing generations to feud until the Griffins picked off the Dragons, slowly, one by one, until there was one left, plus a half if you count Keith."

"You're nuts!" I half laughed at him. "You should be put in an insane asylum! Keith is supposed to be the Dragon? What kind of sick joke are you playing Damon? Because it's not funny!"

Damon looked up at me, his eyebrows knitted together. He took two steps toward me, and I retreated till my back was pressed firmly against the wall.

It all happened in slow motion. Damon's fist slowly pulled back, and I winced before it collided with a sickening crack against my jaw. With a faint cry, I slid down the wall, my hand flying to my jaw.

"You stupid girl. You have no idea who you're messing with, do you? I'm at the head of the prison guard for the largest human city of the Griffins," he said arrogantly, but I had no idea what that was supposed to mean. "I'm in charge of capturing and torturing prisoners." He laughed manically.

"Keith is one of the last creatures with Dragon blood on the face of the earth, besides his mother, of course. He also happens to be a direct descendant of the Dragon that caused all this mess. I've have been looking for an opportunity to capture him for years, and I think I finally have him. My father says I can't capture him until they fix the Artrox, but I'll prove them wrong."

"You're a crazy psychopath!" I knew I shouldn't have gone there, but I said it anyway. Fear took over as I saw his hand twitch to hit me again. All I wanted to do was run, but there was nowhere to go.

Damon only laughed a crazy, fanatical laugh that reverberated off the towering trees of the empty park. "You think I don't have the guts to kill you. In fact, you think I'm just playing a big joke and someone is going to pop out and say 'just kidding'," he leered. "Well, sorry, sweetheart, this is no joke, and by the end of tonight, you will be dead and the only half Dragon in existence will be in my clutches."

I kept quiet. My heart was pounding against my chest.

"Now, we wait for Keith to get here."

I felt a huge ball rise up in my throat as I realized that Damon had only been paying attention to me to get to Keith. His betrayal felt like a punch in the stomach, and I struggled to suck air into my lungs. I pressed my lips tightly together to repress a sob that threatened to break through.

I noticed that Damon was turned away from me, watching eagerly in the other direction. I had no idea what he was waiting for or why. I had no idea how crazy peoples' minds worked.

For a moment, the park seemed silent, apart from my ragged breathing. I closed my eyes and slowly willed myself to straighten and stand up. Damon barely glanced at my movement, so I inched slightly away from the wall, hoping to slip past him.

As fast as lightning, Damon swung around and punched me again, this time in the stomach. I felt the breath fly out of me as I went soaring about three feet into the air and then landed with a loud thump.

The air flew out of my lungs with a loud huff, and I clutched my stomach as I struggled to breath. A small whimper escaped through my clenched teeth as I struggled to stand up.

"Not to worry, he'll show up eventually; they always do." Damon leaned against the wall.

I glanced at him for a millisecond before I ran for my life. Suddenly, I felt my head snap back as Damon stepped in my way and punched me again, sending me catapulting in the opposite direction. I slammed against the wall, letting out a wail of pain before landing in a heap on the ground.

"Nice try, babe," he laughed.

I felt a warm trickle of liquid on my cheek, and I lifted my sleeve and wiped it across my face.

"Don't make me tie you up," he said, as if reprimanding a child for eating too many cookies.

I didn't respond, and in the silence that followed, I heard pounding of footsteps.

"Finally," he muttered, facing in the direction of the footsteps.

I suddenly realized that if Damon was right, and Keith knew that I was there and was coming to save me, then I had to warn him.

Damon grinned like a crazy person. "He can smell us now," he whispered.

I felt a shudder run up my spine as I thought of Damon's reaction to what I was about to do.

I took a deep breath, filled my lungs, and let out a blood-curdling scream, "Keith, stop!" My shout echoed, and much to my relief, the footsteps stopped for a second.

Damon turned, but instead of the deathly glare that I feared, he was beaming wildly. The footsteps were suddenly even faster than before, and I realized my warning probably had the opposite effect of what I intended.

I could see someone running toward us. As the last rays of the sun disappeared behind the horizon, Keith appeared.

"Damon," he hissed, and I was surprised by the way his voice sounded, low and dangerous. "Leave, now."

"Why? We were just getting started." Damon reached in his pocket and pulled out something that I couldn't see. A horrified expression crossed Keith's face.

I struggled to sit straight and see what Damon was holding.

I froze. It was a gun, and he was pointing it at me.

Suddenly Damon took a flashlight and flashed it at Keith, and for the first time I noticed that he was shaking, hunched over with his hands in the corners of his eyes. I felt horror creep through me as a growl ripped through his clenched teeth, and then suddenly his eyes snapped open.

I saw the eyes—the eyes from my dream, the eyes of the painting—staring back at me.

The shudders running through his body didn't stop; they grew in intensity, and suddenly he seemed to get taller and taller. He was at least eight feet tall now and towered menacingly over Damon.

Damon was staring at him with a wicked expression as he slowly crept closer toward me. Keith hissed again, and something seemed to be growing on the sides of his neck. Bright blue scales, the same color as his eyes, grew along his jaw and down to his collarbone. All I could do was stare at him in absolute horror.

What the hell was happening?

Keith let out another growl, and his shoulders suddenly arched backward. Two massive wings tore through his shirt and grew and expanded until they were blocking the entire pathway.

My breath came in low frightened rasps as I struggled to rationalize what I was witnessing.

Suddenly, Keith shouted, "No!" before a shot rang out.

A burning pain shot like fire through my leg.

I screamed and felt a warm liquid spill over my leg and pool around me. Dark spots appeared in my vision as I struggled to remain conscious despite the pain.

I could make out Keith's towering figure lunging viciously at Damon, a growl ripping through him. He seemed to remain suspended in the air for a few seconds as his massive wings picked up the air current and lifted him upward.

Another shot rang through the darkness, and I heard Damon's low voice curse.

"You'll have to fight the old-fashioned way now, Damon," Keith jeered as Damon lunged, struggling to take him to the ground. Keith's wings flapped oddly, as if he didn't know what to do with them.

Damon managed to drag himself away from Keith and run toward me, a manic smile on his face. He took one of his heavy boots and stomped hard on my lower arm. There was an audible crack.

Another one of my screams followed, and I barely had time to register the fact that Keith's face was contorting in a strange way and he was clutching at his stomach. Suddenly a huge flame erupted from his mouth and flew at

Damon and me. Damon dodged it easily, but I couldn't move before it hit my side.

Damon lunged at Keith again, and this time, Damon managed to get his massive frame to the ground. Keith's wings flapped in a contorted way on the ground, churning up huge piles of earth and throwing them everywhere.

I was splattered with dirt but barely felt it compared to the burning in my leg and arm. Damon was thrown backward into the trees, and Keith stood up, another orange glow lighting up the night sky as he sprinted in Damon's direction.

Suddenly, all the pain was too much. I closed my eyes as my body pulled my mind toward unconsciousness.

* * *

I could feel consciousness suddenly break through, and I was aware of the pain that seemed to throb everywhere. I seemed to be sitting in a strange kind of sticky liquid.

I could hear my ragged breathing as I sucked air in and out of my lungs. I felt so faded and tired, as if it would take the strength of a thousand men just to lift my eyelids.

Suddenly, I heard Keith's voice. "Oh my God, what have I done? What have I done?"

I dragged my eyelids open as panic took hold of me.

"Harmony! Oh my God, what did he do to you?" he asked, and his gentle hands slowly moved my sticky hair away from my face. I felt the muscles tense even though I knew that moving would be impossible. With my faded vision, I could tell that his eyes had returned to normal and the strange wings had disappeared.

I forced my lips to move in a whisper that even I could barely hear. "Don't touch me" was all I managed to get out before I cringed with the pain of everything emotional and physical.

I felt him move away from me, and I could hear him make a strange stifled noise in the darkness. Suddenly, my vision was flecked with black.

This time, I let the blackness take me.

Chapter 16

Images flickered around in my head. Were they a flash of a memory? Or just of a dream? The frightening darkness never ended, and the faint pictures that I saw were only shadows.

They were angry and they were fighting, and all the while, there was a pain that never ended. They were images that didn't make sense, with bright lights and things that weren't what they should be.

There were flashes of white that occasionally broke through the darkness, of rushing people who were whispering worriedly, a strong smell that only existed in one place. The sounds of a strange beating from the monitor, of a deep, worried voice that started the cycle all over again.

There seemed to be a faded light in front of me, and I somehow knew that I had to go toward it, but it wasn't easy.

I struggled to swim to the top where there would be light and there would be sound.

The light coming from the surface slowly got brighter, and I struggled harder. Suddenly, I was aware of my body again. I could feel my arms lying heavily against my sides, and I could feel my eyelids.

I dragged my eyelids upward and gasped loudly. I squinted and blinked in the bright light that shone down on my face. It took me a second to associate the strong smell and the stark whiteness with a hospital.

"Harmony," someone said in a very business-like voice with a hint of worry. "How are you feeling?" he said, kneeling down to the level of my bed.

A fiery and aching pain throbbed in my leg, and I breathed in sharply, gritting my teeth together.

"It hurts," I whimpered. My eyes, accustomed to the darkness, slowly adjusted to the bright lights.

"I know. We'll try to give you something to stop that, okay?" he said in a gentle voice. "You had emergency surgery done on your leg. You have a pretty bruised up face and a broken arm and hand. You've also sustained a concussion and have burns in sporadic places along your body." He smiled sympathetically as I cringed at the long list. "The good news is that you'll be able to walk again, although you may have a limp for a while.

"We'll give your mother a call now and tell her that you've woken up. She may not come right away, though. It's about three o'clock in the morning."

"What happened to … Damon?" I said. I was scared that he would somehow find me again. Immediately, the beating on the monitor increased in tempo.

An extremely upset expression crossed on the doctor's face. "If you're referring to the friend you were with, I'm sorry, but no one has seen him since."

I was frightened to succumb to the darkness again, terrified at the images that I might see, but I let my eyes slowly close and heard the doctor quietly go out.

A growl ripping through Keith's clenched teeth. Damon laughing wickedly. Keith arching his shoulders as wings exploded from his back, a yellow flame spilling from his mouth. Damon pointing the gun at me. The dark hole of the barrel staring at me.

The images had no real meaning, occurring in rapid succession one after the other. They swirled around in my head for who knows how much time.

"Harmony?" I heard my mother say, and then her voice faded as she talked to someone else. "Is she sleeping?"

I slowly opened my eyes.

"Oh, sweety," she said, rushing forward to lay a kiss gently on my forehead. She smoothed my hair back and smiled even though she had watery eyes. "How are you feeling?" she asked, settling in the chair next to me and gently placing her hand over mine.

| 15 Stitches |

"Not wonderful," I croaked, struggling to clear my voice.

"You have no idea how worried I've been," she said. She stroked my fingers with a light touch that only a mother could have.

"How long do I have to stay here?" I asked, careful to keep every part of me still in order to prevent the fiery pain from shooting up my leg.

"At least another week till you can come home, and then another week before you can go back to school," she said. She stopped talking and stared into the distance, as if she was debating whether to tell me something. "You know Keith, the boy that you were working on your project with?" she asked.

"Yes," I said stiffly.

I struggled to repress the frightening pictures of him in my head. Even though he had saved me, he was a monster.

"He was here to see you earlier."

"What?" I said as my breathing started to get heavier, thinking of him watching me while I was most vulnerable.

"What's wrong?" she asked, concern etched in her face.

"It's nothing," I said, taking large breaths to try and calm my heart rate. It slowed slightly, but not before the nurse came bustling in.

"Are you feeling all right?" she asked, carefully examining the monitor.

"Yeah," I said, forcing my voice to stay even. "I'm fine."

"You look a little anxious. Is the pain okay? Do we need to give you something for it?"

"No, really, I'm fine," I said.

A nurse entered the room and turned to my mother and said, "Her medication is getting low; we'll have to replenish it. She'll sleep for a while after that."

The nurse walked forward and then injected some medication into the IV.

"It'll take a few minutes before it kicks in," she said, before turning around and leaving the room. I already felt my eyelids droop heavier and fought to stay conscious for a little while longer.

My mom talked about school and how I could try to keep up with the curriculum while I was recovering, but her voice was already drifting out into a faint hum.

The darkness and numbness I felt didn't last long. I heard voices surrounding me, drawing me to the surface and out of that dark safe place.

"Is she asleep?" I heard the deep voice say, and I froze in fear, the voice bringing back the wave of memories that the medicine had repressed.

"I think so," my mother's voice said.

The beating from the monitor skyrocketed, and all the voices stopped.

I resisted, squeezing my eyes shut as if that would make everything go away. I finally allowed my eyes to open, and the throbbing in my head drowned out that of the monitor.

"Harmony," he said, kneeling down next to me. I stared at him wide eyed. His thick black hair hung long, nearly reaching his sharp cheekbones. I saw my mom make an exit out of the room, and I wanted to call out to her, to beg her to stay and not leave me alone with him.

"I'm so sorry," he whispered. "I never wanted any of this to happen. Harmony, please understand." His tortured voice surprised me. I couldn't look at him; I couldn't look at his blue eyes, knowing what they could turn into.

The beating of the monitor continued to whiz frantically along with my heartbeat. I stared at my bandaged hand, struggling to keep myself from completely panicking.

"No!" he practically shouted, startling me. "You have to listen to me," he said desperately, pacing around the room. He ran his fingers raggedly through his shaggy hair. "I never asked to be what I am. You don't have any idea what I would do right now to be a normal person."

"I … I … can't," I murmured, and every instinct screamed for me to run. He was dangerous, and he shouldn't exist.

"Please believe me," he said. "I hate myself much more than you do."

I slowly closed my eyes, hoping that he would realize that I could never look at him the same way again. Just like Damon, my friend had never existed. He too had hidden behind a mask.

I heard the smallest of sobs escape his lips before I heard his retreating footsteps and one last mumbled, "I'm sorry."

Chapter 17

I heard the door close, and my heart rate slowed. I lay there staring at the stark white ceiling. Feeling tears well up in my eyes, I furiously brushed them away.

The heavy throbbing in my head worsened from all the intense pressure, and pain continuously seared up my leg. A nurse quickly scurried in, checking all of the monitors.

"Are you feeling all right, hon?" she asked kindly.

"I don't really know." I was conscious of the fact that I was shaking uncontrollably.

"I think we should start limiting your visitors to immediate family. We want you to stay calm so you can heal," she said with a glint in her eye.

"I'm going to talk to the doctor about increasing your medicine. You seem kind of anxious," she said, sticking a syringe into the IV. "This will help a little bit." She bustled out of the room, and I laid my head heavily against the pillow.

Suddenly a memory appeared before my eyes … *He had Damon's neck in the firm grasp of his hands, and for the first time I noticed that his nails had turned to talons. Keith baring his teeth, the small glow from a flame lightening the shadows of his mouth. Damon's once confidant expression turning to downright fear as Keith turned from cool and distant to a crazed monster.*

"Harmony!"

The monitor alarm was going so fast it was like it was one continuous beep. My breathing came in loud rasps, and sweat drenched the thin sheets on top of me.

An array of doctors and nurses surrounded me, looking at me with concerned expressions. A policeman stood there watching, his arms crossed against his chest. His piercing black eyes surveyed the scene. I looked around frantically for my mother—she was sitting in the chair next to me. Her hand was resting quietly on my shoulder, her dark eyes wide.

"Sweety, the policeman is going to ask you a few questions."

"About what?" I asked, afraid as I stared at the man's dark expression.

The nurses and doctors slowly filed out of the room, and I stared at their retreating backs.

"We're trying to determine what happened and figure out the whereabouts of Damon Caliego," the policeman said.

"Just wait one second," my mom said sternly. "Harmony, do you feel up to this?" she asked, her hand brushing against my forehead. I nodded. I just wanted to get it over with.

The policeman began, "Were you with Damon the evening of Friday, March 15th?"

"Yes. We were at my house."

"What were you doing there?"

"Well, he came to pick me up …"

"What did you do after that?"

I swallowed; we were getting into dangerous territory. "We went for a walk in the park. Damon wanted to go. I didn't want to though."

"Why not?" he asked, scribbling in his notebook.

"It was dark and kind of cold."

"What did you do once you were there?"

"I don't remember," I squeaked, deciding that feigning ignorance was the best thing to do in this situation. I certainly had an excuse for it.

"Do you know who shot you?" he asked, a frustrated tone entering his voice.

"All I remember," I said, pausing and taking a deep steadying breath, "is a loud bang and then pain in my leg … and that's it." I wished that was all I remembered from that horrible night.

"There are signs of a struggle in the place where you were found, but Damon was nowhere in sight. Do you know why that would be?"

"No," I said as I struggled again to keep my heart steady before it would give me away. "I told you all I remembered."

The officer tucked his notebook under his arm and stood up.

"Thank you very much," he said to me and my mom and slowly walked out of the room. All of my energy seemed to leave with him. The minute the door clicked shut, I felt my eyelids droop heavily.

"I'm really tired, Mom. What time is it?"

She glanced at the watch. "Ten in the morning," she said, a soft smile on her face. "Would you like me to turn the lights off?" I nodded.

For the first time, I noticed the heavy shadows under her eyes and the way her skin was a sickly gray color. She slowly pulled the blinds down after turning off the lights, and the room was plunged into darkness.

"I'm going to go home for a little while, okay?" she said.

"Okay," I whispered.

I heard the door softly click shut and fell asleep to the sound of the beeping monitor growing slower and slower.

* * *

My eyes blinked open, and for the first time I felt slightly refreshed. I looked around the room, waiting for my eyes to adjust to the dark shadows. Suddenly one of the shadows moved, and I felt my muscles tense up in fear.

"Hello?" I whispered, feeling my voice tremble nervously.

"Just relax, otherwise the nurses won't let me in here anymore," said the familiar deep voice, and I was beginning to think that wouldn't be a bad thing.

I heard his quiet sigh in the darkness, and my eyes slowly adjusted to see his towering figure watching me from the foot of my narrow bed. "There used to be a time when you were happy to be with me," he stated coldly, and I closed my eyes as the memories came washing back.

"Having seeing what you are changes everything," I said quietly.

"Harmony," he said, "I'm exactly the same person I was before; nothing about your friend has changed at all."

"No," I said tightly, trying to find a way to make him leave. "My friend disappeared when I realized that you weren't who I thought you were."

He came over to the side of the bed and sat beside me.

"I know you don't want me to be here, but I need you to listen to me," he said. "You only heard the story from Damon's perspective. He led you to believe that I'm a monster, but nothing about me has changed. It's just that you know a little bit more.

"Please," he said. "Do you remember that book you read when you were at my house? The small golden one?"

"How could I forget?" I said.

"The story you read was the start of a war that lasted hundreds of years between the Dragons and the Griffins. The Dragon, Zylon in the story, ended up killing the prince of the Griffin hierarchy, and the Griffins vowed to kill every last Dragon. They almost succeeded until there was only one Dragon left, Zylon's sister, Naggyra … She's my mother."

"What? How is that even possible?"

"Wait, I'll get to that part," he said. "The Griffins were cunning, better than the Dragons at evading detection, but they didn't have the natural discovery and problem-solving abilities that humans had. They sought the help of humans, hoping to eventually take them over. They enlisted the help of my father, who is the smartest person that ever lived. Before long, the Griffins had accomplishments that would be considered impossible for our time, and this was in the sixteenth century."

"That was the Middle Ages! Are you crazy?" I could hear my voice turning hysterical.

"Just let me finish," he said. "My father is a genius and developed a serum that stopped him from aging. As you can imagine, the Griffins never forgot about Naggyra. When they finally captured her, they told my father to use her to create a hybrid super species that they could control. Naturally, my dad used his own genes, and, well, here I am, the first human-Dragon child ever in existence."

"God, Keith, your dad made you as an experiment?" I said, finding it hard to believe that the loving man I had seen could be so heartless.

"I know, it sounds horrible," he said. "But he came to realize that what he

| 15 Stitches |

was doing was wrong. He and Naggyra escaped with me, destroying a very valuable piece of the Griffin's technology in the process."

"So, where's your mom now?" I asked, almost afraid to find out.

"She left us that night and disappeared, never to be seen by us or the Griffins again."

"Keith …how do you want me to treat you?" I whispered, blinking furiously at the tears in my eyes.

"You could at least treat me with a little decency," he said. "Why can't you accept this?"

I felt something inside me snap.

"Keith, you *killed* someone!"

"You think that I killed Damon?" he asked, his voice so shocked that I could barely hear the words as they left his lips.

"The last thing I remember is you sprinting after him into the woods and then coming back—that's it. What else do you want me to think? The police said that they can't find him."

"That's not what happened," he said, his eyes pleading with me.

"Then tell me."

"When Damon ran off into the woods, I started to follow him. It's hard to explain … but when I'm like that, it's as if my instincts take over and they're impossible to fight. He was my target, and I had to take him down no matter what." I shuddered at his words, and he grimaced at my reaction. "Then I remembered that you were back by that little shack, and I knew you wouldn't make it if I left you there for too long, so I went back."

"Then what happened to Damon?" I asked, trying to examine his features, but he had turned away to face the window.

"I don't know what happened to Damon. I'm assuming he ran off to one of the Griffin's cities." I didn't even try to decipher what that could possibly mean. I had closed my eyes, trying to block the images from my mind.

Suddenly, a memory broke through of a small symbol of two feathers with a twisted cross, one carved on the shelf in Keith's house, one in the burned woods, and one carved above the tree where my father lay.

"Keith," I hissed, and he faced me, a cautious expression on his face.

"What does that symbol mean, and what does my father have to do with any of this?"

He took a deep breath. "Your father was secretly working for my father for about five years. All those supposed late nights at the company, he was doing work for my father against the Griffins."

"How … what did he do?"

"Well, you know how my mother destroyed something very valuable to the Griffins, the energy source that allowed for all of their technology to work?" I nodded, and he continued. "My father has had suspicions for years that the Griffins are fixing it. He would send your dad to gather intelligence on the progress they were making. If the Griffins succeed in fixing this, they'll have the power to create an army and take over the world, which was their original intention when they created me. Without it, they're relatively harmless."

"Is that why he left us?" I asked quietly.

"Kind of. Your father did everything to keep you and your mother from getting involved in his dangerous job. When your mom started asking questions, he had to leave. He knew how dangerous it would be for you two if you ever found out."

"Oh my God," I said, and I could feel the tears begin to rise in my eyes.

"The Griffins discovered him and … they killed him. The symbol you saw in the forest, the one near your father, with the feathers and twisted cross … that's their symbol."

The tears slowly began to spill. He reached a hand to brush the hair out of my face, but I cringed away from him.

He got up, a bitter smile on his face. "I'm sorry," he whispered before the door shut behind him.

Chapter 18

Nearly a month passed. My leg healed, but nothing else did. Some days were harder than others, and today the pain of loss and betrayal felt unbearable. The total deceit by Damon and how easily he had fooled me was bad enough, but the loss of my dad was worse. And on top of that, the one person I could talk to, I couldn't even accept anymore. Some days, it felt as if it would have been better if Damon had succeeded in killing me and capturing Keith; at least that way I would be free.

I was now having visits with my old psychiatrist about once a month in an attempt to stop the nightmares that plagued me every night. She asked what my nightmares were about, but I refused to tell her.

I had to help myself, and I began thinking more and more that I had to go back and face the point in my life when everything changed. I had to return to Philadelphia and confront Robbie. It felt as if the end of my life started there. Everything was perfect up until that moment. After that, family strife, death, and deception marked my life.

Maybe, if I went back to the place that started it all, the craziness would end.

I had struggled to keep up with all the school work that was piling up, but what I was really worried about with returning to school was seeing Keith again.

I hadn't seen him since I left the hospital, and I couldn't seem to get that horrifying image of his Dragon persona out of my head. If it weren't for my dad's death, I wouldn't even believe any of it. How could my dad have kept what he did from us for so long? Was he really trying to protect us?

The problem was it was far too late to try to switch partners for the ecology project, and I was frightened about the time I would have to spend with Keith. It was almost the end of March, and the due date for the project was rapidly approaching.

"There's nothing to be nervous about. I'm sure that school will be fine tomorrow," Sarah said kindly over the phone.

"I'm just worried that I'll be behind with all my schoolwork," I lied.

"Do the police have any more information about who attacked you?"

"No, not yet …"

"And what about Damon? I can't believe he's still missing!"

I couldn't bring myself to say anything.

"Sorry," she said in response to my silence. "I know you probably don't want to talk about this."

"Yeah, not really. Bye. I'll see you tomorrow," I said, snapping my phone shut. I climbed into bed, curling myself under the heavy quilt.

Despite the warming spring weather, I kept the thick blanket up over my shoulders. It somehow made me feel safe and protected.

When I finally drifted off into an uneasy sleep, the nightmare began.

A furious growl ripped through Keith's teeth the minute he saw me with them. My once childhood friend laughed as he pressed me against the wall.

"He's nothing!" he sneered, assessing all of the heavily-built guys around me. As Keith ran steadily closer, his hair flew away from his face, revealing his eyes, the slits he had for pupils narrow with anger.

All the fear I had seemed to melt away in one instant. He would save me, as he had done before. The only thing I worried about was what he would do to the now terrified people around me.

I sat up suddenly, my heart pounding in my chest. The loud bleating of the alarm seemed to reverberate between my temples.

I took a steadying breath as my heart slowed and the images faded from my memory. I ran my fingers through my damp hair, slightly surprised that it hadn't dried from my shower last night.

"It was just a dream," I chanted to myself, quickly turning off the blaring alarm. I got dressed for school and went downstairs. I sat down at the kitchen counter, nibbling on a waffle and staring into space.

"Harmony," my mother said softly, drawing my attention away from my thoughts of returning to school. "Your leg doesn't feel too bad to walk around in school today?"

"No worse than usual," I said, ignoring the occasional pangs that shot through my leg. My words seemed to placate her enough for now, and she followed me as I walked outside, the unsteady sound of the crutches resounding loudly on the pavement. I wasn't allowed to drive because the leg that I injured was the leg that I would need for driving.

I sighed, tossing my heavy backpack in the car with a loud thump. As my mom turned the key in the ignition, the loud hum of the engine broke the heavy silence.

"Mom, spring is coming!" I exclaimed a few minutes into the drive. I saw the smallest bit of green settling at the bottom of the forest floor as the undergrowth slowly came to life.

"It is," she said, her gaze flickering for a second off the gray expanse of road stretching out before us. Spring was her favorite season.

As we pulled into the school's parking lot, my mom slowed down in front of the towering red brick building. I slid awkwardly out of the car, struggling not to put any weight on the bandaged leg. I slid the backpack down and struggled to carry it and walk with the crutches at the same time.

"Harmony, are you crazy?" asked a familiar voice, and I jumped, my backpack and one crutch clattering to the ground. Sarah, Adrienne, and Jen looked at me with tentative smiles.

"Um," I said, not sure what to say.

"She probably is," Adrienne said as she lifted my crutch off the ground and handed it to me.

"Thanks," I muttered.

"Are you okay?" Jen said.

"Yeah, I'm fine." I scanned the long hallway of crowded students. I could feel the stares as people recognized me, and I could hear the whispers. I wondered what stories were being told, and which ones they believed.

I had the strongest feeling of déjà vu. No more than six months ago, the same thing had happened. The difference was that this time I felt even more hopeless than I did then. Now, I had no hope of making a wonderful new friend who would help pull me through the suffering process. Now, he was one of the people who would disappear from my life forever.

I finally saw him, towering above everyone else. My heart caught in my throat as I quickly looked away.

There was no doubt in my mind that he had seen me. "I have to go to the principal's office," I said abruptly, and I didn't give them time to say anything as I darted away as fast as my crutches could carry me. The last thing I wanted was an encounter with him.

I gulped, scurrying through the hallway. I kept my head down, my auburn hair swinging around my face. I quickly packed up my books from my locker.

As I headed to my classroom, I stumbled over something on the ground and fell, the crutches clattering loudly on the hard floor. I couldn't help the hissed whimper that escaped my teeth when the pain in my leg seared and then receded to a dull throbbing.

"Harmony, are you okay?" I heard his footsteps against the floor before I felt him kneeling next to me.

"I'm fine," I said, struggling to stand up without putting any weight on my leg. I saw that he was offering a hand to me to help me get up, and I had no choice but to take it. He easily lifted me up till I was precariously balanced on one foot. I could feel his eyes raking over my arms, where there were still scars from the burns that his breath had given me.

He grabbed my crutches and handed them to me. I could feel the panic slowly start to leak into my brain, and I had trouble making normal thought processes behind the fear. I couldn't help the way the images flashed across my brain, and the person before me slowly transformed into the monster in my mind.

"Are you sure you're all right?" he asked.

"Yes," I said wearily. "Thanks." I turned away from him and rushed as fast as I could to first period. As I walked in, it took me a second to realize that the room was completely silent.

"Harmony," said the slightly flustered Mr. Arlington, "I'm glad to see that you've returned."

"Thanks," I muttered, walking quickly to my seat. As the announcements began over the loudspeaker, Keith walked in.

I felt his gaze probing me, wanting to make eye contact. I stared at the paper in front of me, ignoring his gaze. I pretended like I didn't notice when he stepped around me to settle in his seat.

I could feel Sarah staring at me, shocked that I didn't even react to Keith. I pretended that I didn't even know he was there. It took me a second to remember that, as far as she knew, we were still good friends. I felt her gaze boring into the back of my head. I heaved a sigh and focused on what Mr. Arlington was saying.

After Mr. Arlington gave me the list of topics I missed, he began a lecture on a novel that we just read. He divided us up into pairs to discuss different chapters of the book. Of course, I would be paired with the person sitting directly behind me.

As everyone around us started moving their desks, he murmured, "You can't ignore me forever." I closed my eyes as I turned my desk to face him, willing for every part of me to relax.

Struggling to steady my voice, I said, "I'm trying to forget everything."

"Would that include me?"

"Yes," I said, and I saw the muscles in his jaw clench. I fought the tears that rose to my eyes; he didn't deserve what I was doing to him.

But what choice did I have? I couldn't pretend that it never happened. It did, and there was no going back.

"If you really feel that way …" he said.

"So … about chapter six," I said. I looked at the first question, hoping I was masking the tears that were threatening to spill over.

We managed to get through all the questions without getting back to the seemingly unavoidable topic. It was just our luck that we were the first to finish. I stared awkwardly at the tip of my paper to avoid his gaze.

"Harmony," he said.

"Yes," I whispered.

"Did I do something to make you hate me? I'm not the one who tried to kill you."

Frustration welled up inside me. I didn't hate him. He just shouldn't exist, and I couldn't get the frightening image of him out of my head. How could I explain this to him? I myself didn't fully understand my overwhelming fear of him. He had explained everything to me, so really, why should I be frightened? All the same, it was impossible to look him in the eye. It was he who saved me after all.

"I don't hate you. I'm trying to get over the fact that you're partially responsible for my father's death," I said quietly.

"He knew what he was getting into. We didn't make it seem as if we were giving him a cushy job to do."

"It's more than that," I said. The truth was I didn't want to admit that I was completely terrified of him.

"Try me," he said. His tone was low and dangerous, as if he was struggling to hold in his temper. Fear clenched my heart, and I suddenly couldn't sit so close to him anymore.

"Mr. Arlington," I said, jumping out of my seat.

"Yes," he said, looking up from grading papers.

"I need to use the bathroom." I headed toward the door, struggling to keep balance on the precarious crutches.

Before the door shut behind me, I heard Mr. Arlington ask, "Should she be moving that quickly?" I didn't hear what they answered as I continued my breakneck pace to the girls' bathroom.

I entered and collapsed against the door, the one place where he couldn't follow me. I glanced at the mirror. Bright red splotches covered my cheeks, crashing horribly with my dark auburn hair. I took cool water and splashed it across my face.

I closed my eyes against the feeling, letting the panic leak out as fast as it had flooded in. I took a deep breath as my face returned to the usual, ghostly pale color.

Chapter 19

I couldn't tell anyone my secret. The minute I said the word *Dragon* they'd drag me off and lock me up. I slowly looked down the long tunnel of time. How had I never noticed how unnormal Keith was? There were so many hints that I had simply ignored. I suddenly remembered Donovan's reaction to my painting, and then there were several little clicks in my brain.

It took everything I had not to tilt my head and laugh so that I wouldn't cry at the complete insanity of it all. I almost pinched myself to make sure this wasn't some extended nightmare. I wished that I could wake up and find that it was my first day back from school in November, or better yet, before last May, when all the madness started.

Unfortunately, the occasional shots of fiery pain in my leg prevented me from denying the truth, no matter how hard I tried to forget. There was only one thing I was completely sure of: I had to avoid Keith at all cost.

The next morning, I purposefully got to school early so that I could talk to Ms. Shelns without being overheard. I approached the door to the classroom and knocked.

"Come in," she said. I pushed against the door and entered the classroom.

I nervously took my slightly frizzy hair in my hands and gently combed it to the side.

"Hello, Harmony, how may I help you?" she asked, looking up at me from the chair behind her desk.

"I was wondering I if could switch groups for the project that's due at the end of this year," I said.

"Why would you want to do that? Is there something dissatisfying about the work that Keith produces? I was under the impression that you two got along very well together." She looked at me with a considering expression, not one filled with pity or concern like the other teachers.

"No, it's not that ... It's just ..." I started, unable to tell her the real reason I wanted to switch groups—that Keith was a monster and I had to get as far away from him as possible.

"It's just ..." she encouraged, staring at me with an intent expression. When I didn't say anything, she sighed heavily. "I'm sorry, Harmony, but unless you have a legitimate excuse for switching to a different partner, then I can't grant your request. We're way too far along in the project," she said.

I nodded glumly and then slowly exited. I went outside and took my light jacket off and laid it on the damp bench. I sat down and stared off into space, struggling to ignore the growing fear. I had hoped that by avoiding Keith, things could return to some semblance of normalcy.

But I now realized that a "semblance" of normalcy was not good enough. I couldn't help but let my thoughts drift back to whose fault this really was. If I had never sought out Robbie all that time ago, things would have been different. I would have been completely normal when Keith transferred to this school, and whatever made him hate everyone else would have made him hate me just as much. The urge to return to the old neighborhood and face my life enemy was stronger than ever. I felt that if I went, I would receive some sort of closure and all the insanity would be over.

* * *

"Harmony," the teacher snapped, pulling me out of my deep thoughts. "Can you tell me who the third general was that the Union hired during the Civil War?"

She knew that I wasn't paying attention and that I had no idea who the third general the Union hired during the Civil War was. I could feel the blood rush to my cheeks as I searched my brain for the possible answer.

"I don't know," I said, staring at my clenched hands in my lap.

A triumphant light flickered in her eyes.

"Would someone like to help her?" she asked, moving her eyes off of me to interrogate some other poor soul. As the bell rang, we all broke for lunch, and I slowly stood.

With dread, I saw my friends approach me in the cafeteria. Sarah turned to glare at me, as I purposefully chose a different table than Keith, leaving him by himself. Her dark eyes held no warmth, and I wanted to scream in frustration. It felt as if all the forces of the world were conspiring against me. I squirmed uncomfortably under their gaze.

"What's with you?" Sarah asked.

"Nothing's with me," I said, but even I could feel the frightened vibe in the air that I was struggling to repress.

"Is there something you're not telling me about you and Keith?"

"No," I said, picking up my pace.

"Then why are you acting like he's the devil?"

"I can't tell you!" I finally exclaimed.

"I thought friends were supposed to trust each other!" she said angrily.

"Sarah, I don't mean to insult you or anything, but it's something I don't feel comfortable talking about right now."

"You seemed able to talk to me about what happened to you before," she said, tilting her chin up indignantly.

"This is different."

"I'm sorry," she said, her wall finally breaking down. "It's just that I'm really worried about you. You were finally beginning to get back to normal. You had a boyfriend, and then you had me, Jen, Adrienne, and Keith for friends, and it just seemed like things were finally beginning to look up for you." I accepted her offer for a hug. "This latest incident seems to have changed everything for the worse."

"You have no idea," I said, releasing a loud sigh.

Chapter 20

"Hello," Dr. Andrews said, giving me the usual warm smile as I sat down in front of her desk.

"Hi," I said, avoiding her gaze as I stared at my hands in my lap.

"You're mad at me," she said without a doubt in her voice. She could read me far too well; there was no way for me to hide anything from her. I finally lifted my eyes and let the full wrath of my gaze bore into her eyes. "Can you tell me why?" she asked, and all of my anger bubbled to the surface.

"Because!" I shouted, too furious to get anything else out.

"Because …" she prompted, unfazed by my outburst.

"Because I know you want to start giving me anxiety medication. *That's* why!"

"The only reason I do is because you don't seem to want to talk about what happened to you. I know you would feel better if you did, and I would be less concerned about your mental health," she said quietly.

"I can't tell you," I said, my voice turning desperate.

"Do you know why you can't tell me?" she asked, and I hated the way she tried to pry tidbits of information out of me. A yes nearly formed across my lips, but then I realized I would have to tell her the reason I had said yes, which I could never do.

"No," I said.

"But there is something you're not telling me?"

| 15 Stitches |

"Yes," I said, and for a moment, I could feel myself warming up to her slightly, the old relationship we used to have starting to resurface.

"Do you want to talk about it?"

"No …"

"Well, your mother tells me that she fears you're shutting her out. You haven't spoken to one of your closest friends since the incident in the park. What happened to you was truly horrific; there is no denying it. This medicine will only help you cope with it better."

Why did she always have to be so logical? Every single word she said was true. I had pushed away one of my closest friends. But it was all over, and it could never go back to the way it once was.

"Harmony, what makes you so withdrawn? You used to tell me everything that was happening."

"Some things are harder to talk about than others," I said, surprised at how cold my voice sounded.

"Well, why don't we talk about something else?" she said, her smile open and friendly again.

"Like what?"

"Something that's less hard to talk about. How are you holding up without your dad?"

The topic she had chosen was hardly less painful.

"He was a jerk, and I miss him." Dr. Andrews smiled encouragingly, and I broke into a rant. "He was completely unsupportive with what happened last May. I mean, it's like how could I ever have loved anyone like that? But he was my *dad*! How could he do that to me?

"He used to actually act like a father. It was only after last May that he started acting all weird. I mean, almost like something else was stressing him out, and he couldn't deal with what happened to me on top of that. But why would he take it out on us? And then, when we found him lying there, it was as if he had never done those things. I couldn't remember anything bad, only the good."

"I'm trying my best to understand. It seems that everything that could go wrong in one life, did," she said. I just nodded, staring at my dark jeans.

"All right," she said, drawing my attention to her face. "You can go now. Send your mother in; I want to talk to her."

I walked out and found my mom.

"How did it go?" my mother asked me.

"Fine," I said.

She walked into the office to hear what Dr. Andrews had to report on my "condition." While she was in there for ten minutes, I waited outside in the soft chairs. I curled my knees to my chest and rested my forehead against the cool material of my jeans. I focused on taking deep, shaky breaths. I held in everything, and not one tear leaked out.

During the drive home, Mom talked about a lot of unimportant things: how the weather was getting warm for April; what she was making for dinner that night. We both knew she was avoiding the topic I didn't want to hear about.

"We're just going to stop at the pharmacy real fast and pick up your medication. I guess we'll start giving it to you tomorrow morning. Does that sound okay?" she said, and I could hear the anxiousness in her voice.

"Yeah, it sounds fine."

When we pulled into the parking lot and walked into the pharmacy, it felt nice to be anonymous. Nobody knew my name, nobody knew my story. We walked up to the pharmacist's desk, and he looked down at me for a moment. Small glasses perched at the end of his long, thin nose. As he read the prescription, his eyes slowly slid from my gaunt face to the medicine's name.

He seemed completely unsurprised that I would need medication like that. I felt a small flame of anger flicker in me, but I suppressed it.

"Did you see that guy's face?" I seethed, once we were back in the car.

"What about it?" Mom asked, her voice unusually high pitched, as if she thought I was a bomb that would go off at any moment. She would be right.

My visit to the psychiatrist had not helped my mood in the slightest. It almost made me feel worse about myself, because her solution was medication. How could she betray me like that? She only wanted to dull my reactions, but I knew that would never help my anxiety. Maybe she wouldn't have if I told

| 15 Stitches |

her about my resolution to confront Robbie, but I couldn't share that with her. If I ever told her, I knew she would tell my mom, who in turn would refuse to let me go. But this was something that I knew I needed to do, despite the fact that I felt sick with worry every time I thought about it. Luckily, I would be off crutches by next week. The following Saturday, I would drive to Philly and find Robbie.

Chapter 21

Sarah smiled as she sat down next to me outside of school the next morning.

"You should be happy to know that the doctor prescribed medication for me," I said.

"What? That's terrible! I can't believe that. It's not like you're insanely nervous or anything. I mean, you're a little jumpy … but that's it," she said, rushing to my defense.

I gave her a weak smile. "Tell me about it. I feel so weird …"

"Are you ready to go to class?" she said, standing up, her gaze drifting in the direction of the parking lot.

"Yeah," I said following her gaze. I had a sickening feeling in my stomach as I recognized the blue sedan. "Let's go," I said, rushing as fast as I could toward the door, hindered by my crutches.

"Harmony, wait!" Sarah called from behind me, but I refused to slow down until I was inside the doors and temporarily out of his sight.

"What?" I said, watching the doors carefully from my locker.

"Don't you want to at least talk to him?" she asked.

"No," I said without further explanation and rushed to our first class.

"I just don't understand," Sarah said, shaking her head as she sat down. I pretended I hadn't heard her, staring studiously at the blank whiteboard.

As the door squeaked open, I ducked my head down. I buried my eyes deep into the literature book, pretending I was reading one of the short stories.

As he began to sit down, I heard him pause, his body turned in my direction. I thought I heard him sigh as he sat down to face the board, and I breathed a sigh of relief when he didn't try to talk to me.

To distract myself, I tried—unsuccessfully—to be absorbed in the difference between romantic poetry and medieval poetry. The bell rang, and every student jumped up, eager to get away from Mr. Arlington's droning voice.

As I walked past Keith, I swore I heard him say, "You can't avoid me forever," which I chose to ignore. I had to give some credit to this medication; it certainly helped me avoid the blind panic that often overtook me. However, I couldn't focus on anything that was happening in class, and it all passed by in a blur. In fact, the next week and a half, much to my regret, passed by in a blur too.

I was finally able to get rid of my crutches. It seemed that I had barely enough time to blink before Friday came, the day before I planned to confront Robbie. I was terrified, but I knew I had to do it.

Despite my eagerness, I was glad for the crutches that kept me from going until now. This way I had plenty of time to mentally prepare myself. I felt queasiness in the bottom of my stomach that warned me against it, but the drugs I was taking obscured the feeling.

Even if I found Robbie, what would I do then? There was no way I could prove the monstrous actions he had done to me. The anger flared up like fire once again in my stomach, and I gritted my teeth. Was there any way that I would be able to exact my revenge? Even if there wasn't, I knew I would have to face him, tell him all the grief that he had brought upon my family.

I walked to my room, listening downstairs to my mother watching some late night show on television. I flung myself onto the bed, arranging my messy covers into some semblance of order before tucking myself under them.

When I clicked the light off, I was suddenly surrounded in darkness so black that I couldn't see my hand in front of me.

I slept restlessly, constantly tossing and turning.

To my regret, an old nightmare returned. *My lungs burned as I strove forward, knowing they were directly behind me. A huge wave of regret seemed to knock me off my feet. However, I had no idea what this regret was for. As I ran, it was a blind panic that drove me forward, and I felt that there was no possible way that I would be able to escape without something terrible happening.*

I felt the sudden pull of reality snap me back to consciousness. I sat up, tossing my covers every which way. My heart still rocketed around in my chest, and adrenaline pounded through my veins. I didn't have to look at the clock to know it was early.

The soft light of dawn, as if the sun had not yet thrown its rays over the horizon, flowed through my window. As my heart slowed, I knew that there was no way I would be able to fall back asleep after that nightmare.

I got up, throwing the covers that had fallen off of my bed into a heap. I walked out of my room and then heard the sound of a door opening and closing. I froze. The sound did not come from my mom's room; it came from the guest room in the other direction.

"Mom?" I called quietly into the dark hallway.

"Harmony?" her soft voice replied, and I breathed a sigh of relief. I stared at her shadowy figure approaching me.

"Mom?" I asked as she got closer.

"Yeah?" she responded. If I didn't know better, I would think that she sounded a little … guilty.

"Were you sleeping in the guest bedroom?" I asked and suddenly realized that I had never seen her go into the master bedroom since dad left.

"Yes," she said. She made it obvious that she didn't want any more questions on the subject. Maybe she was in more pain than she let on.

"What are you doing up so early?" she asked, eyeing me as suspiciously as I had eyed her.

"I was just heading to the shower," I said.

I entered the bathroom and flicked the light on. I forced myself not to look at the mirror, staring straight ahead and walking toward the shower door. I quickly turned the shower on and set it to the temperature that I knew would be perfect. As it heated, I took off my clothes and threw them into a pile on the floor.

When mist started swirling into the bathroom, I stepped into the shower, allowing the hot water to pound against my back. I took my favorite scented shampoo and lathered it into my hair.

| 15 Stitches |

After my shower, I felt panic begin to weave its way into my thoughts as I slowly got dressed. Back in my bedroom, I glanced at the clock. It was six o'clock in the morning.

I was surprised when I walked downstairs to see my mom already sitting there, her shoulders hunched over and her arms stiff. She was staring mindlessly at a cup of coffee.

"Mom, are you okay?"

Her hands started trembling, and her bottom lip began to shake.

"Sometimes I wonder if it ever gets better." She sniffed, and it took me five seconds to figure out what she was talking about. She was staring at a bright yellow coffee cup with three words written on it: Happy Father's Day.

I remember when she gave him that cup. I was probably in fifth grade, and things had seemed much easier and simpler back then.

She let out a small sob as her hands flew to her face. I walked toward her and put my arms around her shoulder and let my tears flow freely as well. After we sat that way for a long time, I looked up at the clock; it read seven thirty.

I felt a deep anxiousness in the pit of my stomach. I hadn't actually told my mom that I had made plans to go somewhere today, and I clearly could not tell her the truth. I felt horrible leaving her like that, but I couldn't back out now.

"Hey, Mom," I said quietly.

"Yeah," she said, and I was glad to hear that her voice was calm and serene.

"I told Jen, Adrienne, and Sarah that I would meet them today." I was surprised as the lie rolled effortlessly off my lips.

"At seven thirty in the morning on a Saturday?"

I faltered. In my eagerness, I had forgotten that it was way too early to go to a friend's house. I shrugged lightly, pretending that I didn't think anything of it.

"All right, go ahead, honey … Wait—don't you need me to drive you?"

I was so glad that I hadn't taken my pills yet.

"I think I can go this one day without the pills, Mom," I said casually and walked out the door, my heart thundering in my chest.

Chapter 22

As I began the forty-five-minute drive into the city, I felt the nerves in my stomach spike higher and higher. Along with the nerves, I felt my rash excitement grow at the thought of seeking him out.

As I got closer, I saw the buildings slowly stretch up before me on the highway. My heart pounded as the panic began to creep in.

I parked my car and headed toward the buses, knowing exactly where I was going. People rushed back and forth, occasionally glancing at me when they saw my pronounced limp.

The doubt seemed to be erased from my mind, and I was filled with a blazing determination that came from deep inside me.

There was no room to sit, so I stood, staring off into space as the bus lurched and swayed. I didn't dwell on what I was about to do, only knowing that I had to do it. My fear was beginning to grow, but I didn't allow it to burn out the fire that was deep inside me, that pushed me forward and told me to keep going.

That fact that I didn't have any sort of plan whatsoever didn't bother me. I would have to make up this whole thing as I went.

The bus stop that I was aiming for seemed to take forever to reach, yet it suddenly came before I was ready, and several people stood up. I forced myself to follow them.

I didn't look around at the once familiar surroundings; I didn't want to see how much things had changed. I didn't want to look upon the place that used to be one of security for me. I knew where I was headed, where I would find him.

That was the good thing about my enemy being a former friend; I knew his habits and where he would be. I felt as if I was walking in a dream, with the edges of my vision slightly blurry.

I stopped outside the deli, the place where he and his friends always hung out. As I stood outside the doorway, I almost choked on the panic as it rose in a new, much stronger wave.

There's nothing to be afraid of, I struggled to convince myself. *It's the middle of the day, and there are plenty of people around,* I told myself. But a smaller voice, the voice of reason, spoke in my ear. *That didn't stop him last time*, it said, and I felt a sudden anger at this voice of reason.

What business did it have telling me what to do? I straightened my shoulders and walked in.

The soft tinkling of the bell announced my arrival, and several heads turned in the direction of the door. As I stared at the four familiar faces, they stared back at me, as if they couldn't believe who they were seeing in front of them.

"Well," one of them sneered, and I recognized that menacing voice. "Look who it is." He stood up, and he seemed just as tall as he had in all of my nightmares. The rest of them followed, and the fear that suddenly rose in my stomach was real—not some figment of my imagination. It seemed stupid now that I should have feared Keith; these were the real monsters.

The four of them advanced on me, and instead of backing up, my anger and want for revenge pushed me forward. They drew closer, and I stood my ground.

"Do you have any idea what you've done to me?" I snarled at him, putting as much venom in my voice as I possibly could. "Did our friendship mean anything at all to you?" I thundered at him.

"You should have known our friendship ended a long, long time ago," he snarled back with equal vehemence. His friends seemed to fade into the background; it was clear that they were going to let him handle this on his own.

"Why did you do it, Robbie? Just because our friendship didn't mean anything to you anymore doesn't mean you had to ruin me." I struggled to keep my voice strong, but it ended up coming out desperate.

"You were meddling in things that you shouldn't have," he said, but I could tell the old person that I knew was beginning to break through, just a bit. His friends saw the change in him and shifted uncomfortably.

"Yeah, because I was just trying to save you from yourself," I snapped at him.

"Robbie, man, are you going to let this little bitch get to you?" one of his friends said, and Robbie's face changed instantly in response, as if he needed to live up to his friends' expectations.

"Oh look," he snickered, his voice taunting and no longer reasonable. "Someone's grown a backbone." Suddenly the anger rose so fast there was no way I was able to restrain myself.

I reached back and put as much power into my punch as I could as it struck against his face.

"You little bitch!" he snarled and lunged forward for me. I jumped backward, every instinct screaming for me to run.

This time, I listened and flew out the door. Fear and regret laced through me. I had accomplished nothing, and now I was in danger once again. I also wasn't as fast as I was a year ago. My leg burned as I struggled to bend the resistant muscles to my will.

People stared as I hobbled by. In what seemed like minutes, Robbie and his friends caught up to me, a much quicker chase than it had been last time.

"Hey!" he yelled as his large hand wrapped around my wrist. "What happened to you?" He jerked me around to face him.

He dragged me down an empty street, and I struggled against his grip. I was so busy trying to get away from him that I forgot to scream. As the realization hit me that I could scream, I took in a deep breath of air and filled my lungs.

As I opened my mouth to let out the loudest scream I could manage, I felt a hand clamp firm against my mouth. I strained against it, writhing under the hands that held me.

They continued dragging me, and the streets appeared much more deserted the further we went.

I managed to release my hands for half a second and raked my nails against the hand that held my mouth closed. I was pushed further and further, and I stopped recognizing street names. The panic rose in my chest.

"When do you want to stop?" one of them grunted.

"Not yet," he growled, and I fought back harder than I ever had. I pulled backward, struggling to keep a distance between me and the unknown destination.

"No you don't," one of them muttered, shoving me forwards, and I stumbled, almost falling to my knees. Then as we reached another street, they let me go, and I fell forwards, too surprised at first to run. Then I took off as fast as I could away from them, my uneven footsteps intermingling with theirs.

I heard their snarky laughs behind me, and I hesitated. *I shouldn't be able to get away this easily.* As I hobbled forward, I tried to ignore their snickers as they echoed down the narrow walls. The day seemed to get darker and darker, and I had the frightening feeling that I wouldn't be able to escape.

I hurried forward as the feeling of helplessness began to overwhelm me. It seemed impossible that this place could be so dark in the middle of the day. I walked forward, and a large brick wall seemed to appear in front of me.

Gray, broken windows were in the back, eliminating my ability to draw anyone's attention. I turned around; my leg had begun to ache with all the running I had done. I kept my weight off of it and stared at the four people swaggering toward me.

"Well," he sneered at me. "Looks like your trapped. Why does this look familiar?" he mocked. "I don't know about you, boys, but I seem to recognize this little scene right here."

I couldn't think straight. The images in front of my eyes seemed to spin and twirl around me, and I couldn't focus on any of their faces.

In a semiconscious state, I laughed at myself for thinking that I could take him alone. What satisfaction had come from seeking and confronting him? None. My attempts at resistance were pitiful as he pressed himself against me. I attempted to kick out at him, but he dodged my leg easily, laughing the entire time.

"Harmony!" a voice roared in anger, and they all spun around to face the approaching person. As I turned toward him, I was never so happy to see anyone. He was sprinting toward us, the wind blowing up his hair to show eyes of the clearest blue.

As Robbie let go of me, I slowly slid down the wall and landed on the ground, my entire body quaking. Robbie and his friends laughed when they saw Keith thundering toward them. They obviously hadn't seen his eyes, or the way his pupils had constricted to barely visible slits in anger.

I gave a slight smirk; even through my fog I knew that Keith would be able to easily beat them. Their arrogance would be what killed them. He barely glanced my way as he grabbed Robbie by the throat and threw him against the wall. I could feel the building shake with the force of his anger.

As soon as Keith slammed him against the wall, all the arrogance left Robbie's face. It was filled with fear and disbelief at what he was seeing.

"Your eyes," Robbie managed to whisper.

His grip on Robbie's neck pressed harder, and Robbie's face picked up a slightly purplish tinge. His eyes bulged out with the enormous pressure exerted on to his neck.

Robbie's friends didn't even try to help him; they just stared in horror at the monster in front of them. I could see Keith's shoulders shaking, and I thought I saw him slowly growing in height.

"Yeah," Keith snarled, his face pressed up against Robbie's, his entire body vibrating with the force of his anger. "What about my eyes," he spat at Robbie, and despite the fact that he was saving me from a horrible fate, I felt afraid of him. "What," he hissed, struggling through his anger to speak. "What business does filth like you have talking about my eyes?" He didn't raise his voice, but it would have been less scary if he had.

Robbie's friends started sprinting away. Keith increased the pressure on Robbie's neck again, causing him to start choking and sputtering. It was the most horrible thing to watch, but I couldn't tear my eyes away.

"Please," he choked, his face darkening with the lack of oxygen. Keith opened his mouth, about to retort, when I interrupted him. I don't know what made me do it.

Maybe a near lifetime of friendship leaves more permanent marks than I thought. Maybe it wasn't revenge I was seeking after all, at least not of this kind.

Whatever it was, my voice rang out in the near silence. "Keith," I said, surprised by the calm in my voice. At the sound, Keith's body froze. He still didn't look at me, but it was clear that I got through his mindless rage. "Don't," I said, and I could see him take a deep, shuddering breath. And the third word that I said was "Please."

The tension in his arms relaxed slightly, and he released his vicious hold on Robbie's neck. He dropped his hands and took a single step backward. Robbie tripped forward and managed to stumble around Keith and down the dark alleyway toward the light.

We were alone, and Keith finally turned his gaze toward me. He knelt down next to me, moving slowly as if he expected me to run at any moment.

"Harmony," he said, his voice hoarse but gentle. "Are you okay?"

In truth, I didn't know the answer. Until that moment, I hadn't realized that my entire body was shivering and my hands were trembling.

"I promise," he said, "I won't touch you, but I need to know if you're hurt."

"I … I … I'm so cold," I said.

"You're going into shock," he said, and then he carefully moved closer to me and looked into my eyes. "But I need to know, did he hurt you?" He put his hands on my shoulders. To my surprise, I didn't panic as I expected myself to.

"Not in the way that you mean," I managed to say through my chattering teeth.

"How did he hurt you then?"

"He didn't … no, he did … I can't talk about this right now," I said, pulling away from him and resting my head on my knees, rocking back and forth.

"You need help," he insisted. "How can I help you?"

"I … need to get out of here." But I made no motion to get up. I didn't think my legs would be able to hold me.

I felt my trembling worsen, turning into a violent shaking that made me shudder back and forth. Keith looked around frantically, clearly at a loss for what to do.

He gently approached me again and bent down. He tucked his hands under my shoulders and my knees and lifted me up, cradling me to his chest.

I closed my eyes and turned my head toward his shoulder.

Chapter 23

As he carried me, I felt the tremors slowly ease. Suddenly, I felt his breath near my ear, and my muscles tensed.

"Are you ready to walk now?" he asked gently. I nodded my head, and he slowly slid me to the ground. The muscles in my knees shook violently, and I rested heavily on his shoulder. "You need to have something to eat," he stated, and supported me as we walked from an empty street and quickly blended into a heavily populated main road.

I staggered through the crowd. His eyes were raised above my head, scanning the windows for someplace where we could eat.

"This looks like a good place," he muttered, more to himself than to me. He steered me inside, and it seemed impossible to me that the gentle hands that held me could easily kill someone. Another shudder ran through me at the thought while he pressed me slightly closer. To my surprise, I was glad that he held me. I felt as if he kept away all the terrible things that threatened to engulf me. An older woman walked toward us, a large fake smile on her face. As she approached, Keith carefully pulled his thick black hair in front of his eyes.

"Table for two?" she asked in a bored voice, and we nodded. We sat down, and I struggled to keep away from his long legs that stretched under the table. I avoided looking at him by staring at my menu, but I could feel him studying me.

After what seemed like a long time, he finally spoke. "Harmony, what could you have been thinking?" I just stared at him. How could he possibly understand the complexity of my thoughts and feelings? He could never comprehend what drove me to return to the place that I once called home.

"I failed," I whispered.

"What?" he asked, but his voice softened. I stared off into the distance and said it again. "Harmony, what are you talking about?"

For the third time, I whispered, "I failed." There was no way he could possibly understand what I was talking about, but the hopelessness I felt was too much to ignore.

"Can I take your order?"

Keith tore his eyes away from me and looked at the waitress. She was young and pretty.

"We're not quite ready yet," he said, and she nodded and walked quickly away. "You should eat something," he said to me.

I shook my head. "I'm not hungry."

"You have to eat. Do you have a cell phone with you? I forgot to bring mine."

"Yes—why?"

"I need to call your mother and tell her what happened."

"What? You can't do that! She doesn't even know where I am," I said, wanting to stand up and run out of the restaurant.

"Harmony, you're scaring me. How could you not tell your mom? We should tell her what happened."

"No!" I knew I was being irrational, but I had failed and there was no way I was going to tell anyone what really happened today, least of all my mom. She would think I had gone completely crazy. "If I eat something, will you not call her?" I asked him frantically, and indecision crossed his face.

"All right," he finally agreed. He called over the waiter and ordered the same thing for both of us.

"I think I'm missing a part of the story," he finally said after studying me for a while.

"Yes," I responded, and I couldn't keep the pain out of my voice. "You're missing a big part of the story."

"Will you ever tell that part to me?" he asked, and I knew he hated that

I kept secrets from him, especially since I knew his biggest secret. I looked up at him, gazed at his face carefully. I remembered all the things that we had been through together. But could I trust him? Would I trust him with my biggest secret?

"I don't know," I said, and I gave him a weak smile.

"Is there a reason you won't tell me what it is? Do you not trust me?"

"That's part of it. I don't know what you would think of me afterward. It's so horrible to think about that I can't bring myself to even say the words." I forced myself to keep my memories firmly locked in the back of my head, where they couldn't hurt me or anyone else.

"I'm sorry," he said, and there was visible pain in his face at the thought of what could have possibly happened to me. At that moment, the waiter returned with our food, and I slowly began to eat. The moment I took my first bite of food, I realized I was ravenous.

"Are you sure you're not hungry?" he asked, lifting an eyebrow at my already half-eaten plate of food.

"Maybe a little," I said, grinning at him.

"I have a question," he said. I watched him cautiously and indicated that he should continue. "When you lived here, did you ever go to the museums here in Philly?"

"No, not really," I said, feeling a blush creep into my cheeks. It must have seemed odd.

"Well, since we're here, do you wanna go visit one?"

I slowly nodded, and a brief smile flashed across his face before he jumped up and paid the check, leaving a small tip on the table. "Let's check out the Academy of Natural Sciences. We should probably take a bus," he said thoughtfully and led me in the direction of the bus stop.

As we walked, I studied his face, his fine sharp features, softened by his thick black hair. I could tell that he felt my eyes but didn't want to meet my gaze. We reached the bus stop and sat down at the bench as we waited for the bus to arrive.

"Why are you so nice to me?" I asked.

"What do you mean?" he asked, turning to face me.

"Well, you do so many things for me, like when you saved me earlier today. And then you took me to lunch. Now, you're going to take me to a museum. All I've been for the past few weeks is nasty to you. I just don't understand, after everything, how you could still care."

"You say that I saved you?" he started, and he brushed his thick black hair out of his eyes. "You were there to save me first," he whispered.

I shook my head. "What are you talking about?" How could I have possibly saved him from anything? He was so big and strong and invincible; there was nothing he needed saving from.

"I'm sure you noticed that I was extremely isolated from everyone in school. Believe me—it wasn't for lack of trying. I have an extreme inability to get close to anyone. You seemed to ignore that wall. You're the only person I've been able to get close to besides my father," he said, smiling. Only at that moment did I realize what my silence must have cost him.

"Keith …" I started to say, but the bus was rounding the corner, its engine roaring loudly. We stood up, and I reached into my pocket to pull out the money needed to get us to the museum. His large hand caught my wrist, and a pulse of electricity shot up my arm. I looked up at his face, and he was giving me a slightly endearing smile.

"I'll take care of it," he said, reaching inside his pocket as the bus pulled in front of us. We climbed the stairs and sat next to each other.

When we reached our stop, we walked out into the bustling streets of Philadelphia.

I stared at the museum in amazement and said, "I can't believe I lived in the city my entire life without ever coming here."

* * *

"At least try to look happy," he teased, grinning at me as I forced a smile. He insisted on taking my picture in front of almost everything that I found remotely interesting. Not once did he let me take a picture of him. The time I spent with him now made me happier than I had been in a long time.

"I don't understand why you insist on taking all these pictures," I said, and he just rolled his eyes at me.

"Hey," someone said to Keith as he was about to snap another picture.

"Do you want me to take a picture of you two?" I opened my mouth to tell him that it wouldn't be necessary, but Keith spoke before me.

"Sure," he beamed. He seemed so happy, as if he didn't have a care in the world. He practically skipped up to me, and I gave him a weird look, which he returned with a shrug and a smile.

He leaned down so he could wrap his arm around my shoulders, and I leaned into him, as if it was the most natural thing in the world. I wrapped my arm around his waist. When he pulled me close, I felt the tremor of electricity pass through me to him. Usually, I would be uncomfortable with our closeness, but I could have stood there with him forever.

"Smile," the guy said, and I beamed the biggest smile that I had all afternoon. The camera clicked.

"Thanks," Keith said, his arm slowly sliding off of my arm to retrieve the camera. As he reached forward, his gaze shifted back to me, a small smile on his lips. *Could he have felt it too?* I wondered, studying him as he took the camera from the man. He handed me the camera, his fingers brushing gently against mine. My heart jolted, but not from fear this time. Without meeting his gaze, I placed it in my pocket as we continued walking.

"You know," he mused, "we really should finish up that stupid ecology project. It's due this coming Friday."

"It's due Friday already?" I gasped.

"Yeah, I know. How about tomorrow? You could come over to my place, and we could have another look at the woods, take a couple of pictures. I'm pretty sure we have all the information we need."

"Yeah, that's probably a good idea."

"Hmm," he agreed. I couldn't believe I was wasting my precious time with him on trivial things like an ecology presentation. It was weird; in one afternoon, my entire perspective of him had completely turned around. I wanted to be with him now and hated the thought of us parting. "When do you need to get home?" he asked as we strolled casually down the crowded streets.

"Soon I guess," I said. The sun had begun to head toward the horizon. Was it just my imagination, or did he seem to regret leaving me too? We walked in silence for a little longer. I listened to the city around us, calm now that he was with me.

I stopped. We had walked almost all the way back to where I parked my car, and I could see it from where I was standing. "How did you know where I was today? And how did you find my exact location?" I asked him, and for the first time I saw a pink tone creep into his pale cheeks. His bright blue eyes met mine, and he smirked, reaching up with his finger to touch his nose two times. An uncomfortable feeling settled in my stomach when I realized that this was one of the extra abilities that he must have inherited.

"Thank you," I said, but the words felt completely inadequate.

"For what?" he asked, and I almost laughed. I couldn't count how many things he had done for me since we first met.

"Just …" I said, searching for the right word. "Just everything."

"No," he corrected me as I began to pull away from him. "Thank *you*."

Chapter 24

"Thanks," I said to the clerk at the desk, who handed me the pictures Keith and I had taken the day before. I walked away, flipping to the bottom of the stack, to the last pictures taken on the camera.

Keith's hair was slightly blown back from the wind, but all you could see was the glimmer of blue from underneath the shadow of his thick black mane. Unlike most people with black hair, his didn't glow brown in the sun; it was so black it seemed to almost glow blue.

It surprised me when I saw the extreme contrast between his white skin and black hair.

His smile was big and genuine as he held me close to him. I looked slightly hesitant but happy with my arms around his waist. My gray blue eyes looked dull in comparison to his. My dark auburn hair, almost glowing red in the sun, swirled around my face.

I quickly tucked the picture in my pocket, knowing I had to keep it from my mother. She would know immediately that something might be going on between us, and obviously that we had been in Philly.

We didn't look like two friends in the picture; we looked like we were much closer than friends.

As I flipped the picture into my pocket, I was surprised to see that there was one more. It couldn't have been take more than a few seconds later, but there was a difference between the first and the second unplanned picture in front of me.

Keith had turned toward me, giving me a soft smile as he reached for the camera. Once more, the wind blew his hair back to reveal the turquoise blue of his eyes, but it did not reveal their true nature. The tender expression on his face took my breath away as I walked through the parking lot to where my mom was waiting in the car.

It took me a long time to pull my eyes away from his face. Had it always been so perfect? I couldn't possibly call him beautiful; his build and features were far too masculine for that term. I looked at my face in the image. I wasn't ugly, but I seemed to pale in comparison with him. I was looking down in the picture, bringing my hesitant eyes away from his face. A soft blush had risen to my cheeks as his arm slowly slid off my shoulders.

I tucked the photo next to the other one in my pocket. I continued to walk to my mom's car and slid in, thinking of the pictures that pressed against my side.

I decided not to take my medication today either. I told my mom that I wanted to drive to Keith's house to finish the project, and that I didn't want to have to depend on her to drive me. It felt good to feel the world again, to see and hear as I was supposed to, and I was eager to see his face.

When I got to Keith's house, his dad answered the door, and again I was stunned by how alike they were. Cyrus was only missing the sapphire eyes. I felt my heart catch in my throat as I realized I was standing in front of perhaps the world's smartest person, but the world knew nothing about his wonderful accomplishments.

His face was much different than the last time I had seen him. This time his eyes were tight and worried. I felt an uncomfortable feeling settle in my stomach as the memory of Keith's words from the hospital echoed in my head. *You know how my mother destroyed something very valuable to the Griffins that allowed for all of their technology to work? Well my father has had suspicions for years that the Griffins are fixing it.*

It seemed to me that the Griffins may have been closer to fixing whatever it was than Keith had let on.

I looked up at Cyrus hesitantly, suddenly reminded of my father and everything that he had kept from our family. It was hard to stand in front of Cyrus, knowing that it was he who sent my father out the night he was killed. But I was sure that my dad knew what he was getting into; otherwise he wouldn't have done it.

"Is Keith here?" I asked.

"Yes," he said, and his smile grew wider and friendlier as he motioned me inside. "C'mon in. I'll tell him you're here."

I was left standing awkwardly in the foyer. I stared up at the towering array of books and felt a shiver run down my spine when I realized that every word that was written in them represented a civilization that I knew nothing about.

"Hey, Harmony," Keith said, suddenly appearing in the doorway. He hesitated slightly. "You okay?" he asked, and I nodded.

"It's just different, that's all," I said.

"What do you mean?" he asked quietly.

"It's just different knowing … you know … that they're true," I said, staring at the books. He smiled before grabbing my hand and led me right back out the door and toward his car. Cyrus suddenly appeared in the doorway.

"Keith!" he called. "Remember to be careful." Cyrus's words echoed around us, and I glanced up at Keith with a curious expression on my face.

"What was he talking about?" I asked.

"Remember what I told you in the hospital?"

"Yes …"

"Yeah well, my dad thinks they've fixed it this time—the technology my mom destroyed. But don't worry; this has been going on for years. Every so often, he'd suspect they were close, and we would get all worried over nothing."

"I wonder if we'll see any changes in the forest," I wondered aloud as the flowering and green trees whipped by in a blur, trying to distract myself from that frightening possibility that the Griffins could take over the world.

"Probably," Keith said, casually resting his arm across the steering wheel.

A few minutes later, we arrived at the barren woods, more pronounced because of the greenery that surrounded them. Nausea clutched at my stomach as we pulled up to the familiar spot, less than a mile away from where my father was found. I could feel all the blood leave my face as I got out of the car with stiff muscles.

"You sure you're okay?" Keith asked me softly with a worried look in his eyes. I swallowed and took a deep breath.

"Yeah, I'll be fine," I said.

We walked toward the woods, and I could already sense a difference. They smelled of life, not death, and the sounds of the woods, though muted, could be heard faintly.

My uneven footsteps intermingled with the sounds of the birds and the soft whispering of the wind. The sun trickled down onto the ground through the still blackened branches, sending the light scattering in all directions.

I wasn't paying attention to the time; I just strolled along, my shoes crunching on the dead leaves. I could hear Keith walking slowly behind me and wondered if my labored pace bothered him at all. Every time I took a step, I swung the stiff muscles in my leg awkwardly.

It was amazing, the life that seemed to fill the forest in just a couple of months! If I looked carefully along the forest floor, I could make out a thin film of green as life slowly began to enter the woodland. Suddenly, I saw a bright splash of color in the sea of black, and I rushed forward, ignoring the spasm of pain in my leg.

"Keith," I said, hearing his footsteps come up behind me.

"What is it?"

I pointed to the small dandelion that was growing at the base of a pitch black trunk. The bright splash of yellow was the first sign of true life that I had seen throughout the entire forest. "That's amazing!" he said, lifting the camera and snapping the picture.

"Hey, are you okay?" he asked, noticing the way I massaged the back muscle on my leg.

"I'm fine," I said through slightly gritted teeth.

"Is it bothering you?"

"A little, after ... well, yesterday." I rested without any weight on it while the pain slowly faded. Then I sat down on a fallen log, and he came and sat next to me. We stayed there for a few comfortable minutes in silence. "I've decided to stop taking my anxiety medication," I said.

"Seriously? That's awesome!"

I nodded but rolled my eyes at the same time.

"What?" he asked at my expression.

"Well, it's not official yet. Dr. Andrews … she's just so nosy about everything!" I exclaimed angrily, and I looked over to see him grinning at me. "What?" I snapped.

"I don't think I've ever seen you that annoyed about anything. It's kind of funny," he laughed.

"You're one to talk. You barely ever smile," I teased.

"I smile when I'm around you," he said quietly, and I was surprised at the intensity of his voice. I felt heat rise to my cheeks as a glimmer of electricity flickered between us.

"Yes," I said, dropping my teasing tone. "You do." My auburn hair swirled around my face, and he took one of his hands and gently tucked it behind one of my ears. My heart quickened.

The soft breeze tossed his hair around, but he didn't bother to comb it perfectly back into place. Again, his blue eyes stunned me with their intensity. He carefully pulled his face closer, until his nose almost brushed mine. My heart thundered against my chest, and my brain was buzzing with electricity.

Suddenly, I glanced up at the tree that was directly above the bright yellow dandelion. I recognized the symbol that I had see the first time I had come into the woods, the same symbol I saw at Keith's and Damon's house, the same symbol that was carved into the tree above where my father's body was found.

"What do they have to do with these woods?" I asked, not sure if I wanted to hear the answer. "I've seen that symbol a lot in here." He was silent, and I could almost feel his frozen muscles against mine. I glanced up at his face, and even though he was right next to me, he could have been worlds away.

I waited patiently, hoping he would answer without any prodding from me.

"There …" he started, but paused again. "There used to be an entrance to one of their underground cities in these woods. That technology that they're trying to fix … well, last June they almost got it, but something went wrong and it overheated, setting off the fire here in the woods. Tons of people in the deep underground city were killed."

"Wait—people?" I asked.

"They have a human city, which is really just a city filled with human slaves. I don't understand it exactly. My dad does, but he won't tell me anything more about it."

"Is there more than one?"

"One what?"

"City."

"Well, there are many cities spread all over the world, a number of which are where they keep humans, but the one closest to us is the center of their technology, where they're trying to fix the energy source."

"Are you sure they haven't fixed it? What if they have this time?" I asked.

"I'm positive. We would know for sure if they had."

"These cities, are they all connected by tunnels underground or something?"

"Yep," he said, and the tone of his voice alerted me that the subject was closed.

I didn't say anything in response, just staring out into the distance of the woods. Suddenly he turned toward me, his eyes shining with intensity once more.

"Are you still frightened of me?" he asked, and I could detect the pain in his voice.

"No," I said. In almost one day he had become a source of comfort for me instead of the fear that was once there.

My heart raced in my chest as he placed his lips against mine. I slowly unfroze and began moving my lips with his. I felt him react and draw me closer. His large hands strayed from my shoulders and slid down to my waist as he pulled me tight against him.

Suddenly my heart started beating in a different kind a way. Panic pulsed through me, and I jerked away from him. I ripped myself from his arms and jumped off the tree. I held my pounding head in my hands as I tried to reason with myself.

| 15 Stitches |

"Harmony," he said as he stood up and walked toward me. "I'm so sorry. I didn't mean … I didn't …"

"No, Keith." I said, walking over to him again. "This is my fault."

"What are you talking about?"

"I should have told you this a long time ago."

"Tell me what?" he said. I sat next to him again, but this time he kept a good foot of distance between us.

"You transferred to my school last September—right?"

"Yeah, why?"

"I wasn't there when you transferred."

"No. Everyone was talking about where you'd gone. There were all sorts of rumors flying around."

"My family chose to keep it confidential. Only the principal and a few of the teachers know—wait, did my dad tell you any of this?" I asked.

"Harmony, we didn't even know he had a daughter; your dad was that secretive."

"Oh … Do you remember that neighborhood where you found me yesterday?" I asked. And he nodded, looking bewildered. "You know I grew up there … and lived there up until a few months ago. Do you remember the four boys?"

Anger suddenly clouded his face. Despite the warm weather, a chill crept up my spine at his deadly expression. "I grew up with them," I said. "Robbie, the leader, was my best friend growing up." I heard my voice break. He looked at me, clearly not connecting what could have happened yesterday, and what happened months ago. "Let me try to explain," I said, realizing there was no way to avoid divulging my entire life's story.

"Please," he said.

"So I grew up in that neighborhood. And Robbie, he was the guy that you were …" I hesitated, not wanting to say it.

"Strangling," he said flatly. "Is that why you stopped me?" he asked quietly.

"Yes. We grew up as neighbors. He was a few years older than me, but we were still best friends. We both went to the public elementary school. When I was ready for high school, my parents were able to send me to this school outside of the neighborhood, and he was already a junior in the public high school. By that time, there was already a change in him.

"He made new friends, and we would all hang out occasionally. I never liked them, and they always made me feel uncomfortable, but I put up with them so I could spend time with him.

"So last May, almost a year ago now, he started to get into some bad things. I didn't know exactly what, but I knew it was bad. He was still my friend, and I cared about him and didn't want him to get into trouble. When we were alone, which wasn't often, I tried to talk him out of it." I stopped again as the pain began to wash over me. I closed my eyes for a second before continuing.

"He got very mad at me. He told me I had no business getting in his business. He cursed at me. It was as if I didn't even know who he was anymore."

"And all this time you had different stuff going on here at school?"

"Yeah," I said, thinking of how I always had to put on a fake face at school while I watched one of my best friends change for the worse. "But I still tried. It was early May, and I had tried to seek him out a number of times before. He had always gotten furious with me.

"He was always alone, but this time, his friends were with them. When I tried to convince him to leave them, he just sneered at me. I then realized that he was going to do something. I left as fast as I could, but I didn't realize they were following me until they were really close. I tried to run. But they were much taller than I was and had much longer legs.

"I ran down this one street that I thought was a shortcut to my street. It wasn't. It was a dead end, and I was trapped." I looked at his expression and smiled weakly. I could feel tears threatening to brim over my eyes, and I blinked them away.

"Would it be weird if I said the rest was history? Let's just say there was no one there to save me that time," I said.

"Then what happened after that?" he asked, almost in a trance.

"Well, they left me there, and soon the police found me and asked me what happened. I told them the same story I told you, but they didn't believe me. They believed someone else had done it—but not Robbie. They thought

I was confused and jealous that he had other friends besides me. They said it was dark and there was no way for me to really tell. It was only because his parents had connections or bribed them," I said with a sigh.

"And your parents? What did they think?" he asked. His pupils had constricted to tiny slits, almost as small as they had been the day before.

"Nobody believed me. My parents were friends with his," I said, the sadness swelling inside me. He hesitantly reached out his hands to me, and I let him draw me to him.

This was different than the kiss. It was like before that awful night with Damon, and when he comforted me after my dad died. He was protecting me from all the horrific things that had happened … and continued to happen to me.

"It's okay now," he said, and I sobbed harder.

His hand gently stroked my hair as my tears leaked onto his shirt.

Chapter 25

It was Monday morning. After my particularly eventful weekend, I did *not* want to go to school. What could I say to Keith?

I felt so confused. I wondered if this had been my fear of Keith all along, not that he was a beast, but that he was getting close to me. I knew deep down that this fear was wrong, but how could I keep myself from recoiling from him the way I had in the woods? Thinking about it now sent small tremors up my spine.

"Harmony!" I heard my mom shout from downstairs. "Are you up?"

"Yeah," I called back and threw on a random assortment of clothes, without even looking in the mirror. I didn't have to look at myself to know that my hair was a disaster. Instead of trying to deal with it, I quickly ran my fingers through it and swirled it into a bun.

I yawned loudly as I stumbled into the kitchen, and my mom gave me a puzzled look.

"Did you sleep okay last night?" she asked, although the answer was obvious to both of us.

"Not really. I had trouble falling asleep." Actually, it was worse than that. I think the most I could have slept all night was an hour.

I was up all night thinking about what happened between me and Keith. My conflicting feelings confused me, and I felt as if two sides of me were warring with each other.

"Ready to go?" Mom asked as I turned away from my partially eaten breakfast. It was certainly an improvement from when I first returned to school. I remembered the completely uneaten dish of food in front of me and grimaced at the thought of those troubled times.

It seemed that I had gotten to school in the space of five minutes, when really it took nearly half an hour to reach the school grounds.

As I pulled in, my heart thudded loudly at the thought of seeing Keith again today, but this time it had nothing to do with fear. I wanted to explain my reaction to his advances yesterday. I wanted to tell him that I could be willing to take this relationship further. When I pulled in, I scanned the cars for the blue sedan that I knew so well.

I didn't see it, and I felt my heart steadily sink in my chest. I got out of the car and slammed the car door shut with a little too much force. I stalked off in the direction of the building when I heard my name called.

"Harmony!" I turned around to see Sarah's tall thin form running toward me.

"Hey," I answered her with a smile.

"Wow," she said, looking at me curiously.

"What?"

"You look like you're in less of a fog than usual. Are you still on your medication?"

"No!"

"Oh my gosh! That's great!"

"I know—right!" I said, falling into step beside her. "Have you seen Keith today?"

"No, I don't think he's here yet."

"Oh." I tried to keep my expression from falling, but I think Sarah saw that my face clouded over. She was scrutinizing me, and I gave her a weird look.

"You are so strange," she said.

"What do you mean?"

"You go back and forth about so many things. It's like one day you hate him, and then the next you love him, and then the next you hate him again."

I thought I hid my confused feelings well from the rest of the world.

"Oh look!" she said, her eyes focusing on something behind me. I turned and felt my heart stop as I recognized his car pulling into the driveway of the school.

I couldn't decide what to do. Should I wait for him here or should I go inside and run into him in the halls or during class? The panic of indecision seemed to settle on me. Luckily, Sarah made the decision for me.

"Let's wait here for him," she said.

"Sure," I said, focusing on keeping my face as blank as possible. My nervousness escalated as I watched him get out of the car. He hadn't noticed us waiting for him yet. It felt good to watch him anonymously, observing the carefulness of his movements.

I watched as the wind tossed up his black hair and his large hand quickly combed it back into place. When he turned our way, I turned toward Sarah, pretending to have been talking to her. I commented dully on the weather, and she responded.

I could hear him approach us, and I began stressing about when I should look up to say hi. I didn't want to look up too soon—he would think I was purposefully staring at him. But I didn't want to look up too late; he would think I was ignoring him.

I ended up staring at Sarah until she waved casually in his direction. I barely lifted my hand in greeting before he waved back, walking toward us at a faster pace now.

"Hey, Sarah, Harmony," he said.

"Hi," I muttered, surprised that I was suddenly overcome by crippling shyness.

"So, Keith," Sarah said. "What did you do this weekend?"

"Not much …" His voice trailed off, and his chin turned slightly in my direction. Even though I couldn't see his eyes, I could almost feel the question in them. I gave him a quick nod, and he continued talking as if nothing had happened. "I ran into Harmony," he said, his voice casual, but I could feel the tension behind it.

"That's cool. Did you guys do anything?" So this is what she was getting at. She knew something had changed and that I wouldn't tell her.

"We hung out for a little … nothing interesting," he continued. I so wished that she would leave. I wanted to talk to him so badly. Unfortunately, Sarah did not allow us to talk privately; she chattered away in her usual fashion.

"If we don't hurry, we'll be late for first period," Keith noted as we ambled down the emptying hallway.

"You're probably right," Sarah said, and she picked up the pace to a brisker walk. When Keith saw I had a hard time keeping up, he dropped back to stay with me.

"You okay?"

"Yeah, my muscles are really stiff—that's all." Then, I playfully added, "I was on my feet a little this weekend."

"Yeah," he said.

"Keith?"

"Yes?"

"I really need to talk to you about … things."

"I do too," he said. The small smile he gave me was sad.

"You said we could go to your place after school one day to work on the project. Would that be an okay place to talk?"

"Yeah, it would be perfect."

We continued walking to class in silence, both of us wanting to say something, but neither of us able to. When we walked into the classroom together, Sarah gave me a questioning glance, but I simply shook my head.

I heard Keith settle behind me as I attempted to pay attention to what the teacher was saying. I glanced at my open textbook to see that I wasn't even on the right page.

Awhile later, the teacher said, "Is everyone finished?" Murmurs of assent swept through the class. "Let's see. Who can answer the first analysis question …" I let his voice fade off in a blur, and I swirled my blue pen around in a random design along the edges of the paper.

The sound of my swirling pen grew quicker, and the intricate blue pattern slowly expanded to fill the whole paper. Finally the bell rang, and we were going to ecology class. I now had an entire period to talk to him.

We walked together in the hall. "What's your favorite book?" I asked him, and he looked at me with a smile.

"I don't really have one."

"What? You must! You have like four gazillion books in your house."

"That's the point. There are so many good books that it's impossible to choose just one as a favorite."

"Fine," I huffed at him. "What are your favorite *books?*"

"I can't tell you that either," he laughed, and I pretended to glare in annoyance at him.

"Let me guess, there are too many to list off?" I said sarcastically.

"You got it. Why don't you tell me your favorite book."

I thought back to all of the books that I read, to all of the cliché romance novels where there's always a happy ending. Then I thought of all the real literature that I had read.

"I'd have to say *The Scarlet Pimpernel.*"

"That's a good one."

"I can't really say why I like it. I hated the beginning, but by the time I reached the middle, I was in love with it."

"It's a really well written mystery. You have no idea who the Scarlet Pimpernel is until the very last minute."

"I guessed who it was really early," I said proudly.

"How'd you manage that one?"

"It was completely random."

We reached the classroom doors and walked in.

"I assume by now most of you have your projects almost completed," the teacher began. I snuck a glance at Keith; our project was far from complete. "Get together with your partners for the rest of the period to discuss final details. Make sure you're not reading from the PowerPoint or poster board. Have note cards, but be sure to know what you want to say so you're not reading the entire time."

The desks scraped loudly against the floor as people arranged the desks to face their partners.

"So," I said, reaching into one of my folders to take out the packet of information. "I can stop at the store today and get poster board and craft supplies."

"That's good. I can get some things too."

"So how do we want to organize it?" I asked, shifting through my papers.

"What do you mean?"

"Like … do you want to present our information independently, or blend it?"

"I think it would be good if we tried to make connections." And the conversation continued. Finally, we had the sequence of the presentation organized, and we knew generally how we would set up the poster board.

"There are so many more important things we could be talking about. A grade is only a letter," I said.

We just stared at each other for a long time, and finally the bell rang. I was relieved when his steady gaze broke from mine as he got up and left the room. I didn't see him much the rest of the day.

Questions roiled around in my brain all night. What could I possibly say to him? Could I trust him? Could I trust anyone? I didn't drift off into a light sleep until the sun was already trying to peek up over the horizon. I felt as if I had just blinked my eyes when my alarm started to ring. I could barely hold my eyelids up as I stumbled into the shower. I glanced at the mirror, taking a moment to notice the big black shadows that hung under my eyes.

Chapter 26

The next day after school, Keith and I met at his house.

"I never asked how you and your dad got your book collection," I said, looking at the towering shelves in his room.

"When we were escaping, my mother … she was very strong, even though she had been weakened by the treatment she had received while she was captured. She was able to carry us and the books to safety." I could tell he was avoiding saying the word *Dragon,* and I was secretly glad.

"So," I said, trying to change the subject, "let's finish this thing already." I poured all of the material onto the floor, including all the papers I had.

He gave me an odd look before sitting down next to me as we started sorting through the information and assembling the poster. He took his hand and brushed his hair out of his eyes. His brow was furrowed in concentration, and I had the sudden urge to tease him, to startle him out of his ferocious concentration. He didn't even look up as I slid next to him.

This was something I used to do to my friends before Robbie changed my life forever. I was known for it, and whenever I would go near someone, like I was doing now, they would run away. But Keith didn't know me then, so he didn't know what I was going to do. I took my hand and jabbed it into his side right below his ribs, where it tickled and hurt at the same time.

"Oh my god!" he exclaimed, jumping away from me. He stared at my teasing, nonapologetic face.

"You're gonna get it for that," he laughed, lunging at me. I squeaked and tried to scramble to my feet to get away from him. I felt his arms snake around my waist and pull me down, till my back was on the floor.

He only used his right arm when he held me to the floor, even though I was struggling against him with all my might. I laughed and wiggled around and heard his teasing chuckle.

"Okay … okay …" I laughed, struggling to catch my breath. Suddenly I stopped laughing and looked up at him.

I felt the sudden electricity pulse between us, and I knew that he felt it too. I slowly slid up into a sitting position, and he slowly backed up, but he didn't move too far away from me.

This time, I did not resist the temptation to reach up and gently comb the thick black hair out of his face. As his soft hair slid through my fingers, I couldn't help but allow a small smile to spread across my face.

He leaned in closer to me. He gently pressed his lips against mine, and a bolt of lightning seemed to shoot through us. I pushed back against him, moving my lips with his and cupping his face in my hands. His hands slid off the wall and gripped my shoulders, crushing me to him.

My nerves were on fire where his hands touched my shoulders. My head was spinning around, and I couldn't feel anything besides the way he felt against me.

I felt my heart rate spike as it hammered against my chest. He began moving quicker, and his arms began to slide down my sides. I felt the flicker of panic spark in the back of my brain as he pushed closer to me. I felt the panic fighting with my burning nerves, trying to take over. I brought my hand down to his chest and could feel his heart hammering against my hand.

The spark of panic in my brain grew, and I had to stop. It was like a bucket of cold water was being doused over my brain. I pressed my hands against his chest in an attempt to push him away.

When he felt the pressure, he began to shift his weight away from me.

"Oh," he said, reading my expression carefully. "Harmony, I'm so sorry! I don't know what happened. I keep making the same mistake—"

I cut him off, laying my hand against his face. "Don't be sorry," I said, smiling slightly.

"But I *am* sorry," he continued in a breathless rush. "I know what happened to you. I should have known you wouldn't be comfortable with something like that. I was going way too fast, and I ... I ..." I had never seen him so flustered.

"Keith," I said, "I can't really explain how I feel right now, but I know I don't want you to be thinking that way."

"What do you mean?"

"I ... I'm very conflicted," I said as he sat back and turned so he was next to me, leaning against the edge of the bed.

"How so?"

"Well, part of me—most of me—really likes you." I placed my hand over his. "But ..."

"But?" he asked, and I could tell this was the very conversation that he had been dreading.

"But there's another part of me that can't allow me to be close to someone again. I barely trust my own mother. It's just really hard."

"So you ... you're not hesitant because I'm ... not like you?" he asked.

"I don't think so ..."

"What does that mean?"

"I'm not scared of you right now. I think, even if you were like me, I would have a lot of trouble with this."

"You trusted Damon," he said, his lips tight.

"I did, but look what happened because of Damon. I let myself trust him—and look what happened. Then look at my dad, the one person of the opposite sex I was sure I could trust. He left. He not only left, but he left because of me."

"That's not really true," he sighed.

"We should really finish that," I noted, pointing to the poster.

"Yeah," he said, and I wiggled out of his hug.

"So, we have to finish gluing down all that information before we start the fun stuff."

"Fun stuff?" he asked, raising his eyebrows.

"Decorating!" I exclaimed.

"Oh, *that* fun stuff," he muttered sarcastically. I gave him a teasing shove before I got back to work. He sat next to me, and we finally had everything glued onto the board. I glanced at the clock, surprised that it was already almost five thirty.

Suddenly, I heard a soft knock, and both of us froze and looked up as Cyrus's face peeking around the door. He barely glanced at me, his worried eyes focused on Keith.

"Keith, can I talk to you for a second?" he asked.

"Yeah," he said standing up. "I'll be right back," he said to me before disappearing behind the door. I couldn't resist sneaking forward and straining my ears toward their hushed voices.

"Dad, you've been worried before. I'm sure they haven't figured it out."

"Keith, listen to me. Even if they haven't gotten it yet, they're much closer than they've ever been in the past."

"C'mon, I've heard this all before," he said, sounding frustrated.

"Look, I really think it'd be a good idea to—" Cyrus started.

"If you actually told me more about what was going on, then I might share some of your concern," Keith said.

"It couldn't hurt to stay a little closer to home," Cyrus said, his voice growing desperate.

"I'm not going to stay cooped up in this house the rest of my life because you *think* they might have fixed something that would allow their power to return."

"Calm down," Cyrus suddenly ordered in a stern voice. "Go cool off before you go in that room and traumatize that poor girl. We'll finish discussing this later." I heard Keith's loud footsteps and a door slam in another part of the house. My heart was thundering in my chest as I realized how serious this was. Cyrus was obviously concerned, and Keith obviously wasn't.

After a few minutes, Keith walked back into the room, his jaw clenched and eyes tight. Luckily, his pupils were perfectly round.

"Now we can finally put the finishing touches on the poster. So, what should our color theme be?" I asked, pretending that I hadn't heard any of their conversation.

"Our what?" he asked, amusement glinting in his eyes as the mask slowly lifted.

"You know—a selection of colors that go together."

"Why don't you do that part?" he said, clearly confused.

"Okay," I sighed. "Clearly you need creative therapy."

"Creative what?"

"You don't know what a color theme is or anything like that. You need serious help."

"Oh, is help what I need now?" he said with a laugh.

"I would think so. Here," I said, holding up an array of green and blue markers, "is our color theme."

"Now, what do you do with that?"

"Look!" I said, grabbing a pipe cleaner that matched one of the colors. I stapled it to the board in a twisted pattern.

An hour later, my stomach was beginning to grumble with hunger.

"What time is it?" I yawned, reaching my arms out to stretch the stiff muscles.

"It's about six forty-five."

"What?" I jumped up. "How did it get so late?"

"Would you like to stay for dinner?" he asked.

"That'd be good." I studied his face as he carefully threw all the things we didn't use into the plastic bag. He looked up and caught me staring at him, his face softening into a gentle smile.

"What is it?" he asked.

"How can anyone be so … nice?"

A slight pink tinge rose to his cheeks as he looked away. He stood the board up, and we proceeded downstairs. Sharp, delicious smells wafted from the kitchen.

"Harmony is going to stay with us for dinner. Is that okay?" he asked his dad, and he beamed at me and gestured for me to follow him into the kitchen. Beautiful cabinets lined the walls, and every appliance was large and stainless steel.

"Sure that'd be fine," his dad said.

After everyone sat down, and then Cyrus turned to me and said, "Harmony, I am so sorry about your dad. I didn't have time to talk to you before." I saw Keith tense up next to me out of the corner of my eye, and I could feel my face turn bright red as I looked down at my lap.

"I don't know if you knew, but we worked together. He was a good man." I didn't know what to say. I glanced up at Keith to gauge his reaction, and he was staring at me with a tight expression on his face.

"He was," I said. It was so nice to hear something good about him. Cyrus simply nodded and turned away. Keith shifted in his chair next to me, and his elbow brushed against my arm. I knew he meant it to be a sign of comfort.

"Are you glad that school is almost over?" Keith asked.

"Yeah, I can't believe it. After this week we have only like two weeks left, not counting finals, of course."

"I know. It seems like I just had my first day yesterday."

"Well, I can't say that my first day back seems like yesterday. When I look at everything that's happened, it easy to believe that it's almost summer time."

"I guess I see your point," he said. This entire time, Keith's father was watching our exchange quietly. I looked at the clock hanging on the kitchen wall, surprised that the time had again gone so quickly.

"I should probably get going," I said, standing up. Keith stood up with me.

"I could drive you home if you want," he offered, and I saw the flicker of hope in his eyes. It filled my heart with warmth at the thought that he wanted to spend time with me.

"No, then you won't have a way to get home."

"Okay, then let me drive you to school tomorrow morning."

"You can do that," I said with a smile. As I turned to leave, Keith's dad got up and shook my hand, a warm smile on his face. We walked out into the warm summer air, and I smiled as I leaned against the car.

"I had a really good time," I said looking up at him.

"You did?"

"Yeah." I surprised him by leaning forward and pressing my lips up against his. I felt his stiff muscles relax against me, his hands moving to cup my face.

I quickly broke away, not wanting it to get as heated as it did earlier. I slid away and gave him a small smile and got into my car.

"I'll see you tomorrow morning? 7:15 at my house?" I asked.

"Yeah," he said, and there was no mistaking the yearning look on his face as I drove away. As my headlights beamed in front of me, I couldn't help the worry that settled in my stomach when I remembered Cyrus's concerned face.

Chapter 27

The next morning was stressful. When I got home, I was so exhausted that I didn't have time to even change into the T-shirt and shorts that I always wore to bed. I got up with my hair piled like a hay stack on top of my head and my clothes all wrinkled. I glanced at the bright red letters of the clock in my room.

It was later than usual. I couldn't believe Mom hadn't woken me up. I ran around the house looking for her, but she wasn't in any of the rooms. I found a small note lying on the kitchen counter.

Harmony,
I had to leave early for work. Have a wonderful day and see you later.
Love, Mom

I resumed my frantic rushing. I took the quickest shower of my life and threw on whatever clothes reached my hands first. As I was scarfing down my breakfast, the doorbell rang exactly at 7:15.

I scrambled to the door and threw it open, pushing my messy hair out of my face. "Hey," I said, beaming him a big smile.

"Hi," he said.

I rushed forward, wrapping my arms tightly around his waist, unable to voice how happy I was to see him. I felt his hand gently brush against my hair. "Slept a little late today?" he asked, noticing my disheveled appearance.

"Only a little," I said. We held hands as we walked to the car, his hand completely enveloping mine. He held the door to his car open for me, and

I felt a blush creep up my cheeks at his courteous behavior. Could it have possibly been only yesterday when I was still debating how I felt about him?

All too quickly, the memory of Cyrus's alarmed voice rang through my head. I debated confronting Keith about his father's concern. By going to school, he seemed to be going against his father's wishes. Yesterday he seemed so angry I decided it would probably not be a good idea to bring it up.

I was resting my hand on the compartment between our seats when I felt the soft touch of his hand and realized why the world seemed brighter today. I looked up at his face to see him looking at me with a soft expression in his eyes.

As we drove around a familiar turn, a memory from a long time ago flashed before my eyes. I remembered driving across this same exact turn, my stomach twisted with nerves. I remembered cutting the turn and smashing into a small blue sedan. I remember looking up in shock to see the now familiar dark blue eyes.

"Keith," I said, suddenly nervous about hearing the answer.

"Yeah?"

"Um, do you remember the day when I first returned from school?"

"I'll never forget it," he said.

"Something happened when I was driving that morning that I was never really able to explain. That morning, I had a dream that you were saving me from those four guys, but how could I possibly know about you because I had never even met you? Later I thought I got into a car crash, and I'm almost positive the driver was you because I saw your eyes. But then everything disappeared, so I assumed I made the entire thing up because of stress."

He shifted in his seat uncomfortably as he stared out into the distance, seemingly lost in thought. I waited a long time for him to speak. I was about to open my mouth to tell him to forget I said anything when his voice broke the silence.

"That's hard to explain and will take a long time," he said, and I could tell he was tense and guarded. "I don't really understand it. My dad gets it better than I do, but I'll do my best to explain. Dragons often have a certain effect on people that can bring on hallucinations and dreams."

"What?"

"For example, when the Griffins set out to capture my mother, my dad was having dreams about it for months. He even thought he saw her in the tunnels before they actually brought her. It doesn't happen to everyone."

"Keith, I overheard some of that conversation with your dad yesterday," I said quietly.

"I wouldn't worry too much about it, even if they have fixed it. My dad says that they won't kill me, even if they do capture me."

"Why doesn't he think they'll want to kill you?"

"Mostly because I'm very valuable. I was a really expensive science experiment that went awry. If they ever caught me, Dad thinks the worst they'll do is lock me up." He shrugged, as if it was no big deal, but I couldn't help feeling that it was.

I got out of the car, dragging my heavy backpack full of books with me. I saw Sarah, Jen, and Adrienne standing in the distance, expressions of shock on their faces. I knew they would be waiting to ambush me. Dealing with them seemed so trivial after my tense conversation in the car.

As we walked over, Jen strolled forward, glanced hesitantly at Keith, and said, "Hey, guys." She smiled brightly but gave me a look that told me we would talk later. "Can you believe that school is almost over? Everything went so fast! Next year we're going to be seniors! It's so exciting!"

"Dude," Adrienne said suddenly. "That means college! And freedom!"

"I know!" I said, rushing into the conversation as Keith hung back, as usual. As we walked past the girls' bathroom, all three of them dragged me toward the door.

"I'll be right back," I said sheepishly to him. I saw his ghost of a smile before his face disappeared behind the door.

"Okay," Jen said, frowning at me and beginning to tap her foot.

"Yeah," I said slightly hesitantly.

"What's going on between you and Keith?" Adrienne demanded.

"I don't exactly know ..."

"I don't buy that," Sarah said.

"Well, yesterday I went to his house so that we could work on the project. And I guess we sort of ..."

"Did you kiss?" she asked, and only then did I see the excitement in her eyes.

"Maybe," I giggled. The memory erased any dark thoughts that had been lingering in my brain.

"Oh my God!" she squeaked, and she ran forward to hug me. I didn't need a mirror to tell me that I was beat red. "You have no idea how long I was waiting for that to happen."

"What?" I asked, surprised.

"It was just so obvious! And it was so frustrating watching you two constantly avoid it. And then you started going out with Damon, and then, after that terrible thing in the park, things got all weird. I'm so happy for you!"

"I don't really know if it's going to go anywhere yet."

"Of course it will! You guys have the entire summer, and you live right near each other, so it should be easy!"

"Yeah, I guess," I said. Grabbing their arms, I added, "C'mon, we're going to be late for class." They followed me out the door, and we quickly raced through the halls so we could make it to class on time.

The rest of the week passed quickly. Keith picked me up every day. We did not kiss again the entire week, but it didn't matter to me. I was so happy just to be near him.

He didn't tell me anything more about the Griffins or the machine they were supposedly fixing, and I didn't ask. The normal routine of life made the whole thing fade out of reality.

It was Friday, the day of the big ecology presentation. As usual, I waited outside near the end of my driveway for Keith to come pick me up. When I saw the small blue sedan slowly pull up the driveway, I couldn't help but smile.

"Hey," I said, jumping into the car.

"Hey, yourself." He studied me carefully as I fidgeted around in my seat and twirled a hair tie around in my fingers.

"You look nervous," he observed.

"Yeah, well, I've never been that skilled at public speaking."

"You know what?"

"What?"

"Neither have I," he said, starting to drive into the road.

"Well, at least our poster looks good." I turned around to look at the well-decorated poster in the backseat.

"Keith?" I asked as we began pulling into the school's driveway.

"Yeah?"

"I was wondering. You know how your dad is like a super genius? Are you really smart too?"

"I'm pretty smart, but I wouldn't call myself a super genius like he is—just an average genius," he laughed.

"Where did you go to school before this?"

"I was home schooled actually. It took a really long time to know for sure whether or not I would be able to keep my temper under control. We finally decided that this year was as good as it was going to get, so I decided to enroll." We walked out of the car together in silence. He carried the poster in one hand. My black and white charcoal drawing with the wind picking up dead ashes was glued to the center of the board. That first drawing seemed like such a long time ago.

"Wow, guys, that looks amazing!" Sarah exclaimed from behind us.

"Thanks," I muttered nervously.

"Our poster doesn't look nearly as good as that," she said.

"Don't worry about it. I'm sure it looks great," I said.

"It looks okay …" she murmured, looking wistfully at our poster again.

Keith didn't say anything. I turned back to look at him, but his face was vacant, and he was staring off into the distance. His gaze shifted to mine, and he smiled slightly, but his body remained stiff and tense.

"You okay?" I asked him, and I reached out my hand and gently brushed it against his fingers. For a moment, the entire world had faded into the background, and it was just him and me together.

"Yeah," he said hoarsely. "I'm fine." I looked at him, not completely believing his terse words. As I turned away, the rest of the world came racing back. Sarah was watching us, her eyes puzzling and her brow furrowed. I felt my gaze shift back to his face again; I could watch him forever.

When we settled down to class, my stomach began to twist and turn.

I simply stared off into the distance as I struggled to keep my nerves under control.

The slower I wanted the time to go, the faster it went. It seemed I only had to blink and it was time for ecology class. I stopped outside the door as I waited for Keith. I didn't want to walk into the classroom without him. I scanned the hallways for his tall frame, and suddenly I saw him turning around the corner. He gave me the smallest of smiles, like the kind he first gave me when we first met.

"Ready?" I asked, glancing down at the poster in his hands.

"Ready," he said.

"Okay," the teacher called, struggling to get the students settled. "Everyone, settle down and sit in your seats. The sooner we start the presentations, the sooner we will be able to finish." The noise around me slowly quieted until everyone's attention was focused on the teacher. "Now," she said, surveying everyone, "we will do this in alphabetical order, so there's no confusion about who goes next." She named the first person on the attendance list and settled down to listen to the presentations.

Finally, she called our names. I felt the tension rise in the room as we both stiffly got up and walked to the front of the classroom. I suddenly remembered that moment in the forest, all that time ago. I remembered seeing those charred woods, how the haze from the fire still lingered in the trees, how the ashes still lay heavily on the ground. I remembered likening myself to the empty black trunks, because that's really all I was, an empty shell. Now, I realized as I stared at my first charcoal sketch, that I was more like the live woods on the other side of the road, just beginning to bloom with life on the eve of summer. I glanced at Keith and gave him an encouraging smile. Even now, people barely heard Keith speak and were expectant with curiosity. I could tell, as he stared out at the classroom, how hard this was for him.

I hoped that I had diverted some of the attention from him when I started talking, and as I paused to look around the room, I was grateful to realize that I had. Finally, it was his turn.

I heard him take a deep, slightly shaky breath before he began speaking. His deep voice reverberated around the silent classroom, and I could feel him grow more comfortable as he talked. Finally, after what seemed like an eternity, we were finished.

"Harmony, did you draw that picture of the woods? The one in the center?" Someone from the classroom asked. I felt a blush rise to my cheeks, and I looked down at my shoes.

"Yeah."

"It's so amazing, like there's more to it than just a sketch. I never really saw them in that light."

"Thanks," I said as Keith and I walked back to our seats and the next group went up.

"God, I'm glad that's over," he said. All the tension seemed to lift from his face as he gave me a beaming smile.

"I know. I didn't think it was as bad as I thought it was going to be."

"No, it wasn't terrible," he agreed.

"Now that that's over, I feel like school's going to fly by."

"I know. Me too."

And fly it did.

Chapter 28

Right after our last final exam, Keith came over my house.

I had placed the two pictures of us from the city on the shelf. He was studying the pictures carefully, an unreadable expression on his face. After a long time, he turned his face to study me. The minute he looked at the clinging tank top and short shorts, I suddenly realized he had never seen me dress so casually before.

"Let's go," he said, the blush on his face slowly getting redder before he turned away. "You wanna go to the park?" he asked me as we exited the house.

"Yeah, it's such a gorgeous day. It'd be a shame if we didn't enjoy it."

"I agree," he said. He glanced down at our two hands, our fingers gently brushing against one another.

So many feelings coursed through me at once. I had known him for a long time, but it felt like I was just meeting him. I could feel hesitation, but at the same time I felt eager and wild. The clinging anxiety remained in the back of my mind, and the fact that he might be in danger practically took my breath away.

We walked in silence, our hands swinging between us. We approached the park and settled underneath the shade of a tree near the lake, which was so still it could have been glass. The trees were reflected on the still surface.

"Keith?" I asked, and I felt my heart accelerate at the thought of what I was about to ask.

"Yeah?" I could feel his eyes on me, but I did not look up.

"Could I ask you something?"

"You know, when you're ready, you can ask me anything."

"Well, I only have about a million questions."

"I'm sure we'll have plenty of time to cover them all," he said, and his voice was the warmest I'd heard it in a long time.

"I don't really know where to start …"

"I can't really help you there, seeing as I don't know what they are."

"Okay, I have one."

"Yeah?"

"Do you like … age differently? And if you do, how old are you?" When I finished, I could almost feel him sigh in relief at the easiness of my first question.

"Dragons do age differently because Dragons can live forever. They age until they're fully grown and mature, and then the process slows down and eventually just stops. I had the normal growth patterns of any human until I was fourteen, and then my dad noticed that my growing was slowly falling behind what it should be for the average person my age. He realized immediately what was happening and didn't get too worried. So, technically, right now, I have the mental and physical maturity of a sixteen-year-old even though I'm more like nineteen."

"That's really cool," I said. I was beginning to worry that he was much older than I was.

"I can't get over how old your dad is."

"It's pretty crazy, and it's still hard for me to believe that he was able to create that serum."

"I shook hands with someone who was around during the medieval period," I said, shaking my head in disbelief. I could feel his body rocking with laughter at my observation. I suddenly felt my stomach rumble with hunger.

"Oh, I forgot to have lunch," I said, glancing at my watch. I couldn't believe it was already almost four o'clock. "I should probably go home. My mom is going to get home soon," I said, a sudden shyness making me look at my feet instead of his face.

He gently took my chin and pulled it up so my eyes met his. He had brushed his hair away from his face with his fingers, and I could almost drown in the blue ocean. He leaned down toward me and I knew what was going to happen.

His lips pressed down on mine gently. Lightning seemed to strike where his skin touched mine, and my body reacted before I was ready.

I moved my lips with his, surprising myself by leaning into him and tangling my fingers with his hair. One of my hands moved to his chest as a heat that had nothing to do with the summer sun coursed through us.

I clutched him closer to me, and I could feel that he was just as stunned as I was at my bold move. His large hands moved to my shoulders and clutched me even closer to him.

He held me so tightly that I couldn't tell whether it was his heart thundering against my chest, or mine.

I didn't want this day to end. We talked all the way home about nothing in particular, but our conversation meant so much more than what we were actually saying.

I walked in the door, and I felt as if the entire world had been lifted off my shoulders. My heart was so light that it could've flown out of my chest.

Everything in the world seemed to be brighter; even the shadows seemed to glow vibrantly. I wanted to dance and sing and jump around. I wanted to skip down the street and show everyone the way my heart wanted to fly.

I couldn't sit still. I kept jumping up and down and repeating in my head everything that had happened that afternoon. I kept bringing up his face in my mind, and the way his crystal blue eyes had melted when they looked at me.

I couldn't let go of the feeling of his thick hair as it slid through my fingers. I grabbed one of the pillows from the couch and grasped it to me, wishing it was something else completely. I finally was able to sit still.

I sat by the window in the living room, which faced our backyard. I still held the pillow to my chest and stared blankly at the green trees and grass without really seeing them. I couldn't stop the images that swirled in front of my eyes, and I didn't want to.

For the first time in a very long time, I was happy just to delve into my memories and stay there for a long time.

I repeated our conversation over and over in my head and was again shocked to find that I wasn't repulsed by his answers to my questions. When my mother walked in, almost forty-five minutes later, I was still sitting there, staring out the window, imagining that his arms were around me at that moment.

"Harmony?" she called into the house, and I resentfully pulled away from the blissful memories.

"In here," I told her, and I turned to see her walking into the room.

"How was your last exam?" she asked me, and I could've laughed. Was it only this morning that I had taken a two-hour test? I couldn't even remember what subject it was on.

"Fine," I said, turning to the window.

"You okay?" she asked, and I turned to see her giving me an odd look.

"Yes, I'm much more than okay." She continued to stare at me with an odd look when the ringing of the phone interrupted the silence between us. "I'll get it!" I said, jumping up. Could it possibly be him? The sharp anticipation in my chest was so hard it hurt. I tore the phone off the hook and held it to me ear.

"Hello?" I said, forcing the sharp expectation out of my voice.

"Harmony?" Keith asked, and at the sound of his voice, I felt a strange release, as if chains were suddenly lifted from around me.

"Yeah?" I answered, not able to keep the happiness out of my voice.

"I was wondering if you were free tomorrow."

"Of course! It's summer."

"Did you want to hang out again?"

"Yes," I answered, and I was so happy I wanted to cry.

After that, a routine began to develop, and Mom was always at work, so she didn't know how much time I spent out of the house.

Every day, we would go to the park, and we would often walk around and talk for hours. Sometimes, we would go under the same tree as the first day and we would kiss, hidden from the world.

He seemed to know when I had had enough and would always pull away first when he thought I was getting nervous. Sometimes, we would just sit there, with me leaning up against his shoulder. We wouldn't say anything; we would just stare out at the lake.

Weeks passed, and the most perfect summer that I had ever had was suddenly interrupted by what I had feared. It was the middle of July, and the weather was sweltering. I stared at the clock in anticipation. Keith was much later than usual. As the time passed, worry began to settle in the pit of my stomach. I began to pace anxiously around the house, barely able to tear my eyes away from the bright letters of the clock.

The uneasiness seemed to crawl up my spine and settle in my chest as more time passed. In my mind, I saw Cyrus's worried face entreating Keith to be careful. I couldn't get Keith's confident face out of my mind, so sure that he had nothing to fear. I paced back and forth in the house, debating whether or not I should try to call him.

I didn't want him to think I was hovering, but he said nothing yesterday about our routine changing. I forced myself to take a deep breath and relax. If anything bad happened, Cyrus would call me. Wouldn't he?

After what seemed like an eternity, the doorbell finally rang. I rushed forward and jerked open the door, all the panic and worry lifting off my shoulders when I saw Keith standing in front of me.

But that was before I looked at him closely. He was completely covered in sweat, his thick dark hair plastered to his head, and his shirt clung to his muscular torso. He was breathing hard, like he had just run very far and very fast.

My heart twisted in fear when I saw his eyes; his pupils had narrowed and elongated until they were vertical slits.

"Keith, what's wrong?" I asked when I stepped aside to let him in.

"My dad …" he huffed, "is driving me … crazy."

"What happened?"

"This morning, he forbade that I leave the house, and when I tried to sneak out, I realized that he took my car keys."

"Really?"

"Yeah, I was so mad I nearly burnt the house down," he said, and from the look on his face, I knew he wasn't kidding. "Instead, I decided it would be a better idea to run here, but that's why it took me so long."

"Yeah, probably," I said. He had never talked so bluntly about his temper before.

"Do you mind if I have a glass of water?" he asked, his pupils slowly returning back to normal.

"Of course not," I replied, leading him to the kitchen. He guzzled down the water in one gulp, his breathing slowly returning to normal. "Keith, if your dad is so worried, don't you think it would be a good idea to listen to him? I don't mind going to your house to visit—" The minute the words left my lips, his muscles tensed up again, and his pupils began to change.

"You don't understand. I don't care if the Griffins are returning to power, even if my dad is right. They're going to regain their power and technology sometime, whether it be now, five years from now, or twenty years from now. I want to be free to live my life, without being in constant fear that they *might* be regaining their power."

"But the problem is," I argued in a soft voice, "if they do return, you might not be free to live at all."

Chapter 29

"Do they let people swim in that?" I asked on a particularly hot day, gesturing to the goose infested pond. The aftermath of our discussion the week before was still fresh in my mind, but it seemed to have faded from his. He had to sneak out of his house every day to come and see me, although I had no idea how his dad never found out.

"I don't think you'd want to," he said, wrinkling his nose in disgust.

"Why?"

He pointed toward the surface. Three ducks were swimming across, causing the glasslike surface to ripple.

"I wish there was a pool around here. It's so hot!" I exclaimed.

"This might make you feel better," he said, raising his water bottle. I barely had time to recognize the teasing glint in his eyes before my head was doused in water.

"Jerk!" I exclaimed, and raising my own water bottle, I jumped on top of him and sprayed him in the face.

"Oh!" he called out, and he pretended to fall over, his wet hair plastered to his face. In order to stop myself from falling on his face, I gripped his waist with my knees. We landed in a position where I was sitting on top of his stomach with one knee on either side of him. His knees were raised so that they would have been supporting my back if I was sitting up straight. But I wasn't sitting up straight. I had fallen over with him, and my hands were on either shoulder, and our faces were very close.

The smile slowly faded from his face, and I felt the sparks of electricity between us. He propped himself up on his elbows, pushing his face even closer to mine.

He raised his lips to meet mine, and we sat there for a moment; the only part of us that was moving was our lips. Without taking his lips from mine, he slowly shifted me so that I was sitting on his lap, with my legs pointing in the same direction.

I raised my hands so they knotted through his thick hair and pulled his face to mine. His hands, which were resting on my waist, gently tugged me closer.

"I love you," he said, and I jumped slightly with surprise. This was the first time he had said that. I slowly lifted one hand and raised it to his face, gently brushing his hair away from his eyes.

All I could do was smile at him and say, "Me too." His face changed, and the hard lines became sharper with intensity. He leaned down again and pressed his lips to mine.

This kiss was different; it was much more forceful and passionate. His hand pulled my waist in toward him until I was all but fused to his body. My skin seemed to tingle and burn wherever he touched me, and it felt as if he were everywhere at once. I shifted so that I was straddling his waist with my legs, and I could feel him respond. I didn't resist this time when he gently encouraged my mouth open.

My heart seemed to want to fly straight out of my chest it was beating so hard. My hand slid down so that it was resting on his chest, and I could feel the way his heart throbbed under my hand. I couldn't think, and the world seemed to be spinning dizzily around me. One of his hands remained on my waist while the other moved up and down my face, sending sparks along his fingertips.

I could barely breathe as he knotted his fingers in my hair and pulled us impossibly closer.

He pulled away and stared into my eyes, gently smoothing down my messed up hair. We both seemed to look away at the same time, staring out into the lake.

"Hey," he said.

"Yeah?"

"I never want this summer to end," he whispered.

"I agree, but we're going to have to find some sort of pool or something, 'cause it's getting really hot."

"I was wondering ..." he started, but then he looked down.

"What?" I asked him, trying to catch his eyes again.

"Does your mom know about us?"

I looked at him carefully and could see how much this meant to him, despite all the other turmoil that surrounded him.

"No, she doesn't," I said quietly.

"Would you want to tell her?"

"Of course, but I've been trying to wait for the right moment."

"Trust me ... there is never a right moment."

"Did you tell your dad?"

"He pretty much knows everything," he said. "There aren't very many people I can talk to. There are only two in fact."

"Who's the second?" I asked, even though I was almost sure of the answer.

"You," he said, gently bringing his hand up to run his fingers through my hair again.

"I should probably go home," I said, noticing the setting sun.

"Yeah," he said, and he sounded just as unhappy about it as I was. We both stood up, brushing the grass and dirt off of our legs. "I think I know where we can swim tomorrow."

"Sounds good," I said. I tried to tell myself that he wasn't risking anything by coming to see me every day like this—that he was right and Cyrus was wrong.

"I'll walk you home," he said.

When we arrived at the front of my house, we stopped outside. I looked around to see if any people were around; the street was deserted. "I love you," I told him, and the smile he gave me was so big that his skin crinkled at the edge of his eyes.

"Me too," he said, and I gave him a smile that rivaled his. I had the urge to repeat Cyrus's words to be careful, but I resisted, knowing they would only make him mad. With huge regret, I turned away and walked into my empty house. Before I turned to shut the door, I waved at him, and he smiled again, more sad than before. When I closed the door, I quickly rushed to the window with the best view of the street.

He was slowly strolling down the road, in the direction of his house. Every once in a while, he would turn and glance at my house. As he walked, the street seemed to crowd with more cars and people.

Soon, he was too far for me to watch anymore, and I turned away from the window. Every afternoon, I felt as if I was in a strange kind of limbo until I saw him again.

As I paced randomly around the house, I heard the key turn in the door as my mom came home. "Hey, Harmony," she called to me.

"Hi," I said distantly, and I was glad she was too busy to notice how out of it I was. Suddenly, I was sure that I had to tell her about Keith. I knew that it would make it more real, that it wouldn't just be a dream.

"Hey, Mom?"

"Yeah?" she said, walking into the kitchen, flipping through the mail.

"Do you remember that guy that I worked on that ecology project with?" I asked her nervously, twisting my fingers together.

"Yeah …" she said, watching me carefully. "What about him?"

"Well, we're kind of going out. We've been hanging out in the park every day since school ended. I'm going to see him again tomorrow."

"Oh really?" she said, looking slightly surprised for a second. "He seemed nice," she continued before starting to flip distractedly through the mail again. Realizing she was preoccupied, I wandered out of the kitchen and continued staring out the window, waiting for the sun to fall behind the horizon.

Chapter 30

I saw his car pull into our driveway. My heart raced, and I paced around the foyer area as I waited for him to ring the bell. I tried to ignore the guilty feeling in my stomach when I realized the trouble he probably had to go through to get the car. Neither one of us believed that Cyrus was actually fooled. Cyrus was probably frightened about what Keith would do if he really tried to restrict him.

The ringing of the doorbell echoed throughout the house. I raced to the door and threw it open, my face breaking into a smile the minute I laid my eyes on him. "Do you want to come in?" I asked him awkwardly, and he gave me a slightly nervous smile as he walked through the door. However, there was something in his expression that made me think that something else was bothering him. I tried not to let the worry show on my face when I introduced him to my mom.

"Hi, Keith," Mom said casually as she walked through the kitchen door.

"Hello," he said nervously. He looked at the ground and self-consciously ran his fingers through his hair.

"So, where are you guys going today?" she asked, and I was grateful for the ease with which she smiled at him, glad that she still seemed to like him.

"There's this pool that's about a ten-minute drive from here. Since it's been really hot, we decided to cool off there for today," he said. The entire time he was staring at his feet.

| 15 Stitches |

"That's good. So I guess I'll see you guys later," she said, waving us off as we slowly exited. As we climbed into the car, I could see him visibly relax.

"Do you think it's going to be crowded?" I asked.

"I hope it's not too bad," he said.

"Yeah, me too." I looked at him for a second, studying his near perfect profile as he stared out into the road. "Are you feeling okay?" I asked him, and he glanced at me as we stopped at a red light.

"Yeah, fine why?"

"You seem upset about something, that's all."

He sighed loudly and smiled.

"You know me too well."

"What? What is it?" I asked, feeling anxiousness creep into my voice.

"It was really hard for me to get these keys. I hope he doesn't try to follow me; knowing him, he probably put some tracking device on the car."

"What did he do?"

"He's just freaking out about his whole Artrox thing."

"What exactly is an Artrox?"

"That's the name the Griffins gave to the device my mother destroyed."

"Oh my god, Keith. I heard that word before … when Damon and his dad were talking about capturing someone." All the pieces fell into place.

"I avoided telling you because I didn't want you to freak out or anything. But my dad's 100 percent positive they've fixed it, and he's like having a nervous breakdown."

"Seriously, Keith, if you're in danger out here, then we should go back to your house."

"God! You sound just like my father! Nothing is going to happen! I refuse to live in fear for the rest of my life!" he shouted, his pupils narrowing to slits. This was the first time he got angry with me, and I fell quiet, my heart beating loudly in my chest.

I stared out the window, clasping my hands together to prevent them from shaking. Suddenly, I felt his soft touch at the top of my arm, and I turned around stiffly.

"I'm sorry," he said quietly. "I would never lose my control with you, not ever. Do you understand?" I nodded, but that didn't stop the tips of my fingers from trembling. "It's just that the last thing that I need right now is the Griffins ruining my summer, and if I stay locked up in my house, it would be like admitting defeat."

"I have a question about the Griffins," I said, letting my curiosity get the better of me.

"Go ahead," he said very quietly again, as if he was trying not to scare me.

"Well, when you talked about them, you made it sound like they were unbeatable and nothing could harm them. But then your mother was able to escape and they haven't really bothered you. And what happened with Damon suggests they're not all-powerful. Why haven't they sought you out sooner? And surely they have a weakness."

"You're right," he said. "They do have a weakness, but it's not one thing exactly. They're biggest weakness is their overdependence on technology. They make us look like cavemen who've only invented fire. This could be an advantage for them, except they don't know how to survive without it.

"When my mother destroyed the Artrox, the Griffins suddenly became incapable of doing the things they used to. Their tracking devices didn't work at all. All the technology that they would use to contain me if I was captured became defunct and still is ... unless my dad's hunch is right."

"How do Donovan and Damon have anything to do with this?" I asked, hesitating to speak Damon's name.

"The Griffins installed Donovan as my dad's replacement. Donovan is smart, about the level of Einstein, but he still doesn't come close to my dad. They found him a year after Damon was born."

"That's really scary," I said, and I felt a shiver creep up my back at the thought.

"Yes, to be perfectly honest, I'm surprised they haven't fixed the Artrox already. Fifteen years is a long time."

"How was Damon able to find you?"

"A remote possibility is that it was by chance that we happened to fall into the same school. It's more likely that Donovan was able to do some basic detective work to figure out where we were. It still scares me to think he tried to kill me only months after I started in the school."

"Did you know who he was?"

"Yeah, almost right away, but my dad told me not to do anything, and that leaving would cause much more trouble than if I stayed. The fact that he was alone proves that he didn't have any support for his actions. He was probably going against his father's wishes. If the Artrox was working, that would mean they had the right technology to contain me, and there would have been plenty of people to back him up."

I felt another shiver creep up my spine as my memories from that night took on a different perspective.

"Don't worry," he said wrapping a hand around my shoulder. "I still don't think they could have fixed the Artrox. Well … here we are," he said, pulling into the parking lot, which was about three-quarters filled.

"I'm kind of excited; I haven't gone swimming in a long time," I said. We walked up to the front desk, and I tried to ignore the way people seemed to stare at the bright red scar on my leg. We found two chairs together and put our stuff down. I was wearing my bathing suit under my clothes, and I carefully tugged my shirt up over my head. I glanced at Keith shyly to see him staring at me with his mouth slightly open.

"Do you need sunscreen?" he asked me, eyeing my pale skin.

"Oh yeah," I said, gently rubbing it all over me so that I wouldn't get burned.

"I'll help with your back," he said, taking the sunscreen from my hands. I shivered slightly as his strong hands rubbed the sunscreen up and down on my back.

"Don't you need sunscreen?" I asked him. "You're paler than I am."

"No, I've never burned in my entire life," he said, giving me a significant look. I saw him reach down with his large hands and pull his shirt up over his head. I unconsciously sucked in my breath as I took in his muscular back.

"You ready?" he asked, turning around to face me.

"Yeah," I said slightly hollowly, not able to take my eyes off of his chest.

As we walked down to the pool, almost every girl over the age of twelve turned when they saw him. They barely seemed to recognize that I was there with him as they gawked openly. I watched his face carefully to see if he noticed, but he didn't seem to. He led me over to the deep end of the pool.

"Watch this," he said, and he flipped his hair. He dove in, his body creating the perfect arc as he hit the water. As he surfaced, his thick hair was plastered to his face. "Come on!" he called to me, holding his arms open for me to jump into.

I leapt off the edge and into his waiting arms. The water swirled around me, plastering my hair to my face and shoulders. As I surfaced, I quickly flipped it away from my face.

He was standing easily in the water, which came up to his shoulders. I struggled to keep my head above water as I treaded. "Why do you have to be so tall!" I joked as I continued to struggle. Suddenly, I felt his arms around me and his face close to mine.

"You can hold onto me," he said, and he started walking around in the pool, with me clutching at his broad shoulders.

As we sat in the corner of the shallow end, I noticed a particularly pretty girl eyeing him up and down. She strode over to us confidently as he was talking to me, and I glanced at her a bunch of times, trying to figure out what she was up to. She walked up to him and then stood off to the side.

Suddenly she exclaimed, "Oh!" and practically fell on top of him. The minute she touched him, he jumped away, a shocked look on his face. His arms immediately reached out to catch her so she wouldn't fall face-first in the water.

"Excuse me," he said blankly, the voice he used to use while we were at school.

"I'm so sorry," she said in a chirpy voice. "I was walking past, and I tripped on one of the toys," she said, giving him a dazzling smile. He just stared at her blandly, his features hardening.

"I'm sorry that you tripped," he said with forced politeness. He reached over to me, grabbed me by my hand, and began leading me away. He stopped when we were in the deep end of the pool, a murderous expression on his face.

"I hate people like that," he growled, glaring in her direction.

"Me too," I responded, surprised that he was as mad as he was. I saw him take a deep breath, and his face visibly softened. "Just try to ignore her," I suggested, and he gave me a smile.

The rest of the day passed slowly, but I wished it could have lasted forever. I loved surprising him by suddenly splashing him with water and seeing the first initial shock wear off to teasing as he splashed me back.

We stayed until closing time. The sun had started to set, and purple and orange swirled around in the sky.

One of the lifeguards walked up to us to tell us that we had to leave. When we walked out into the parking lot, the blue sedan was the only car there.

"I had an amazing time!" I said, climbing into the passenger seat.

"Me too," he said, and I yawned, only just realizing how tired I was. We rode home in silence, just enjoying each other's company. We finally arrived at my house, and he stopped outside the front step.

"Thanks for finding that place," I said, smiling. He leaned forward, and I did as well, closing my eyes as our lips touched. We stayed there for a moment; the only sound was our heavy breathing. As I slowly pulled away, I felt another question bubble to my lips.

"Do you have heightened senses? Can you hear and see better than a normal person?"

He smiled at me and said, "Yes, I do. In fact, I can hear your heart speeding up right now. I can see the blush spreading across your cheeks."

"You're obviously stronger, but are you faster also?"

"I'm not inhumanely fast, but I'm faster than most," he said, and I could tell that he was amused by my questions. "You should probably go in," he said, leaning down for one more kiss.

Chapter 31

A few days later, we went for a walk in the trails. It was at least shady and cool. "My dad is really stressing," Keith said quietly, and the calmness didn't match his words.

"Keith, don't you think that maybe you should go back to where it's safe? I don't mind coming to visit you," I said. I glanced around at the trees, suddenly terrified that every shadow would turn into someone that would want to hurt him.

"Relax. You're worse than my dad. I don't think anything is going to happen, especially now. They're going to be too busy getting their act together."

"Are you sure?"

"Of course I'm sure." His reassuring words eased my worry a little bit, but the clenched feeling in my stomach refused to go away.

"You know, I kind of like hiking here better than I like walking by the lake," I said after a while of silence. The birds whistled, their loud calls echoing in the canopy of leaves above us.

"Really? Why?"

"I guess it just seems much more natural and real. Like the lake is perfectly round, and there's barely ever a ripple, and the trees are perfectly trimmed, and the path is paved smooth. But here, everything just seems much wilder I guess."

"I know what you're saying; this is very removed from the rest of the world." We continued to walk together, not really paying attention to where we were going or how long it took us to get there.

"Keith," I said after a while.

"Yeah?"

"Can we rest for a little bit? My leg is starting to bother me."

"Of course. I'm sorry if I took you too far. Look, there's a bench over there where we can sit," he said, and he scooped me up into his arms and cradled me to his chest as we walked toward the bench. We sat there for a while, with me leaning up against him, his head resting against mine.

Suddenly, Keith's entire body seemed to stiffen, and he jumped up and pulled me behind his back.

"Keith, what's going on?" I listened hard, but the forest was eerily quiet. Not one bird's voice rang above us. Even the air around us seemed still with tension.

"Oh my God," he said, backing me up and pushing me behind him. Fear clutched my heart as I realized there was only one thing that would terrify him this much.

"What is it?" I asked him again, but he didn't respond.

There was the smallest rustle of leaves from behind me, and Keith whirled around, keeping me firmly behind him. I had no idea what was going on, and I started shaking with fear.

I was about to ask him what was going on for the third time when I suddenly felt a hand wrap around my mouth and drag me backward. It felt like half an instant, but I was suddenly about ten feet away from him.

Panic raised its ugly head and threatened to overwhelm me. I kicked out and struggled and writhed in the hands that held me, until I felt the cold barrel of a gun press against my temple.

I froze, the overwhelming panic prohibiting my body from even trembling.

At the sound of my scuffling footsteps, Keith turned around quickly, not even seeming to realize that I was gone until he turned to face us. The anger in his face quickly morphed into complete terror and panic. The small amount of color that remained in his cheeks quickly drained.

For the fourth time in my life, I saw Keith's pupils constrict until they were barely visible vertical lines running through hard blue crystal. A new fear and panic began to settle in me, but it wasn't fear for myself; I was scared for him and what he might do to get me out.

But surely there was only one person; he could easily take him without getting me shot in the head. The second the thought crossed my brain, I quivered again and felt the man's grip on my hands tighten behind my back.

I closed my eyes, keeping my head and neck in a stiff odd angle as I strained away from the barrel of the gun as far as I could. Keith and whoever was holding me seemed to be having some kind of stare down. Suddenly, I felt fingers grasp the end of my hair and pull sharply, and a small whimper managed to escape my lips.

As soon as the sound left my lips, Keith's fury seemed to explode, and the tremors started to rack up his massive frame. He grew before my very eyes until he was a towering eight feet. He stretched his neck from side to side, and I could see the glimmer of bright blue scales at the base of his collarbone.

His shoulders were shaking violently, and before the huge pair of wings could spring from his back, he clutched his stomach, and I had a sudden memory of that night in the park with Damon.

His hands flew to his mouth, and I could see him try to keep it closed. He failed, and as his mouth opened, a huge torrent of flame erupted.

He seemed irrational, but he continued to stare at me with longing on his face. I knew that if I spoke, I could ease the burning anger inside him. I knew that I could calm him, but I was in no position to do so. I knew that the minute the words left my lips, the fingers that held me would press on the trigger—and that would be the end.

It looked like a torrent of flames would erupt from Keith's mouth again, but instead were words with the deadliest tone I had ever heard. "Put her down. Now." I shivered at the terrifying sound of his voice.

"I don't think you're in a position to negotiate." I froze as I recognized the voice, sounding once so tender and dear to me. I couldn't believe it. I thought he was gone from my life forever, but here he was. Damon.

As he spoke, at least fifteen people seemed to materialize from thin air, surrounding us in a large circle. Each one of them had a gun, and they were pointed at either Keith or me. I saw him freeze as he realized the hopelessness of the situation.

"You make one wrong move," Damon said, "and this bullet is going straight through this pretty head of hers." Keith's face turned to a sick, gray color. "But if you come quietly, no harm comes to her." Dread filled me as I realized the choice Keith would have to make.

He could fight and escape, but then I would die. But if he saved me, he would give himself up without a fight and go with them.

He was staring at me, a pained and torn expression on his face. My chest ached as I recalled that, only a few minutes before, he was laughing and happy. I begged him with my eyes, *Don't listen to him. Please.*

I could feel my heart slowly breaking in two as I saw a blazing determination cross his face.

"Damon, please," I whispered quietly, and his grip tightened on my arm. I had to struggle not to whimper.

"One wrong move, sweetheart, and both you and he are dead." His voice was cold and indifferent. Keith was looking at me, and his head was slowly shaking. That one motion of defeat told me that it was all over and there was no hope.

Keith was going to leave me unharmed and sacrifice himself so that I might remain safe. I wanted to shout, to scream at them, to fight and writhe in their hands. I wanted to rush over to him and replace the heartbreaking expression on his face with something happy.

I bit my lip hard as he tore his gaze from me. He didn't look at me again as he said in his strongest voice, "I'll come with you." All I could do was stare at him with a mixture of horror and admiration.

Three of the men broke from their circle to rush toward him, jerking his arms behind his back and handcuffing him.

He wasn't fighting them; he didn't even try to resist as they forced him onto his knees on the ground. He didn't even look at me as they all swarmed around him to make sure that he was secured properly.

"We just need to give you something to make sure that you stay calm," Damon told him as one of the guys approached him with a needle.

"Wait," he said, and again his voice rang strong. "Let her go first, and then you can do with me what you want." As he said those last words, his voice quivered slightly, and hysteria threatened to overcome me.

My breathing was fast and shallow as they all paused and looked at Damon, clearly waiting for him to decide what to do. "Fine," he finally said, and he jerked me to my feet. As I rose, I saw Keith had finally turned to look at me one last time.

Chapter 32

I stumbled through the trails and felt utterly alone, as if the entire world was spinning around me. I couldn't think straight, and I all I could see were the blurred lines of the trail as I struggled to walk through my blind panic.

I could only think of three words: *oh my God*. They were the words that he said when he realized that he was wrong, that they were coming for him after all. There was no doubt in my mind who they were and what they were there for.

What was I supposed to do now? I couldn't just do nothing; that was not an option. But who could I tell that would believe me?

I saw the end of the trail ahead and looked up at the sunlight; it was trickling through the trees and hitting the graveled path. How could he possibly be so strong and fearless in the face of so many enemies? As I knelt down in the dirt, my breath came in and out in wild frantic gasps. I tried to tell myself to get a grip, but it felt impossible. My entire body was shuddering, and it felt as if the entire world was trembling around me.

The biggest pain of all was the huge ache deep in my chest. I felt as if there was a piece of my heart and lungs ripped out, and I couldn't breathe properly. The worst part was the knowledge that it was my fault that he gave up without a fight. If I hadn't been involved with him, he would have fought them with everything he had.

He had saved me so many times. I had been able to become myself again because of him; I had learned to be happy again. And now, he was in danger, and I felt like there was nothing I could do.

But I had to try. I had to try to repay him for all he had done for me.

I had to reach Keith's dad. The pain pulsed through my leg as I tried to pick up speed, and I struggled to ignore it and move as quickly as I could.

I feared facing Cyrus. How could I explain this to him? Would he put the blame rightfully on my shoulders? Was there anything he could do?

These questions and others swirled in my head as I stumbled through the streets toward my house to get my car. I ignored the odd stares people seemed to give me. When I reached my house, I walked up the steps, wiping my sweaty forehead with the back of my hand. I reached into my pocket for the key. I could barely put the key in the lock because my hands were shaking so badly. I headed straight for the garage. Every second that passed was a second longer that Keith was in the hands of the Griffins.

I was startled when the sound of the engine broke the silence of the garage. It felt as if every noise was too loud, the sun was too bright, and the shadows were too dark.

When I finally pulled out into the road, my eyes darted everywhere, seeing an enemy in every face that I passed. I could feel myself falling apart, and my breathing quickened to low shallow breaths, coming in and out of my mouth in violent gasps. *Calm down,* I told myself. *His house is only a few minutes away.* Thoughts of his house flashed across my brain, wonderful memories of the last time I was there. Tears began to roll down my cheeks, and a loud, painful sob racked my throat.

I pulled my car over to the side of the road, pressing my forehead against the steering wheel as I struggled to pull myself together. After I stemmed the steady flow of tears, I took a deep breath and pulled out into the road once more.

I finally reached my destination and almost gave in to hysteria again at the sight of his house, perfectly unchanged. When I reached the end of the driveway, I didn't pause as I jumped out of the car. I reached his front door and knocked, struggling to keep myself calm. After about thirty seconds, the door opened.

"Harmony? What's—"

| 15 Stitches |

The minute I saw his face, the face that looked so much like Keith's, I completely broke down.

"I ... I ..." My voice sounded high pitched and hysterical between the violent sobs.

"What happened?" he asked.

"He ... he ..." I couldn't force myself to say the words.

"He who?"

"Keith!" I burst out, curling up into a tiny ball and rocking back and forth.

"What happened to him?" I could hear the terror in his voice.

"They ... they ..." But again I couldn't get the words out.

"Just take a deep breath," he said in a calming tone. "I'll go get you a cup of water." He walked into the kitchen. I clutched at my stomach and my chest, as if my hands would be able to heal the gaping holes I felt. He came back quickly, holding a small plastic cup with water in it. "Before you drink, I want you to know that I put something in there that will help you calm down a little," he said. I paused for half a second before I gulped down the water as if it were a life source. The minute it went down my throat, I felt my heart rate slow and my breathing deepen.

"Feel better?" he asked.

"What is that?" I asked him.

"It's something I developed a little while back; it has calming effects better than what doctors prescribe today, and it doesn't give you that drugged-up feeling," he said, smiling gently. "Now," he said, worry creasing the lines on his face, "do you think you can tell me what happened? If Keith is in trouble, I need to know what happened so I can help him."

"Well," I said, "we decided to go for a walk on the trails this morning. Then, my leg was starting to bother me, so Keith found a bench for me to sit on. Then, while we were sitting there, Keith got really tense and jumped up and put me behind him. All he said was, 'Oh my God,' when I asked him what happened.

"Then Damon grabbed me from behind and put a gun to my head. It felt as if they just appeared out of nowhere. One moment there were only three people—Keith, Damon, and I. The next moment, about fifteen people seemed to materialize around us. Every one of them had guns, and they were pointed at Keith and me.

"Then, when Keith told Damon to put me down, he only laughed. He said if Keith came quietly with them, they would let me go, but if he made one wrong move they would shoot me in the head." My voice quivered as I remembered the feeling of the cold medal pressed against my temple.

"And he chose to go with them and save you," he said, his voice low. All I could do was nod, and even the medicine didn't stop the tears that began to spill over. I was frightened that he would blame me for what happened, and I knew that he would be right.

"How much did Keith tell you about us?" he asked. I looked at him in surprise. What did this have to do with saving him?

"I know what he is. I know what happens when he loses his temper, and I know that he can breathe fire. I know that you used to work for them and that you used your own genes and the genes of a Dragon to create him to be a super race," I said.

"I never told him the whole story. There was an error in Keith's makeup." His eyes were glistening with tears.

"What was your mistake?"

"He was supposed to be a mindless robot that would be part of the army for the Griffins. Keith was never supposed to have a soul. Did he tell you anything about how we escaped from there?"

"Yes, he said that his mother destroyed something very important to the Griffins' operations—that by destroying it, their technology became impossible to use."

"Yes, the Griffins had an incredible technology that was built around one core development. It gave them boundless power. Here's something I never told Keith," he said. "I built it."

Chapter 33

"What?" I said. I was under the impression that the Griffins had the advanced technology long before Cyrus came into the picture.

"The Griffins were cunning and very smart, but it was my genius that allowed them to become the overwhelming superpower they were—and I assume are again. That's what allowed them to capture the last Dragon … my genius."

"But what is it? What does it even do?" I asked, wondering if it could be the key to getting Keith out of there.

"It's what the Griffins call the Artrox, but its function is difficult to explain. It's based on something called string theory. Basically everything in the universe is made of tiny vibrating strings … Well never mind that," he said when he saw my blank expression. "What's important is that I was able to harness the most fundamental energy source in the universe with this invention." Cyrus didn't seem happy about all of the things he had done; his voice was filled with bitter regret.

"The Griffins used it to try to take over the world, until Naggyra destroyed it," he said, and he looked numbly into space, staring without seeing. "Naggyra … that was Keith's mother."

"Yes, I know," I said, remembering what Keith had told me. "Why did it take them so long to rebuild?"

"Because Donovan Caliego, my replacement, and the Griffins didn't truly understand the concept behind it. It didn't take them as long as I would have hoped," he said, again looking dismayed.

"But I don't understand. What does this have to do with saving Keith? Why did he even need to be captured in the first place? Why do I even have to know all this?" I asked, feeling my voice rising with hysteria once more.

"The Griffins have this mentality where nothing with Dragon blood should be roaming around free. Second of all, they like to have physical representation of all their experiments and inventions. As to why do you need to know this? When you go into the lair, the only way you'll ever escape is if you destroy the Artrox."

"Wait—aren't you coming with me? What is their 'lair' exactly?" I squeaked.

"The Griffins live in cities connected by an extensive system of underground tunnels, designed to seem like they're above ground. No, I won't be able to go with you. They'll recognize me."

"Won't they recognize me too? Especially if Donovan and Damon are there?"

"Damon's not going to be in this particular city because he's going to the capital to receive a reward. I don't think you'll see Donovan because he's still trying to bring the Artrox to its former power."

"If the Griffins are so unstoppable with the Artrox, then why did you want Keith to stay in the house? Would it have made any difference?" I said, feelings of guilt surging through me.

"I developed a security system. It wouldn't have been foolproof, but it certainly would have been safer."

"I don't understand what lured you to them in the first place?" I regretted my curiosity when a pained look crossed his features.

"What else besides wealth, power, glory? The society I had lived in hadn't even begun to tap into what you know today. I knew I was greater and better than that, even in my forties. When the Griffins found me, it was everything that I had been looking for."

"Why did you change?" I asked, hoping he wasn't annoyed with my stream of questions. I had already heard Keith's reasoning, but I wanted to hear the words from him.

"When I saw the face of my son, I couldn't help but love him more than anything in the world. I loved him more than all of the wealth and all of the glory that I accumulated over nearly four hundred years," he said, his pale gray eyes looking past me to a world that I didn't know.

"You have to understand," he said looking deeply in my eyes, "this is going to be very dangerous, and you might not make it out." At his dark words, I felt a shot of fear course through me, but with it, another shot of determination.

"I understand," I said firmly, pushing the fear and panic behind me.

"Now it's going to take me a long time to hack into the computers, but we cannot plan anything unless I do. This way we have all of the information possible; it will make things much easier and less risky."

"Okay," I said feeling better that he had a plan; the responsibility was taken out of my hands. We would save him. We would get him back.

But that knowledge didn't stop my hands from shaking as I slowly drove back home.

* * *

It was a very long week. Ever since school ended, I had slept well every night, but now I barely slept at all. When I did sleep, I would have frightening dreams, forcing me awake crying and shaking.

I dreamt of all of the horrible situations possible, that everything went wrong when I went in to get him back, that I was too late. I struggled to hide these horrible dreams from my mother.

I pretended to sleep late, so she wouldn't see me when I got up in the morning, having just woken up from a nightmare. As hard as I tried, I couldn't get his face out of my head. I couldn't get his last sad expression with his glistening blue eyes to leave my brain. I tried to remember all of the good times that we had before then, but that only made the pain in my chest much worse.

I couldn't force the raging guilt from my mind either. I knew it was my fault that he didn't fight back. Sometimes I would just curl up in a corner of the house and cry for hours, thinking of all he had done for me, and how it seemed impossible that I could ever pay him back.

The only thing that gave me a glimmer of hope was Keith's dad. I called him almost every night to see how the progress was going on hacking into the Griffins' information system.

"Hello, Harmony." He knew the exact time when I called by now, and he always sounded weary and slightly bitter.

"Mr. Draykon?" I asked, knowing that he already knew what I was calling for.

"It's getting closer every day. Don't worry. I should have it done within the next couple of days."

"You're sure?"

"Yes, don't worry. I'm sure they won't do anything fatal to him."

But his words were always laced with worry, and he sounded like he was trying to assure himself more than he was trying to assure me.

"Thank you."

"You're very welcome."

"Bye."

"Bye." And as soon as I clicked the phone shut, the hopelessness and anxiety seemed to hit me like a tidal wave. The only time I quit my endless pacing and worrying was when my mom was home.

I kept my face bright, even though my gut was twisting in odd contortions inside of me. Sometimes I think she saw through my mask. As painful as it was, I let her believe her natural conclusion—that Keith and I had broken up. It gave me an excuse for my behavior.

It was almost a month since they had captured him, and I was frantic with worry. Finally, at about two in the afternoon, the phone rang.

"Hello?"

"Harmony?" When I heard his voice, I could have cried with relief.

"Yeah?" I said, clutching at the phone as if it were a lifeline.

"I finally got it."

"You did? I'll be there in a few minutes."

I practically sprinted out into the garage. A weight lifted from my shoulders when I realized I would actually get to do something instead of waiting around. Finally, I would be able to save him.

When I reached the car door, I almost fell over; my knees were shaking so badly. I scrambled into the front seat, trying to steady my trembling fingers so that I could put the key in the ignition.

Finally, I managed to pull shakily out of the driveway. The minute the tires hit the road, I pressed as hard on the gas as I could, and they squealed as the car raced forward. I was glad that the neighborhood wasn't very crowded as my car rocketed through the streets.

I braked hard when my tires hit the gravel on his driveway, and I launched myself out of the car, leaving it at a crooked angle. The minute I reached the door, it swung inward, and I looked eagerly at Keith's dad's face.

From the sound of his voice, I wasn't surprised to see that he had big dark bags under his eyes. His hair was a ruffled mess. He smiled weakly.

"Okay, so now what do we do?" I asked as he led me through the house to a room where I'd never been before. A big metal door, at least a foot thick, barred it. As he swiped his hand across the door, it seemed to come to life, illuminated by a huge touch screen

"Whoa," I said, my eyes widening in surprise as I stared at the huge screen.

"It only recognizes my handprints," he said as his fingers flashed across the screen in a long complicated code. As he finished, the door swung open. When we entered, I was surprised at the large expanse of the area and the fact that it contained several rooms.

The room we entered contained numerous huge bottles filled with mysterious clear substances. A large metal table was in the middle of the room, which was immaculately clean and did not have a single fingerprint on it.

"Be careful not to touch anything. If it registers any other fingerprints besides mine, the entire place will close down, preventing the thief from leaving until I can come and see whoever it was that tried to break in." As he spoke, I wrapped my arms around myself and shivered, goose bumps rising on my arms. We continued forward into the next room.

Unlike the previous room, big screens covered every single wall. Large projectors lined the ceiling and floor, pointing in opposite directions around the room. He walked briskly over to one corner, seeming to come alive now. I stayed in the middle of the room, careful to keep my arms firmly against my sides. I watched as he waved his hand in front of another screen and the entire room came to life.

I was expecting the familiar whirring of a computer as the machines turned on, but it was silent. If I had closed my eyes, I wouldn't have known that anything was turned on at all. Again, I saw his fingers flashing across the screen as he entered a long complicated code into the system.

"Okay," he said, grabbing my arm and gently guiding me to where he was standing. "The Artrox has been moved to a different underground location, but luckily it's near where Keith is being kept. There will be a bit of a drive to the entrance gate, because it's no longer near the burnt woods. The first thing we need to do is get you familiar with the way the place is laid out. I have to say, I'm surprised; they haven't changed it much."

"How am I supposed to be familiarized with the place if I'm not even there?" I asked, feeling my voice begin to get desperate.

"Easy," he said casually. "They have tiny cameras covering every square inch of the entire place. With this," he said, gesturing at the screens around him, "I can access those images and have them projected so it's like we're actually there. The fact that these cameras are even working means big trouble."

"Really?" I asked, and the nerves slowly crept into my stomach as the reality of the situation began to hit me.

"Yes," he said as he strode over to the screen once more and pressed several buttons. Immediately, the light created by the screens was extinguished, and I couldn't see a single thing. My breathing began to increase, and I was sure that he must be able to hear my heartbeats in the silence.

I heard a faint tapping as he pressed a few more buttons, and then the faintest click, as if two pins had bumped against each other. Then, we were suddenly surrounded by light, and the images around us spun and twirled. I clutched my stomach as the dizzying movement caused my gut to protest loudly. Finally, the images began to slow, and it was as if we were transported into a different universe.

We were in a complicated, twisting labyrinth with bright artificial lighting.

The area had sleek white tile flooring, and the walls were made of something that looked like stainless steel. Instead of standing near a screen, it appeared that he was standing a few feet farther down the tunnel.

All I could do was stare at him in shock.

"Now, I know it's a little disconcerting at first, but you'll have to get used to it quickly; we don't have much time."

"Okay," I said, and my voice sounded strangely far away. "Do they know we're here?" I whispered, looking around nervously.

"No, because we're not; this is just a projected image. An illusion, you could call it. Now, when I walk, it'll be like we're actually moving through the tunnel, but you don't really have to move at all." I was surprised at the ease in which he talked, as if this was something that he did every day.

"Did you invent all this?" I asked, and he hesitated, looking back at me.

"Yes, including all of these cameras."

"Wow," was all I could say as he began to walk forward. As he explained, it felt like I was actually moving along the tunnel, except it was like gliding because I wasn't actually walking.

"Now, we're about to enter the main town area as you could call it. We are not actually going to see any Griffins because they're holding Keith in one of their human cities where the human slaves run operations and staff the prison.

"The room where the Artrox is kept is much too small for a Griffin to do any maintenance in, so they use human robot slaves to do it for them. This is where almost everything happens that we're concerned about, but I'm warning you, it's going to be quite a shock when you first see it." He continued walking, and we headed through a doorway.

As Cyrus predicted, I was shocked by what I saw. There was a huge cavernous area about the size of a small town. Everything was so bright and white as if it were open to the outside world, which I knew it wasn't. Everything was bustling and busy, with people walking in every direction. But there was something very strange about these people; their expressions were blank, and they moved oddly and stiffly.

A cold feeling settled at the base of my stomach when I realized what these strange people must be. I glanced at Cyrus's face, and there was no denying his guilty expression as he watched their robot-like movements.

"Watch them carefully because when you're actually there, you have to behave like one of them." I stared at their awkward movements.

"There's one problem," I said as he walked through the wide expanse.

"What?" he asked with a hint of worry in his voice.

"I have a limp." Suddenly his expression cleared, and he smiled.

"Don't worry. That's an easy fix," he said, walking as I followed along behind him.

"Are there no Griffins in the entire city?" I asked.

"There are a few … just to make sure everything is working properly," he said quietly, his eyes distant with ancient memories.

"This way," he said quietly. "This is where you'll find him, except they don't have views of any of the cells, so I don't know which one he's in. As beautiful as that area was back there, you're about to see a terrible part of their lair. Because you can't see the cells, it's not that bad now, but when you're actually there, it's terrible." There was no misinterpreting the agony in his voice as he led me through another doorway.

"There aren't any cameras in the prison cells?" I asked.

"No …" he said, sounding distracted.

"Don't you think that would be smarter? To have cameras where the prisoners are?"

"So you would think …"

He continued to lead me through the city in his virtual computer world, explaining everything that we came in contact with and helping me find my way around. Soon came the test, when I was to try to lead him around.

I got lost a few times, but eventually I was able to find my way around the enormous area. He showed me what the entrance looked like, from inside and outside of their lair.

"Good," he said, and I was happy at the reassured tone in his voice. Soon he walked away from me, and the scene moved with him. "Now time for the plan."

Chapter 34

I tried to keep my face relaxed as I lied to my mom. I said I would be going to the beach for a couple of days with Sarah, Jen, and Adrienne along with Sarah's family. She studied me for a long time before responding.

"Sure you can go," she said finally, and I breathed a sigh of relief. I felt conflicted about keeping so much from my mom. I couldn't stand to be with her, yet I couldn't stand to be without her. I wanted to tell her everything, but I couldn't tell her anything. I wanted to be alone, and yet I wanted her company.

My nerves roiled around wildly within me, and it seemed impossible that the day had finally arrived, the day when I could save him, when he would be safely with me again. Cyrus and I had rehearsed the details so many times over the past few days that I felt I could recite the plan in my sleep. Yet, my hands still shook as I took a shower and got dressed that morning. "Bye, Mom," I said, trying to keep my voice light and happy. I had to keep up the charade for a little bit longer. I don't know how I drove to his house; I could barely think.

I knocked on the door. Keith's dad opened it, a tight smile on his face when he saw my nervousness.

"Maybe you could use some of that medication?" he asked me, but I shook my head. I wanted to do this myself, without any help. "You know I can drive you only so far, but then you have to walk the rest of the way?" I nodded. We had been over it a thousand times. He brought me into the living room and directed me to put my injured leg up on a table. He grabbed a shot and gently injected it into my muscle tissue.

"By the time we arrive at the city entrance, it should have stopped the limp completely," he said, and I nodded. We got into his car, and my leg was already starting to feel different, the muscles looser and more flexible.

We drove in silence, and I reviewed the plan over and over in my head.

I could do this. For Keith, I would do anything.

I stared out the window as the sun slowly rose in the sky, until it was directly overhead.

"Are you hungry?" he asked me.

"I think if I ate anything, I would barf." He nodded and continued driving, as if he felt the same.

We drove on.

"Try to get some sleep," he suggested.

"What about you?" I asked.

"Don't worry about me. I can go almost a week without sleep—and believe me, I have." With this reassurance, we fell into silence again, and I leaned my head against the cool glass. It helped soothe my raw nerves, and my eyelids drifted shut. I fell into a light, restless sleep.

A short time later, I jerked myself awake, my heart beating like a freight train.

"Are we almost there?" I asked.

"We're very close," he said in a tight voice.

"What happens if I get caught?" It was the one question I had been avoiding the entire time we were planning. Now that it was too late to turn back, I had to know what might be in store for me.

"You'll be put in prison and probably tortured until you tell who you're working for. Then, they'll either put you in a cell where you'll stay with minimal food and water for the rest of your life, or …"

I couldn't fail. I would not fail.

The road we were driving on wasn't paved, and the tires rattled loudly. The coarse noise frayed on my already delicate nerves.

The car slowly slid to a stop, and my heart immediately pounded into overdrive as I realized that from now on I would be on my own. Keith was counting on me, and his father was counting on me to bring his son home.

I slowly slid out of the car wearing the perfect disguise, the standard human slave uniform of the Griffin world.

"Whatever you do," Cyrus warned me with urgency in his voice, "do not deviate from the plan one millimeter. If you do, this will never ever work." I nodded, and with bravery that I didn't know I possessed, I quickly strode away from the car into the cover of the woods.

I kept my footsteps as quiet as possible, with my eye constantly on the road next to me for any sign of action.

There wasn't any.

I felt as if I were in a dreamlike haze, not really thinking, not really feeling, just moving. I had to act this way. I knew that if I felt anything, I would break down and wouldn't be able to complete my mission.

So I walked, focusing on every twig in front of my feet and the dirt road next to me. I could hear the sound of my footsteps crunching on dead leaves, joining with the sounds of birds echoing above me. I smelled the summer air around me, even though it was already late August. The bright summer sun didn't suit the turmoil of emotions that were churning around in me.

I walked at a steady pace for fifteen minutes, and then I began to look around for the end of the road. I adhered to the plan precisely and didn't emerge from the woods until this time point had passed.

It seemed like an eternity, but it was more like a half hour of walking before, finally, I saw the end of the road. I froze; the entrance to the Griffin's lair was much more obvious than I thought it was going to be.

Two massive trees stood representing columns that extended into the sky far higher than any of the other trees. On each tree, there was an intricate carving of two bird-like creatures with four legs. They had massive feathery wings that extended from their backs as they reared up on their hind legs, facing each other.

As my gaze slid lower down the columns, I couldn't help but feel horrified at the images. Several Dragons were lying dead underneath the feet of the Griffins, and I had to momentarily look away.

The Griffins seemed to be looking up at a familiar symbol, two feathers surrounded by a twisted cross.

I shook off the feeling of nausea in my stomach, and I waited, as the plan dictated.

Soon, I heard footsteps from far away, and I looked up, frozen in the shadows. I continued watching the area of the woods where two trees were bent oddly toward each other, where I knew the footsteps were coming from. I held my breath as someone emerged from those two trees, the person I was waiting for.

It had to be this particular person, Keith's father had said, because he was the only human slave who had access both to the prison where Keith was kept and to the area where Artrox was kept safe.

As he moved closer to where I crouched, I slunk toward him to cut off his trajectory. Thanks to Cyrus, I knew exactly where he was headed. It shocked me more in real life than I thought possible, seeing the odd stiff gait and the blank expression on the person's face as he did the Griffin's bidding.

As he walked past me, I grabbed him by the shirt and pulled him down toward me, clapping my hand over his mouth in case he made a noise. He didn't make a peep, just as I expected.

I grabbed a syringe with shaking fingers and pushed it into his arm, a serum that would make him sleep for several days. I grabbed his watch, which would alert me to the times of all his tasks, something I would need to play my part properly.

I knew that if I took too long, the Griffins might begin to suspect something was wrong. I rushed to the small clearing and grabbed a bucket full of grain, which was now my duty for the next few days. I held my breath as I approached the two trees, my heart in my throat.

I could've thrown up as I held my hand up to the tree on the left, waiting for it to register my handprint. Keith's dad had managed to program the system so that it recognized my handprint as well as that of the man I left in the forest. The shadows between the two trees flickered, and I knew I was in.

I breathed a little lighter as I headed into the darkness. The floor under me slanted downward slightly, the area behind me getting darker and darker.

I continued to move at the same pace, working on keeping my expression as blank as possible before I encountered anyone else.

I counted my steps, and as soon as I reached the number fifteen, I held up my hand again, and something in front of me slid open, revealing a bright white light that emanated from the main town area.

I kept my face blank as I walked forward, staring vacantly in front of me, even though seeing this area for the first time with my own eyes was just as shocking as the first time in Cyrus's virtual room.

But I didn't show any of this on my face, keeping the pace of my walk even just like everyone else. Unlike everyone else, my heart rocketed around in my chest, and I was frightened someone would be able to hear it.

No one did.

I finally reached the second door, where all of the prisoners were kept, and I stepped inside, immediately feeling the mustiness of the air. I kept my eyes straight ahead as I waited for the dull lights to turn on.

When they did, I snuck a glance at my watch, the one I had taken; I had twelve minutes until feeding time. I was perfectly on schedule. As I walked, I looked up to see lines of cells in the dingy brown light of the tunnel.

I felt my heart hitch slightly when I realized that Keith might be only a couple hundred feet away; I wanted to run to him and drag him out of this horrible place. But I didn't. I stuck to the plan.

I went into a room where I knew the human slaves stayed when they were between duties. I sat down on my bed and waited for the small bell to ring on my watch. Many other people were seated in a similar fashion, staring at the ground with blank expressions.

In any other situation, I would have fidgeted, but I didn't. I was perfectly motionless. I didn't even glance at my watch again as I waited for it to ring. I played my part perfectly.

Don't do anything, he had said. *Once you're in, act your part until exactly twenty-four hours later. It must be exactly the right time. I will be able to watch you from the computer in my car. Just stick to the plan.* Knowing that he was probably watching me was comforting as I sat there staring at the floor. I didn't even take a deep breath; I kept it steady and even.

When someone else's watched beeped, I forced myself not to react. I didn't even follow them with my eyes as they walked at the same steady pace out the door.

Finally, I heard my watch beep. Instead of jumping up and sprinting out of the room, which was what I wanted to do, I stood up and walked out the door using the stiff even walk I had practiced.

I walked at the same pace to the room right next to me, took a wheelbarrow filled with disgusting brown mush and a large scoop. I pushed it out, straining slightly at first under its weight, and then pushed it forward.

I felt my heart banging against my chest as I put the scoop into the brown mush and slid it through the bars into a disgusting looking bucket. I struggled not to gasp in horror at the smell coming from the cell.

At first I didn't think there was anyone there, but the minute the food sloshed in the bucket, I heard the dragging of chains as someone moved to the front. I paused for less than a second to try to determine if it was Keith.

As the dragging chains got closer, I felt my hope lift until I saw a tangled white beard. My heart filled with pity when I saw the man before me, but I knew there was nothing I could do to save him.

I turned to the next cell and continued down the aisle, always waiting that extra half a second to see if it was Keith that slinked out of the shadows. As I walked down the aisle, I felt my heart sink lower and lower as the inhabitant of cell after cell wasn't him.

My soul swelled with enormous pity at these emaciated men who wolfed down the disgusting slurry that I gave them. I wanted to save them, but it was impossible. I had to stick to the plan.

Finally I reached the last cell in the aisle. I heard a strange buzzing noise that seemed to come from the bars of the cell. Puzzled, I slowly reached my hand up to the bars. As they got closer, a searing heat seemed to be growing at the palm of my hand. I snatched it away, surprised that there was a bright red, throbbing mark at the base of my hand.

A memory from a long time ago flashed before my eyes, and I involuntarily hissed through my teeth at what these sizzling bars might mean.

The door to the exhibit opened again, and Donovan was standing there, gesturing for Damon to come out of the car. Damon sighed quietly and said to me, "I'll be right back."

Their voices drifted through the window with the wind, and I strained my ears to listen.

"Dad, I don't understand something. Why can't I take him?"

"Because, who knows if we have the resources to contain him without the Artrox? Just wait until I have it working again."

"You've been working on it for more than fifteen years! I know you've come a long way, but how much longer can we let him roam around uncontained?"

"You will listen to me, and you won't act until I have the Artrox working. Understand?"

The dragging of chains across the dirt floor snapped me back to reality. If I squinted, I could see the moving of black shadows. I held my breath, and my heart nearly stopped when I saw a figure emerge from the gloom.

There was no mistaking the black hair, but instead of being soft and healthy, it was matted and knotted. It was longer than I was used to seeing it, brushing just past his chin. Just like everyone else in the cells, he was emaciated, with every one of his bones protruding from his body. It seemed impossible that someone could lose so much weight in such a short period of time.

I wanted so badly to call out to him so I could see his sapphire eyes, but I knew I couldn't—not yet. I waited longer than I did with the others, wishing he would look up and see me, but he didn't. He kept his hidden eyes on the excuse for food now in the pail.

From under his tattered shirt, I could see the beginnings of hideous scars that stretched across his back. Some of the unhealed wounds had taken on a greenish color, and I could tell that they were terribly infected. Bright red burn marks, similar to the one now on my hand, ran up along his face, arms, and hands.

His restraints were different from those of the others. Most of them had the chain wrapping around their ankle, and that was all. Keith had varied constraints that clearly prohibited him from moving properly. I began to worry about the buzzing bars. I felt the beginning of nausea in the pit of my stomach when I began to wonder if I would fail to save him.

But then, his father's words flowed through my mind. *There might be extra protection around his cell instead of just a lock and key that will obviously rely on the Artrox for power. The computer drive that I gave you will disable all the extra protections around the cell first, just in case. All of the chains and constraints on him are powered by the Artrox, so after a few minutes, they should unlock themselves.*

I just prayed that whatever the drive was programmed to disable, it would disable the heated bars first. I had to stick to the plan, but I had to get Keith out of here quickly. I feared that, the way he looked, he didn't have much time left.

As I turned away from him, I had to struggle to walk upright. I wanted to break down right there and completely give up, but I didn't. I could stay strong; I had to stay strong for him.

I walked back to the feed room and put the wheelbarrow into the exact spot where I found it. I then proceeded back to the room with the beds and waited for the watch to ring a second time. The next ring, I knew, would be more important than the first.

My job would be to examine the Artrox for any faults or problems, and if there were any, to report them immediately. I knew I only had to do my part and appear to be paying close attention to the way the machine operated.

This was the time when, according to my plan, I was supposed to identify where I would insert the small flash drive, now in my pocket, which then would catalyze the entire escape plan.

It felt like it was harder to wait now that I knew Keith was suffering immensely a mere hundred feet away from me. I wanted to start everything now, but I knew I couldn't.

This part is crucial to the plan, Keith's dad had said. *The waiting is going to seem like agony. When you enter, they might suspect something is not right if you do things even slightly differently than a slave would. So you must do exactly what we rehearsed, but it is critical that you locate the socket to place the flash drive with your eyes, and your eyes only, so that tomorrow your motions can be fluid as you insert it. Remember, today will give you confidence for tomorrow.*

I recited these words around in my head for what felt like a long time. I couldn't give in now; I had to wait. Patience was never a virtue of mine, and this entire thing was an exercise in patience.

So I concentrated on my breathing and measured the time by the number of my breaths. I kept my breaths long and slow to make it seem as if time was passing faster. I could tell it was late, as many of the slave people had already gone to sleep because they didn't have another task until the next morning.

Soon, almost everyone else was asleep, but I still sat up, waiting for my bell to ring. I wanted to risk glancing at the watch to see how much time I had left, but I didn't, remembering how cameras seemed to cover every inch of the place.

Finally my watch rang out, and I got up slowly and walked steadily out of the room, turning away from the aisle of prisoners. I kept walking down the winding tunnel until I reached the main town area. It was frighteningly quiet, and it threw me off. With all the bustling noise, it seemed easier to blend in, but now that I was alone, I didn't feel so confident in my deception.

I kept walking, careful to keep my steady pace. I reached a door that was much more obscure than all the others, with a much more complicated opening system.

I raised my hand, and it recognized my handprint. But instead of opening, the door brightened, revealing a touch keypad, very similar to the one that Keith's dad used to guard his room. With sweating palms, I ran over the code once in my head before I began gently pressing the buttons.

I cringed, almost expecting a loud siren to ring and warn them of my actions. Instead, there was a faint click, the door swung inward, and I walked forward. Claustrophobia threatened to come upon me as the door shut behind me, leaving me enclosed in absolute blackness.

I took a deep breath and walked forward, as if I had walked this way hundreds of times before. My footsteps echoed loudly on the marble-like surface. As I walked, bright lights lit up along either side of the tunnel. Their vivid light was reflected on the stainless steel tunnel.

I could see that I was approaching another door, and I wanted to run toward it, to get out of the frightening hallway. I didn't; I kept an even pace and headed toward the door.

There, I had to move my hand across it and enter another code. I held my breath as the door clicked and swung inward for me again. The next time I would be at this door, I would be in much graver danger.

I quickly walked into the huge expansive room and stared around in shock. None of the trips that I had taken through the cameras had helped to accustom me to what this was like. The huge machinery nearly filled the large room, leaving a three-foot space between it and the wall.

The gears and engines were all whirring quickly. The room was frighteningly bright, and I had to squint before my eyes adjusted to the dazzling light. The majority of the light was coming from the center of the Artrox, with the high wall of the machine blocking my view of the tremendous energy contained within. I had the sudden urge to see what was behind the high wall, to see what created enough energy to keep an entire underground civilization going.

I resisted the urge and continued walking slowly and looking at the frantically whirring machinery. I pretended to pay close attention to the way the smooth metal parts glided past each other, but I was only pretending.

Really I was looking closely for the socket in the computer, and finally I located it, a small slit in the side of a small rectangular box under the central monitor. I touched the small flash drive in my pocket. I knew it would be twelve hours from now before I inserted it into this massive machinery.

I returned to the room with the beds and curled up, yearning with my whole heart to go out to Keith and take him out of this terrible place.

I tossed and turned, not able to sleep because of the nerves that clutched at my heart. I remembered Cyrus's many warnings and replayed them over and over in my head until I finally drifted off into an uneasy sleep, despite the hacking coughs coming from the prison aisle only feet away.

Chapter 35

I woke up to the ringing of someone's watch, and I almost jumped out of bed before I suddenly remembered the past twelve hours with horror. I repressed the terrible images that came rushing back to me of Keith and all those poor men that were with him. Guilt racked through me when I remembered that there was no way I could save them all. I forced the tears from my eyes when I realized that not one of them deserved the fate that they had been given.

I slowly rose to a sitting position and stared at my lap, mimicking the other people in the room.

"What are they?" I remembered asking him one day about the strange slave people.

"They're people, but they've been given injections that clear their brain of any personal thought. They're more like robots really." His angry face stopped me from asking who had created those injections. I already knew the answer.

My brain returned to the present, and I yearned to stretch out of this stiffening position, but I did not.

My heart thundered in my chest as I realized with a strange kind of joy that today was the day he would be safe with me again.

I kept repeating that over and over in my head, which is what allowed me to stay in that rigid position as I waited for the feeding bell to ring on my watch.

Having him with me was all I wanted, and the thought that he was so nearby both comforted and horrified me. I still had so far to go to accomplish my mission, but it was so close that I could touch it. I kept my eyes blank, refusing to let the tears come.

To occupy the time, I thought of the happy times we had together. I remembered our long conversations and laughs. I remembered the walks by the lake and the beautiful kisses under the tree, where we felt protected from the world. I remembered the way his blue eyes softened when they looked at me, and the way a smile slid unconsciously onto his face.

It seemed like an eternity, but my bell finally rang. I methodically took the wheelbarrow of food as I had the day before and brought it to the cells.

Unlike yesterday, I did not wait for the men to emerge from the shadows; I couldn't bear to see their hopeless faces, knowing I couldn't save them.

Finally I reached Keith's cell, and I waited for him to emerge from the shadows, again sickened by his terrible condition. I knew that if we ever got out of here, he would never be the same again, and neither would I.

He didn't even glance at me but wolfed down his food. I wanted to reassure him that soon he wouldn't have to endure any more of this. I wanted to reach out to him and comfort him, but I didn't. After staring at him for one more long moment, I turned away. Again, I was hit with a horrible pain deep in my chest, and again, I had to fight the urge to curl up in a ball and give up.

Finally, I was able to sit down and get control of the deep wound in my chest that was invisible to everyone but me. I kept telling myself that I could get him out of here, that he would be saved.

I rehearsed what I was supposed to do in my head, making sure I had the sequence of the steps clear. I wanted to close my eyes to focus on what I was about to do, but I knew that I couldn't. So I stared blankly into the distance.

When my watch rang for the last time, my heart seemed to batter against my chest so fast that I couldn't determine the individual beats. I struggled to keep my breath slow and even and keep all of the emotion off my face.

It was time.

Just like yesterday, I walked across the main town area, my mind completely blank, except for everything I was about to do. It didn't bother me that the area was empty now; it gave me space to think.

And again I walked through the frightening hallway, knowing that the blinking lights wouldn't be working much longer.

When I reached the large room, my breath became shallow, and I felt like I couldn't get enough oxygen. It was coming out in wild gasps, and I paused as I headed toward the socket on the side of the computer.

I could do this. For him, I could do anything.

I pulled out the flash drive and looked directly at the insertion point. I hesitated before putting it in, realizing that as soon as I made that move, they would be alerted. But it would be too late. Cyrus's words echoed loudly around in my brain.

"This," he had said, holding the small rectangular drive out to me, "is the key for this plan to work. It contains programming that will cause the Artrox to self-destruct. The second that it goes into that computer, there is no reversing it, even if you take it out half a second later.

"After it is inserted, you have half an hour at most before the entire city shuts down and you won't be able to leave. You have forty minutes before the entire city is destroyed, and that will be the end. You'll know it's working when you see a small red light blinking."

I stared at the small piece of metal in my hand, and with every bit of determination that I had, I inserted it into the computer. I waited half a second to make sure that I saw the red light blinking.

And then I was running. I sprinted as fast as I could out the door, knowing it would take me at least five minutes before I reached his cell, and who knows how long before I could remove his shackles. Remembering the loud buzzing bars, I prayed that whatever that drive was, it worked fast.

The person waiting to hear the report of the Artrox didn't say anything as I roared past him. I had never run so fast in my life. I ran through the dark hallway with the chilling lights on either side of me, ignoring all sense of secrecy. It didn't matter what happened now; all I had to focus on was getting him out safely.

Again I was relieved when the town area was empty, knowing it would be only minutes until it was filled with people. But that was what I needed to escape; I needed complete chaos. I didn't pause when I walked past the sleeping people and ran straight to Keith's cell.

"Keith!" I shouted the minute I got there. I almost started crying when I heard no response.

I turned the key in the lock and was relieved when it swung open. The lights above us began to flicker, and I rushed into the cell with renewed urgency. He was hunched at the back of his cell, his long legs bent to fit into the small space. I saw him slowly move to face me, a guarded expression on his face.

I froze and stared at him in horror. I expected to see his crystal clear blue eyes, but in their place were faded, milky gray eyes. It was as if a gray film had covered the eyes that I loved so much. I suddenly realized why he hadn't seen me before and why he didn't look up: he was blind.

"Oh my God, what did they do to you," I whispered.

His emaciated face was covered with burns and scars. I felt a furious anger course through me, an anger that was lit by the fire of revenge. Whoever did this to him should pay—and dearly.

"Harmony?" he croaked, and he slowly extended a shaking hand in my direction. I reached forward and took his coarse hand in mine.

His hand traced up my arm, rested on my shoulder, and crept up to my face. He took his second hand and cupped my other cheek, and I could see tears brimming over in his milky eyes. I could feel his hands trembling against my cheeks as he traced my face with his thumb.

For a moment, I completely forgot where we were and what was happening. It was just the two of us, reunited at last. His thumb continued to trace my face as one of his hands slowly slid down my neck.

Suddenly his arms came crashing down on my shoulders, and he pulled me close. I could barely take in a breath the way he was holding me. I reached up to tangle my fingers in his hair and crushed myself closer to him.

He whispered, "Oh, Harmony." I shivered as I felt his breath along my collarbone. It felt as if we were transported miles away to a much brighter, happier place.

"I can't believe you're here," he whispered, and as the words left his lips, the dull lights in the aisle began to flicker. I could hear the bleating of an alarm, and I knew that the chaos was starting.

"Keith," I said, praying that he would be strong enough to walk. "We have

15 Stitches

to get out of here." I moved away from his hands. The clasps fastening the heavy restraints on his body started to unclick, just as Cyrus had promised, and I began tearing at them. "We're going to get you out of here."

"What's happening?" he asked in a voice barely above a whisper. "Where are you?" His hands reached out searchingly for me as the last chain fell off of him.

"There's no time to explain now," I said, pressing my lips against his hand, and I began to pull on his arm. Suddenly, all of the lights went off again, and we were surrounded by complete darkness. Ten seconds passed before they came back on again.

"Oh my God!" I squeaked as a strange siren echoed around us. The entire place seemed to shake and tremble. Suddenly, people were rushing by us, not even noticing the open cell door. Perfect—that was exactly what I was waiting for.

"What's going on?" he croaked again.

I just grabbed him by the arm and struggled to haul him to his feet.

"Just follow me," I said, breathing heavily under his weight. He stumbled along beside me, clearly too weak to use the muscles himself. I glanced at my watch. Ten of my precious thirty minutes were gone!

There was shouting and screaming as people came pouring into the central town area from all sides. I just prayed that one of the Griffins in charge wouldn't come out; that was the last thing I needed. As I dragged him through the crowd, the lights went off and on again. I stormed through the mass of people. The entire place shook again, and I hurried faster.

"Keith you have to help me," I breathed as I pushed through, my eyes glued to the exit that would lead to our escape. I suddenly felt his weight lessen, and his feet began moving more steadily. "That's it!" I encouraged him.

I was so focused on the objective ahead that I ran directly into someone, and I silently prayed that it was just another robot. The plan had gone off without a hitch so far, and we were so close to the end that I could feel it.

I looked up at the face of the person I ran into, and I felt my heart freeze in terror. Donovan Caliego stood directly in front of us, his golden eyes bulging when he saw Keith. His dark, graying hair was sticking up in different directions, and he had black soot all over him. Keith had no idea who we had just run into, and I could feel him wondering why we had stopped our frantic run.

"What the hell are you doing—" he started, but then his eyes fell on me. "You!" Donovan shrieked, and his words echoed around me, despite all of the noise and chaos. "What the hell did you do!" he screeched at me, approaching me violently. "How do I fix it! Tell me!" he yelled, lunging at me.

I didn't respond to his wild yells, my eyes straying toward the inconspicuous passage to freedom that couldn't have been more than twenty yards behind him. I slowly started to walk backward as his expression turned maniacal. He walked toward us with a frightening smile on his face. I pulled Keith backward with me, my eyes not leaving Donovan's face.

"Harmony—" Keith started, but I quickly shushed him. I heard Donovan laugh as his arms slowly reached toward his belt to pull out a knife.

It glistened in the flickering bright lights around us, and I felt my heart thunder against my chest in fear.

I felt Keith freeze against me, and I heard his low voice hiss, "Donovan." Suddenly the trembling in his body became much more concrete. I knew that he had recognized Donovan's voice and was about to lose his temper.

Donovan lunged at me—not Keith, as I was expecting. I jumped to the side, but not before the wickedly sharp knife sliced against my arm.

I let out a gasp as I dragged Keith away from Donovan, feeling the panic overwhelm me as I realized that we might not get out in time. Blood poured from the slice in my arm and dripped over onto Keith's hand.

He slowly lifted it up and, to my surprise, took a deep breath and smelled it. Keith's frantic trembling increased in tempo, and I knew what was going to happen before it did.

A low hissing escaped his lips as his shoulders rocked wildly back and forth.

Keith suddenly grew about a foot and a half, and I could see the hint of scales begin to grow on his emaciated collarbone. Instead of hunching his shoulders and fighting the transformation, he pulled his shoulders back, and the dark blue leathery wings exploded and expanded from between his shoulder blades.

| 15 Stitches |

"Ha," Donovan laughed. "You don't stand a chance against me. You can't even see!" Keith let out a roar and lunged forward, his huge wings suspending him in the air. He obviously couldn't see where Donovan was exactly, so he guessed by the sound of his voice. He jumped slightly to the right of Donovan, clipping him in the shoulder.

Donovan swung around, the glistening knife aimed directly at his neck.

"Keith!" I shrieked, and he jumped to the side just in time.

"Harmony, get out of here!" he shouted, and I was shocked that he had enough strength to master that kind of volume.

I suddenly realized what I had to do. I knew Keith wasn't nearly strong enough to take on Donovan, and there was no way that I was going to leave him.

But we didn't have much time left.

Chapter 36

I rushed through the chaotic town center and back toward the prison. I clutched at the deep cut in my arm, blood dripping onto my fingers. I didn't feel any pain, but I knew it would eventually come.

I swung my hand at the access door to the prison. It took a long time before I heard a faint click and the door slowly swung inward. I rushed past all of the prisoners and into Keith's cell, grabbing one of the huge chains that had been used to bind him.

Sweat was pouring down my face from anxiety and effort as I dragged the heavy chain along. My huge wound began to burn wildly as blood continued to pour over my arm and down my shirt, running onto the chain that was grasped in my hand. My faint cry was lost in the tumult that was everywhere.

I searched frantically around as the once bright lights dimmed and blinked. Their power source was running out of time.

And so was I.

I searched frantically around at the rushing people as they tried to figure out what to do. My heart was thrumming against my chest, as if a hummingbird was frantically trying to leave its cage.

I couldn't find Keith and Donovan. They seemed to have been swallowed by the chaos that surrounded me. My arm felt like it was on fire as I struggled to stem the bleeding and search for Keith at the same time. I wanted to lie down and curl into a ball and wait until it was all over.

But I couldn't. I knew Keith was counting on me, and that alone was enough to keep me going. I dragged the heavy chain, the muscles in my arm screaming in protest. I forced my brain to think past the searing pain.

I rushed around the panicking people, crashing into them left and right. I thought I would be able to find him easily, that his outrageous appearance would lead me to him. But I was wrong.

"C'mon!" I yelled. As my eyes searched the crowd, I wondered if I might run out of adrenaline or faint from loss of blood.

The only thing that kept me going was the memory of Keith and the look on his face when he realized that I had come to save him. The fire for revenge kept my fading energy from dying out.

Suddenly, my eyes locked on something that was happening on the ground, and I realized I had found them. I could have cried with relief as I rushed forward as fast as my aching limbs and burning arm would let me. I paused as I took in the horrific situation.

Donovan had managed to get Keith down, and they were wrestling on the ground. Keith's wings were flapping frantically against the marble flooring, causing a huge circle of people to begin to form around them.

Donovan had the huge knife pointed downward at Keith's chest as Keith's hands were bracing against Donovan's muscular arms. I could see the knife trembling as Keith's already weak muscles threatened to give out.

"No!" I screamed and rushed forward, throwing the heavy chain randomly in their direction, praying that it hit Donovan. I saw the end of the heavy chain collide with Donovan's unsuspecting temple, and he suddenly slumped over, knocked unconscious. "Keith!" I screamed, rolling Donovan's unconscious body from on top of him.

He was slowly transforming back. The scales were fading from his neck, and the huge wings were steadily retracting back between his shoulder blades. His eyes were shut, and I could barely see his chest moving faintly up and down.

"Keith!" I screamed again.

His milky eyes opened. He smiled slightly. "I can't do it."

"No!" I yelled at him. "I didn't come this far for you to give up!"

A pained expression crossed his face, and he attempted to get up. I grabbed his hand and dragged him upward, every muscle in my body yelling in protest.

"That's it!" I encouraged, straining against his weight so that he wouldn't have to support himself that much. Suddenly, he took his hand off of my arm, and his fingers were dripping with my blood.

"Harmony ..." he said hoarsely, a horrified look crossing his face.

"It's nothing, Keith. I'm fine," I lied, continuing to rush forward. Finally, I reached the small insignificant looking exit that led to the outside world. I held up my palm to the sensor and waited for it to light up.

Nothing happened.

"Come on!" I screamed. I glanced at my watch; my half hour to escape was almost gone. It finally gave a click and swung open.

I pulled him through the door, not pausing to see if it shut behind us. The lights went out again, and the place shook for five seconds, nearly toppling us over. I felt the ground tilt upward slightly, and I could have cried from happiness. I only had to pass through one more door.

I reached it and swung my hand in front of it.

Again, nothing happened.

"Please," I cried at it and swung my hand again. Nothing. The entire place shook again, knocking us off balance. "Please!" I begged again, flinging my hand at the sensor. Finally, it lit up slightly, letting me know that it registered. There was agonizing slowness in the response, until I finally heard a faint click.

"Yes!" I shouted, sweat pouring down my face. "Please!" I shouted again as the door swung open and I dragged him out through the tunnel. The ground continued to rise, and I was running against his weight, with him still stumbling next to me. We finally passed through the two trees, sprinting across the dirt road.

I dragged him across it until we were safely in the forest. A huge moon hung overhead, and it seemed impossibly close to the earth. It cast a silvery shine on everything it touched. The serene atmosphere contrasted oddly with the adrenaline pumping through my veins.

I knew that the night would not be peaceful much longer.

"Get down," I said, pulling him down with me as I felt the ground shake under us. I kept my injured arm off of the dirty ground to prevent it from getting infected. I ripped my shirt and pressed a piece of the rough cloth onto my arm as I struggled to stop the bleeding. A hiss escaped my teeth as the burning pain shot up to my shoulder.

He lay down on his stomach. His eyes were closed, and his breath came out in wheezing rasps. I forced the tears away; I still had to be strong for him.

The ground shook violently again, and I heard the animals in the forest screeching wildly as they sensed that something terrible was going to happen. The shadows of birds against the moon fell over the night as they struggled to get away.

I glanced at my watch, knowing that there couldn't be much time left. Then I remembered that the power source that made the watch run was dying—and quickly. I wiped the blood off of the watch and observed it with a sick sort of fascination. The entire thing was blinking and beeping.

I could see what was happening underground by watching the small device on my wrist. When the watch went black, I knew that everyone underground was surrounded in blackness. When the watch's light blinked brightly and then flickered, I knew that the lights flickered underground.

I reached out to Keith and held him close to me, gently running my hands over his matted hair. The dark liquid on my fingers smeared across his pale face. Keith's condition was far worse than mine. His breathing was ragged, and he was shivering and trembling. I glanced at the watch again. It was black, and it didn't come back on this time. I knew a huge explosion was only minutes away.

I wanted to be as far away from there as possible, but I didn't think Keith would be able to move fast enough. I felt my body tremble as I thought of all of the poor people down there I couldn't save.

I held my tears back again as I ran my hands down his side, careful to avoid the ugly cuts on his back. I reached out with my other hand and put it in one of his, and he grabbed, squeezing it forcefully. I struggled not to cringe when I saw that my hand covered his in blood. I reached out again and moved his black hair away from his face.

Suddenly the ground quivered again, but it didn't stop, and I knew this was it. I ducked down next to Keith and pressed my eyes shut as the frantic shaking grew more intense. I could barely breathe, but it wasn't because I was scared; Keith was holding me so tightly that I could barely expand my chest.

I reached down and rubbed my hand up and down his arm as the shaking underground caused the earth to throw us back and forth. When I pressed my ear against the ground, I thought I could hear shouts. I thought I could hear the machine revving wildly with effort, people yelling, and frantic footsteps.

A strange cracking sound came from under us, and I realized that the ground would not hold up against the force of the blast. "Run!" I screamed as the earth began to buckle and sink. I dragged Keith to his feet and sprinted forward, refusing to let go of my deathlike grip on his hand.

I couldn't hear anything but the explosions under our feet. The strong smell of burning and ashes and melting metal surrounded us. I had no idea how far we would have to run until we were safe.

I knew that the force of the energy would explode throughout the labyrinth of cities and tunnels created by the Griffins. How far the destruction would reach, I didn't know, but their primary energy source would be gone.

Finally, it felt as if the shaking underneath us was slowing, and the way the trees swayed around us wasn't quite so frightening. The earth continued to tremble, but it was slowly fading, until it was still and everything was silent. I tried to block out the faint echo of screaming people. I ducked down and prayed that the enormous tree that we were under would hold up. I closed my eyes as Keith pressed his face into my hair, his body shaking almost as much as the ground had.

Now there was only the sound of our breathing. Suddenly he curled himself into a ball, and I heard a strange sound coming from his lips. It took me a second to realize that he was sobbing. I sat up and slowly encouraged him to do the same, until his upper body was resting in my lap. His entire body shook with the force of his tears. I held his body close to me, rocking back and forth, and made comforting noises.

His tears soaked my shirt, and I remembered when our positions were reversed—when I was the one needing comfort from him.

| 15 Stitches |

I lifted my head, looked around, and realized that I had absolutely no idea where we were. In our frantic attempt to escape, we left the road and had gone running into the woods. I had no idea how to find the road or Cyrus. I knew we needed to find him fast; otherwise we might not survive.

"It's okay," I said, keeping the trembling out of my voice. "We have to get out of here," I told him.

"I can't," he whispered, shaking his head. "I can't make it."

"Yes, you can," I said, letting every ounce of hope I had fill my voice. "You have to," I added, when I thought of the unbearable alternative. "I …" I said, not able to hold back the tears anymore. "I wouldn't be able to live if you were gone."

"Will you help me?" he asked. When I looked at his face, I wanted to burst into tears again because of his frightening gray color. But I didn't. I stayed strong.

"Harmony," he said shakily, "don't lie. How badly are you hurt?"

"I'll be able to make it to your dad's car," I said quietly, avoiding his question. I didn't mention that I really didn't know where his dad's car was. "Keith, we have to find your dad," I said quietly, looking around for anything familiar.

An expression of extreme pain came to his face as he slowly tried to get to his feet.

"Wait, why don't we just sit here for a few minutes to get our strength and then start walking?" I said.

He didn't say anything in response but lay down next to me.

Despite the hard uncomfortable ground and the fear of being lost, I could feel my eyelids try to slide shut. I fought against them with all my might. I knew that the chances were slim that I would wake up in the morning if I let myself sleep now. I turned around and saw that Keith had already fallen asleep, his expression peaceful for the first time since he was captured.

I finally lost the battle, and my eyes slowly slid shut.

Chapter 37

Relief overwhelmed me when I saw his milky eyes open the next morning and the awakening sun splashing colors against the early fall sky. With the dawn came new hope, and even though I didn't know where the road was, I was able to tell what general direction I should be going in.

"Keith," I whispered. I looked at the horrible cut on my arm that was now oozing a dense yellow substance.

"Yes," he croaked. He made no move to get up, his filmy eyes staring away at nothing. I slowly ran my fingers down his long matted hair, and he closed his eyes again.

"C'mon," I said, letting eagerness slip into my voice as I stood up. I ripped off another piece of my shirt to press against the wound on my arm.

I grabbed his arm and let him lean heavily on me. I didn't show how tired I was or how heavy he was or how much my arm burned. Every time I looked at him, I pushed away pessimistic thoughts and replaced them with others: *We made it. I succeeded. I got him out.* I knew that he was strong, that he could handle a lot of things, but the way his face was clenched frightened me beyond belief.

He stumbled again, and I knew he couldn't go on. We needed to find his dad—and fast. I gently guided him down until he was sitting. "Are we almost there?" he asked me.

"Yes," I said, remembering the same tree bent at an odd angle from when I passed it two days ago. I could almost distinguish the road about a hundred yards in front of us, but I also knew we had longer to go than he could walk. "Yes, we're very close." *But not close enough*, I thought.

I looked closer and saw the faint shadow of a car through the dense trees. It got closer and closer. I lifted my hand, frantically waving in the direction of the car.

"We're almost there," I said, straining as hard as I could against Keith's weight. I wanted to carry him over there, where I knew that his father would be able to take care of him properly. Finally, I saw the door open, and Keith's dad got out. He started sprinting toward us.

"Keith, your dad's coming," I whispered.

A small smile lit his features. "He is?" he said.

"Yes, he is."

Cyrus reached us and immediately grabbed Keith in a huge hug.

"I thought you guys didn't make it," I heard him mutter.

I stepped back and watched, trying to give them space.

"Thank you," he said, turning to me with glassy eyes. I muttered something in response, too exhausted to form a coherent reply.

"C'mon, son," he said, turning so that Keith was leaning on one of his shoulders. The minute they took one step, I could tell that something was wrong. I rushed forward, already knowing what was going to happen. When they took the second step, Keith's exhausted muscles gave out, and he began to topple over.

"Easy, easy," Cyrus said, catching him just in time to lower him to the ground. I could tell how hard it was for Cyrus to keep the fear out of his voice. I knelt beside him, feeling the tears begin to rise in my eyes.

His eyes were closed, and his breathing was worse than it had been a few seconds before. "I'll bring the car over," Cyrus whispered, and I could tell he was trying to mask the panic. He suddenly looked up at me and saw that I was covered in blood.

"Oh my God, Harmony, what happened to you?"

"It's nothing. Let's take care of Keith first," I said, and he nodded. He sprinted over to get the car.

"Please," I whispered to Keith, clutching his hand to my chest, "just a little longer." He reached up with one shaking hand, and I gently guided it to my face. His hand traced my face, and his fingers lingered on my lips. I closed my eyes against his touch, praying that he would have the strength to hold on.

He lifted his lips slightly at me and whispered, "Yes," and at that moment, Cyrus pulled up with the car. He rushed over and brought a stretcher that would fit in the back of the car.

We slowly worked together to get Keith on top of it. Cyrus grabbed an oxygen mask, and for the first time, I noticed the huge tank in the back of the car. Keith lay there, his milky gray eyes staring up at the sky without seeing it. His wheezing breath eased considerably as he breathed pure oxygen. Then Cyrus inserted an IV into one of his arms and hung a bag above Keith's head.

"This will hydrate him." As Cyrus leaned away, I could see the way his hand trembled. "Don't worry," he told Keith. "You're going to be okay."

"Cyrus," I said.

"Yes?"

"Is there anything that you can do for his eyes?" I whispered, hoping that Keith wouldn't be able to hear me.

"I don't know," he said quietly. He had huge tears in his eyes. "I don't think I can thank you enough," he said. "You did it." I smiled at him as he reached forward to pull me into a hug. When he let go, he pointed to my arm and said, "We really need to take care of that. It's horribly infected. What happened?"

"We ran into Donovan and he had a knife," I said quietly.

He rummaged through the trunk of the car. "This is going to burn a little," he said, holding up a bottle with a clear liquid inside. He put a drop of it on a small towel and pressed it against my arm. I couldn't help the small cry that escaped my lips as the burning sensation seemed to penetrate every nerve.

"You must have lost a lot of blood," he said, concern in his voice as he examined my arm. He took out another container with a white powder inside. He squeezed some into his hand and spread it onto my shoulder. He then took a clean bandage and wrapped it up.

"This should last you the rest of the car ride, but we'll have to treat it again when we get back to the house." I just nodded, too tired to do anything else.

| 15 Stitches |

There was nowhere to sit in the backseat—Keith was temporarily using it as a bed—but there was no way I was going to spend that car ride away from Keith. I climbed in, settling on the floor of the car and resting my head against the seat. I saw Cyrus smile slightly as he started the car.

Suddenly, the torrent of emotion that I had used so much energy to repress burst forth, and a huge sob broke from my lips as the tears began to flow. I was so exhausted that I didn't have the energy to hold it in anymore.

All the worry, anxiety, fear, anger, pain, and grief seemed to cover me in a blanket of emotion. I felt Keith's hand rest gently against my head, his fingers stroking back and forth against my hair. It only made me cry harder; after everything he had gone through, he was still thinking of me.

We sat like that for most of the car ride, tears streaming down my face, and his hand moving gently back and forth against my hair.

We finally got back to his house, and Cyrus carefully lifted him out of the car. I followed, suddenly so tired. I felt as if a heavy weight were pulling downward on my eyelids, and I knew there was no stopping it. I followed Cyrus inside. After Cyrus put Keith down on the bed, he turned to me and treated my wound again.

"You need to stay here for tonight. You've been through so much," he said to me, and I turned and walked to the bed that Keith was sleeping in.

I felt Keith's arms wrap around me. He was breathing fine now, and Cyrus had taken the oxygen mask off of his face. It looked like he was staring at me with his milky eyes, as if he were willing his eyes to see. I lifted my fingers and traced his face, letting my fingers hesitate over his lips.

"You don't think I'm hideous?" he whispered, and I laughed softly in the dark, though the situation was far from funny.

"You are the most beautiful man I have ever met," I said to him. I slowly pressed my lips to Keith's, wrapping my arms up and around his shoulders. Keith and I were safe and together, as we should be.

As we lay there, it felt like the world had been lifted off my shoulders. I suddenly felt accomplished; after everything that had happened to me, after everything I had done, I had succeeded.

The final stitch had been pulled through the gaping hole, healed but leaving a scar that would last forever.

CPSIA information can be obtained at www.ICGtesting.com
Printed in the USA
BVOW021109190412

288041BV00001B/80/P

9 781469 790930